WAKING UP RICH

JAMES ROBB

First Edition

For Hal. "Running Bitcoin."

CHAPTER ONE

Perched on the side of a hundred-meter-high cliff in Uluwatu, Bali, Agent Jake Hunter sat in the baking heat. He was lying on a white sun lounger overlooking a beautiful, blue infinity pool. Today's target for the CIA Quantum team was Alexei Averin, a dangerous arms dealer. Jake watched from across the pool as Alexei sipped a glass of champagne.

'The target looks like he could be moving soon,' Jake said into his radio mic. He adjusted his Panama hat with an air of nonchalance.

Alexei's, Hawaiian shirt had the first three buttons undone and showed off his hairy black chest. He danced wildly in one of the VIP cabanas at Bali's premier venue, The Omnia Beach Club, and was surrounded by tanned, bikini-clad women and other acquaintances. He was on display. From both sides of the cabana, his eight-strong security team, dressed in perfect black suits, protected him.

'Transport confirmed, Agent Hunter. The drone has picked up a convoy of SUV's moving towards the front of the beach club,' announced a voice over his radio. 'As for Alexei's henchmen, they look heavily armed, Jake.'

'You two look like you're having fun there, Jake.' A different voice came over the radio. 'Love the disguise,' said Tom Thacker, Deputy Director of the CIA. He was in the Operations Room. He watched events unfold from the comfort of CIA headquarters in Langley, Virginia, USA.

'Is that a hint of jealousy I hear in your voice, sir?' replied Jake. 'I didn't think you'd be sitting in on this one. How's the weather back in Langley?'

'We've been chasing this arms dealer around the globe for close to a year, so I wouldn't miss this for the world,' Tom replied. 'And it's raining and cold here as usual, by the way.'

'Can we focus?' Agent Jennifer Beck cut in as she climbed the steps of the infinity swimming pool looking over the Uluwatu cliffs to the Indian Ocean. She wore a revealing red bikini and walked to Jake's double sun lounger to lay down.

As Jake watched Jen's athletic body approach, he was distracted.

'You still with us, Jake?' crackled Tom's voice over the radio. 'You're meant to be watching Alexei.'

'Still here. We have two contacts approaching Alexei's cabana. One is carrying a metal briefcase.'

Jake and Jennifer watched three of Alexei's security team step forward to pat down the two visitors before allowing them into the cabana.

Waving a couple of dancers away, Alexei greeted his visitors. He took a seat in the corner of the cabana, away from the dancing crowd.

'Do we have a potential identification of the newcomers?' Jake peered over his sunglasses, straining to see.

'Negative, sir,' Langley replied. 'The net curtains around part of the cabana are obscuring our camera view.'

'Can we try and get better audio on this?' Jennifer asked, adjusting her earpiece and straining to hear what was being said. 'They are taking out a laptop.'

'No usable audio available, I'm afraid,' replied another analyst in the Langley Operations Room.

'Damn, guys. We've worked for weeks to get coop-eration with the Indonesians, so we can't blow this.' Who set this up?

'Look, team, we've spent all afternoon surveilling Alexei, and, as you all know, he's one of the CIA's top pri-ority targets. It'll be a wasted afternoon if we can't confirm the deal, so get the damn audio sorted.' Jake studied Alexei, and the flapping curtains only gave him sporadic glimpses.

'Their music is blocking the audio, Agent Hunter. I can't seem to filter it out,' the analyst said.

'Has Quantum confirmed any transactions? We need to know that the bitcoin has been transferred before we make our move.'

'Hang on. Yes, it looks like Quantum just confirmed a transaction's taken place, Jake.'

Tom leaned over the analyst's shoulder, typing in a frenzy, as the screen flashed green.

Quantum was the CIA's top-secret computer system used to track bitcoin transactions, break cryptographic systems, and monitor other sensitive data. It was active twenty-four hours a day. Quantum analyzed almost infinite amounts of chat, commerce, internet traffic and intelli-gence data from around the globe. The CIA, working with the NSA, had achieved quantum supremacy. Still, only a select few knew of this secretive project within the CIA. Companies such as Google and IBM were still trying to reach a milestone, but they were a long way behind the CIA.

'Has Quantum matched the bitcoin address to Alexei's identity and location?' Jennifer asked.

The analyst waited as the screen ran calculations, mapping data and bitcoin transactions. 'Yes, it's a match. We have it. It's definitely him. Quantum has confirmed lo-cation and address, everyone.'

To the outside world, bitcoin was created by Satoshi

Nakamoto. Even those without security clearance of the Quantum team assumed that Satoshi Nakamoto was a pseudonym the CIA created. They had conceived the idea of bitcoin in late 2007, and the first trade took place in 2009. The CIA created the pseudo-currency ten year's ago. What started as an experiment run by elite technologists in the organisation was now one of the CIA's critical tools in fighting organised crime and rogue nation-states. Getting Alexei Averin would be another feather in the Quantum team's cap.

'Is the ground team in place?' Jake asked, looking around the beach club and pegging other undercover agents mingling with guests.

'CIA ground team confirmed. They are in position. Waiting for your go-ahead, Agent Hunter.'

'Black Ops, are you in position? Jake reached into the leather bag beside his sun lounger and checked his SIG Sauer P226 firearm.

'Everyone in position, awaiting your command,' The Black Ops leader reported.

'Remember, we want him alive. This guy has traded enough weapons to run the Syrian war. We need what intelligence he has,' Tom said.

Jennifer slung her handbag over her shoulder, and Jake followed her down the terrace. 'Moving on the target.' They walked towards the cabana. Several of the Black Ops team, accompanied by the Indonesian Special Forces, closed in along the sides of the building near the bar closest to the pool area.

'Alexei.' One of his personal guards shouted. He pulled a gun and fired a staccato of shots.

One of the Indonesian Special Forces had moved too early and broke cover onto a balcony overlooking the cabana.

'Get him to the cars,' shouted another of Alexei's bodyguards. Alexei pulled a Heckler and Koch MP5 and shed forty rounds. He hit two Indonesian Special Forces and killed them where they fell. A third bodyguard pulled a couple of large tactical bags from under the cabana's bed while Alexei's acquaintances reached for their concealed weapons.

'I'll follow Alexei. You get the laptop,' Jake yelled over the blaring music and gunfire. Jennifer took cover behind a marble-topped bar. Counting to three, she rose above the bar and pulled the trigger twice— a double-tap—that hit one of the bodyguards in the chest. He slumped but didn't bleed.

'They are wearing body armour,' she shouted as the bodyguard got to his feet, winded but otherwise okay.

Screaming guests scattered, and some took refuge by diving into the pool. Others tripped over chairs and sun loungers as they fought to escape. Amid the melee, Jake saw Alexei and two bodyguards charge down a narrow path between the main swimming pool and the cliff edge.

'Come with me,' he said to one of the Black Ops soldiers who reached him behind a concrete sculpture. They broke cover and followed Alexei to fire across the swimming pool, but too many panicked guests were crossing their line of sight. 'There's nowhere for them to go. They're cornered.'

'Sitrep, Jake,' Tom's voice came over the radio as he watched the chaos unfolding on the Operation Room's giant screens.

'Kind of busy at the moment, sir.' bullets whizzed past his head and smacked into the wall behind him. Shards of concrete stung his neck, and he motioned to the Black Ops soldier. Go to the sunken pool bar, and we'll flank them on the left.' In the middle of the crescent-shaped pool running along the cliff top was a glass bridge. It led to another bar, elevated and protruding over the Uluwatu cliffs like a hovering platform.

As the Black Ops soldier reached the bridge, one of Alexei's bodyguards emerged from behind the pool and shot him twice in the chest. Jake returned fire, a headshot, and the bodyguard's limp body splashed into the pool. His blood spread, discoloring the blue water.

Reaching the downed member of the Black Ops team, Jake grabbed him by the vest and pulled him towards cover behind a heavy, stone table in front of one of the empty cabanas. 'You okay?' he asked as he fired at Alexei and his bodyguard. Jake ran out of ammunition and grabbed the Black Op's M4 Carbine. He fired another volley, hitting the bodyguard next to Alexei.

'I'm good. Lucky the body, amour caught it. I'm just winded,'

On the other side of the beach club, Jake saw Jennifer, supported by the black ops team. She was embroiled in a blazing gunfight with the last few bodyguards. Alexei moved from behind the pool wall to the exit, but incoming fire pushed him back to the glass bridge and overhanging cliff bar.

'Cover me,' said Jake. 'I'm going for Alexei.' Jake ran out from behind the table, making for the bridge and reached it just as Alexi did. Grabbing him by the ankle, they fell onto the steps. Alexi kicked him twice in the face, and Jake released his grip.

Alexei tried to run as Jake fired a single round, hitting the glass bridge. The sound of breaking glass ricocheted off the whitewashed walls and fed back into the area to mingle with the cacophony of gunfire and screaming. Jake jumped on his advantage and fired again, hitting Alexei in the thigh. The target screamed and grabbed his leg in agony.

'There's nowhere to go, Alexei. Give it up,' Jake yelled as Alexei limped towards the end of the bar. He looked around for a means of escape. His head jerked, and his eyes were wild. The bridge would have provided his only route in or out. He was trapped, and there was nothing below but ocean and cliff. Jake fired again, hitting Alexei in the arm, and his target yelled in pain as he fell against the metal struts that were all that was left of the bridge. He was bleeding from the arterial wound in his thigh, and a slick of blood pooled on the floor beside him.

Minutes before, Alexei was partying. Jake saw his confusion as the loss of blood made Alexei sway. He watched the last members of his group surrender. They were cuffed behind their backs and taken into custody. Alexei stared at the ocean and the waves crashing against the cliffs a hundred metres below.

'Give up, Alexei. There's nowhere to go.' Jake inched closer to the wounded target. 'Let me take you in. We can strike a deal.'

'Fuck you. I'll never give up. Nothing can stop the organization I work for, even if you take me out. I'd rather die than give them up.' Alexei raised his gun to fire. He was weak and disorientated, making it a feeble effort. His movement was slow, a last-ditch show of bravado leading to an almost certain suicide. Jennifer, who had come up silently at Jake's back, squeezed off two rounds, striking Alexei in his shoulder. The impact sent him over the side of the bar. They ran to stop him from falling over the cliff, but his body plunged into the ocean.

' Tell me I didn't just see our target go over the cliff,' Tom said over the radio.

'Damn it, sorry,' Jennifer replied. 'He didn't leave us much option.'

'Shit, Jennifer, we needed this one alive. Especially after the fiasco in Tokyo. At least we have the laptop from his villa. The team are recovering some interesting data. They're uploading it for deeper analysis now.'

'What did they find?'

'It looks like Alexei wasn't the kingpin, we thought. Hang on, images feeding through. Okay, we've got mug-shots, locations and some relationship links that will make the big boys very twitchy. His organization goes deeper than we suspected. This proves he ran one team of many across the globe.'

'Interesting, do we know what the organization's called?'

'Doesn't say. We'll need a few days to comb through the data to get an idea of the extent of the organization and its roots.

'Okay, thanks, sir. Let us know if you find anything we need at ground level, and we'll see you in a couple of days.'

'Safe flight, you two. Get back to Langley for a de-briefing, and we'll go through what we've got then. And well done, guys, I'm putting this one down as a success.' The Deputy Director signed off, and the link with Langley terminated.

'Well, that was a hell of an afternoon. Dinner tonight to celebrate? I'm thinking lobster on the beach at sunset would be nice.' Jake said.

'I'm up for that. We have multiple reasons to cele-brate now, right? So, when are we going to tell the Deputy Director?'

'We can tell him as soon as we get back. We've only just found out ourselves. We can't have you behaving like a ninja on any more missions now that you're pregnant. This was the last one for you for a while, Jen. Tom will under-stand. We've worked together for five years. I'm not made of iron, and with you as beautiful as you are, what did he expect? Jennifer Hunter. I like the sound of that.'

'I'll be sad to leave the Quantum team. We've achieved so much, and yet, I feel that this is only the tip of the iceberg.'

'You'll have a few months behind a desk before we sent you home to knit baby bonnets, yet. I know you hate the idea of desk work but having somebody like you running the data while I'm out in the field will boost my confidence. Quantum is amazing, but I like the human touch. A super-computer can't go on gut feelings and intuition, which is key to a successful operation.'

'Yeah. Anyway, let's get out of here and back to the hotel.' Jennifer wrapped a sarong around her waist.

They were packing up to leave when a Black Ops soldier came over. 'Sir, there's a status update for you.'

'Go on.'

'We've got three of Alexei's men in custody, and we're about to process them for interrogation. Two were injured and are being treated over there. Medical staff are attending to the two men. And those guys behind them are the Indonesian Special Forces. 'Neither of the prisoners suffered life-threatening injuries, and they are both stable. Alexei's visitors are both dead. We believe they were North Korean nationals.'

'North Koreans? Interesting, I wonder what they were up to. 'You're the Korean expert, Jen. What are your thoughts?'

'We've seen an increase in activity recently. They could be after anything from oil to arms for their military. With the Russian connections Alexei had, it might be replacement parts for their fleet of MIG jets. We know that only a small proportion of the North Korean air force is operational due to part shortages.'

'Okay, I want to ask them a few questions myself. Alexei mentioned a spinoff organization. I want to know who they work for.' Jake gave Jennifer a rueful shrug.

'Well, I guess that dinner you promised me can wait a while longer.' She followed Jake to the bar where the prisoners were treated amid broken glass, bottles and up-turned chairs.

As they approached, one of the prisoners shuffled nervously.

'I think I recognize that guy, Jen.'

'Yeah, you're right. It's the one we tracked in Geneva a couple of months ago. I recognise the tattoos on his neck, and I'd like to know how he managed to give us the slip. He had inside help somewhere.'

There was a commotion, leading to a yell from one of the medical staff. A struggle broke out between the tattooed suspect and one of the Indonesian Special Forces guards. The muscular man overpowered the soldier, grabbed his weapon, and sprayed bullets across the beach club. They ran for cover, and within seconds, the suspect was shot dead. The area had been cleared, and the only people left on the terrace were med-tecs and trained ops.

'Fucking hell. That was close. Thanks for that,' Jake said, turning to the Black Ops soldier.

'Well, I owed you for helping me out earlier. Now we're even.' As he spoke, his eyes jerked to something over Jake's shoulder.

'What's wrong?' Jake followed his gaze. 'Jennifer,' he shouted as he ran to where she lay motionless. He dropped to his knees and cradled her in his arms. 'come on, baby, speak to me.' While he spoke soothing words at her, he assessed the wound in her chest.

Her eyes opened. 'Jake? Our baby.' She moved her arm, trying to cover her stomach as blood oozed with her breath.

'Get a medic over here.' Jake yelled to a couple of CIA agents running over to help.

'Jake. I'm sorry,' Jennifer gasped for air. 'You're going to have to let me go.' As she struggled to breathe, tears flowed down her face. 'Promise me that you'll finish this,' she reached for his hand.

'You'll be okay, Jen. Just hold on. The medics are here. You're going to be fine. And we're going to get married.' He held her in his arms and kissed her forehead. Her hand went limp, and her body stilled.

'No. Fucking no. This is not the time,' he yelled, rocking in his flood of grief, as he held her limp body in his arms. The agents bowed their heads in silence.

Rage surged through Jake. He looked at the other suspects sitting up by the medics. He clenched his fist and marched over to them. Pulling out his SIG Sauer, he pumped three rounds into the man propped against the wall, smirking at him. Blood spraying over the shocked medics as they leapt out of the way. Jake grabbed another suspect by the throat.

'What is the name of your fucking organization?' he yelled into his face. 'Who the fuck do you work for?' He repeated the question, then, without hesitation, he shot the man in the knee. The suspect let out a cry of pain.

'We going to stop him?' asked one of the Black Ops soldiers to the CIA agents watching.

'No chance. You don't want to mess with him when he gets like this.'

'Who do you work for? You're not going to give me anything then, are you?' Jake pistol-whipped the side of the man's skull with the butt of his handgun. They heard the crack of bone, and the man collapsed. Before he lost consciousness, he coughed out a few words.

'What was that?' Jake headbutted the man, breaking his nose. 'Fucking, repeat it.' He pushed the barrel of his gun into the man's destroyed knee, and the suspect howled.

He was almost unconscious, and his head was covered in blood. He whispered something, and Jake moved closer so he could hear. He released his grip from around the man's neck and threw him to the ground.

With a spray of blood across his face and his white linen shirt, Jake spat, 'Load that motherfucker on the jet, and we'll take him to one of the black sites. I'm not finished with him. I swear, the bastard will never see the light of day.'

'Jake, what are you doing?' One of the young agents in Jake's team confronted him. The others, who knew Jake well, stayed well clear.

'What's wrong? Don't like what you see? We've done far worse than a bit of a beating and killing, and you know it. We're the fucking CIA. Now, pay off the Indonesians, and we're out of here. I'm going to get every one of the fuckers for what they've done to Jen. We have an organization name now. They call themselves Wraith.'

Jake promised himself that if it was the last thing, he did, he would get every last member in the organization and bring down Wraith.

CHAPTER TWO

Tom Thacker left the Langley Operations Room and went to his office. He didn't see what happened minutes after Alexei Averin fell into the ocean below the Uluwatu cliffs in Bali. It had been a successful day, he thought. There was one fewer arms dealer in the world. He'd wanted him alive, but how could his death be a bad thing? His preference was to capture Alexei for questioning—but either way was a result.

'Deputy Director, you have David Johnson, the new head of the Intelligence Committee here to see you,' Tom's secretary said.

'Here? Right now?' Tom checked his iPhone for appointments. 'There's nothing in my diary.'

'Well, he's in your office, waiting for you. I wasn't about to say no to somebody like that. He was insistent that you see him.'

Tom went into his office. A short, bald man in a suit stood in front of one of his paintings with his hands behind his back. 'Mr Johnson, what a pleasant surprise.'

'Good day, Deputy Director. And let's not pretend this is a pleasure for you. Nobody likes it when I visit them, I know that.'

'Fair enough. So, how can I help you?' Tom watched the fat man take a seat.

'As you know, I've taken over as head of the Intelligence Committee. I'm reviewing the special programmes that I don't think give the American taxpayers value for money.' He looked at the piles of paperwork strewn on the Deputy Director's desk.

'I can assure you that we provide outstanding value for money for the American taxpayer and everybody else. Have you tried the FBI yet?' He laughed.

David Johnson was stone-faced. 'Tell me about the Central Intelligence Agency's Quantum programme, Deputy Director.'

'Sure thing. What do you want to know?'

'Everything. I want to know what you do and where all the money goes. It would appear that the Quantum project is like an agency within an agency, and even your own people know very little about it.'

'I'm aware of your security clearance, so let me start from the beginning. The programme spawning the Quantum team came after nine-eleven. After the Twin Tower attacks in 2001, the complexity of terrorist and drug cartel activities increased. The CIA is always looking for new ways to defeat rogue nations, terrorists, and cartels.'

'And after nine-eleven, was it a coincidence that you had a huge increase in the budget?'

'We had an increase, yes. The Quantum programme came from an offshoot of ARPNET. The American government thought a budget increase was appropriate at the time. It grew into its own programme when it was deemed a success.'

'ARPNET? The Advanced Research Projects Agency Network?'

'Yes. ARPNET invented the internet in the 1960s and 1970s, and they are why we have the internet today. The United States pretty much runs the internet and decides protocols, policies and other factors around its usage.

'I thought ARPNET was decommissioned in the 1990s?'

'Publicly, yes, it was. However, it has continued as an undercover operation. It was so successful that we kept it. The US government funded many key developments and new technologies by partnering with technology companies and start-ups.'

'So, then where does Quantum come in?'

'The Quantum programme was a partnership with several companies to develop a supercomputer capable of tracking and processing vast amounts of data that conventional computers couldn't handle. When it looked like we might make big breakthroughs, we terminated the partnership and completed the project independently. Though, of course, we didn't tell the big technology companies that.'

'And where does bitcoin come in?'

'The idea of an imaginary currency named Bitcoin sounded like a joke when it was presented to me in 2007. One of the young technology analysts responsible for developing Quantum came up with the idea of a virtual currency and, I thought it was crazy. But, I let him carry on with the research. It was a wise move. The agency wouldn't be anywhere near as successful without it.'

'Are you telling me that the United States government is responsible for the creation of bitcoin? Have you thought about what would happen if that ever got out?'

'Yes, the CIA created bitcoin. We didn't think it would be as successful as it has been. Back in 2017, when bitcoin passed the $20,000 mark, we had a scare with a couple of leaks. However, we managed to plug them. If it got out that the United States government created it, its value would likely drop to zero, as there would be a complete lack of trust in it and the system around it. We could always blame China or Russia if people get too close to the CIA, though.'

'The bitcoin price is far higher than that now.' Johnson noted.

'Yes, the price is much higher. I'm aware that investors, governments, and even regular folk are confused by bitcoin. They wonder how something that is based on thin air is so valuable? With most assets there's something to show for your investment, but bitcoin is different to assets like gold, silver, commodities and stocks because there's no hard underlying product or asset.'

'So, what about these leaks then?'

'We took care of them, don't worry. As an example, we had one employee leave to start a crypto exchange in Canada, and he threatened to reveal the CIA programme to the world.'

'What happened to him?'

'Let's just say that while he was on vacation in India, he had an accident he was unable to recover from.'

'Understood. Messy business. So, you say this started in 2007? How do you measure its success?'

'The idea inception was in 2007. We took precautions to make it seem as if it was created outside of the CIA. We created numerous false trails around the web as a means of misdirection. The first bitcoin trade that the public knows about was in 2009, with the genesis block. Back then, you could purchase bitcoin for a few cents. In 2012, it hit parity with the US dollar. Our measure of success is the list of criminals we have to apprehend over the years through their use of bitcoin.'

'Where do you see the price going now?'

'The sky's the limit. It could be $100,000 or a million. We don't know. The analyst who created bitcoin used to talk about it being a world currency, maybe even replacing other currencies in time. He speculated that bitcoin might hit ten million per coin if it became a global currency. Once bitcoin is fully mined, that could happen, but who knows?'

'This is incredible. However, I agree with you that the price would fall considerably if the public found out that the CIA created it.' Johnson looked concerned.

'Yes, it could happen. I imagine a huge amount of trust would be lost. Most of the criminal organizations using it would move onto something else. Probably, to something like Ethereum.' Tom motioned to a screen on the wall showing the prices of cryptocurrencies. 'Don't worry, Mr Johnson, we're hedging our bets on these, and there are a few other crypto currencies we're involved in funding. We syphon them through our shell companies or our agents, so people never know it's us.

'What about security and hacking? What kind of protection do you have in place?' Johnson seemed captivated as he watched the prices ticking over on the screen.

'Mr Johnson,' Tom laughed. 'The Central Intelligence Agency is the only one that can effectively manipulate bitcoin. We control the Blockchain and have the computing majority and required power. Nobody outside the CIA can detect it. Massive computing power is required to control bitcoin. Obviously, as the United States government, we are the only organization with the capability.'

'So, we, as the United States government, have hacked our own currency?'

'Yes, we do it all the time. To avoid directly funding terrorism as much as possible, we own and can manipulate bitcoin by returning confiscated coins when we apprehend certain groups or individuals. The public refers to this as a 51% attack.' We have seen the need for instances such as "double-spend" scenarios, where we con individuals or groups into believing we are transferring them large amounts of bitcoin when, in fact, it is a double-spend, and they will have something worthless. We can only do double-spends for extremely short time periods, though, due to technical limitations. Then there's the risk of the manipulation being detected by the outside world. As we control bitcoin, hold quantum supremacy, and have the computing power required, it means the outside world is unaware of it.

Watching Johnson's body language, Tom thought that the little fat man was coming around to the idea of the Quantum programme. 'It might not be evident to the outside world, but bitcoin has been so successful for the CIA that they have found direct correlations between the bitcoin price and the amount of illegal activity that the CIA and other government organizations monitor around the globe.'

'What do you mean by correlations? Are you saying that the Quantum supercomputer does analysis on this?'

'To see the correlations, you don't need a supercomputer, as it's pretty obvious. You could use Google and check yourself. Take, for example, when the United States puts sanctions on countries like North Korea, Iran or Venezuela. During these periods, the price of bitcoin sees a massive increase. The public could draw conclusions for themselves, but they and never prove them. With Quantum, the CIA tracks everything, and we see where who, and what is being done when a bitcoin transaction occurs. Countries with sanctions appear to buy into bitcoin each time they are hit to avoid the restrictions. They think they can trade using bitcoin when we see everything they do. Bitcoin is pseudonymous, which is as good as anonymous when trading on exchanges with no identification checks or transferring to another contact's wallet, peer-to-peer. Bitcoin, combined with our messaging and location tracking platforms and apps, have infiltrated criminal operations.

'Are you sure they have no idea? It seems as though you're saying the price increase has almost all been driven by criminal activity.'

'You're right. Most of the traffic is through illegal transactions. The CIA pick and choose the groups we go after. We would never round up everybody in one hit, as it would be too obvious and scare users away from bitcoin.' Tom picked up a piece of paper from his desk and passed it to Johnson. 'These are the successes this month.'

'I was sceptical when I came into this meeting, but what I'm seeing is incredible. The United States has created a fake currency worth a trillion dollars, and you can cherry-pick the targets you choose.'

'Cherry-pick would be one way of putting it. It isn't just governments that use bitcoin. It's the dollar of choice for drug cartels, arms dealers, and terrorists. For years, illegal groups have avoided money laundering charges through banks, and now we've given them the perfect platform to operate. We funnel criminal activity into a single place where we can control and see it. There's no more chasing hundreds of banks and filtering trillions of transactions. I liken bitcoin to a Trojan horse that we've inserted into the criminal underworld. We have also done the same with messaging platforms by creating apps that criminals believe are encrypted. Quantum can read everything they do in real-time.'

'But this could be a disaster if the cover's blown it?'

'We would deny it, Mr Johnson, just like we do with everything else. The CIA has been in bed with so many countries, cartels and terrorists, that even if it came out, it would be old news in a day or two. Take the Iran Contra-mess or Bin Laden as an example. The CIA trained Bin Laden and his associates for years. We brainwashed them to fight in Afghanistan against the Russians, eventually years later resulting in the biggest terrorist attack on the United States. Yet, the fact we trained them is a small footnote in history that nobody remembers. Besides, we've been running bitcoin for over a decade, and nobody has found out yet. We keep a small, close-knit group in the know. These agents comprise the Quantum team. Every so often, we throw out some fake news about the bitcoin origins or a mysterious founder to keep the press away. We are adept at handling the secrecy aspect. We even invite public figures, and bitcoin experts, to the CIA to give lectures on the dangers of bitcoin. It's the biggest joke ever. A few months ago, we threw out some data saying that the Russians created bitcoin. Six months before that, we did the same and said it was WikiLeaks. There's no way this is getting out. Any published reports claiming it was to do with the CIA would be discredited. And anybody outside the organisation that is in the know. Ahem,' he looked pointedly at his visitor, 'would be ruined—and then silenced before they could close their briefcase.'

Johnson nodded as he took in what the Deputy Director was telling him. 'Governments and monetary institutions are asking for the regulation of bitcoin,' Johnson observed, recalling an earlier meeting. 'How are you dealing with that?

'Regulation is not coming anytime soon. The CIA Quantum team use it to chase criminals for years to come. It will be an unavoidable part of the global future of financial technology.'

'You don't think regulation can harm your success?'

'Bitcoin can't be regulated. It's seen as decentralized and doesn't get impacted by country borders. If a country tries to take down a bitcoin exchange, it moves to a new country. We financed the creation of many of the bitcoin exchanges by the way. Even our own CFTC and IRS can't agree on what bitcoin actually is.' Tom laughed.

'They would be fuming if they found out that a branch

of their own government created it.' Johnson mopped his brow. 'This is a lot to take in.'

'Trust me, Mr Johnson, bitcoin is the best programme the CIA has ever created, and I've been involved in a lot of others over the decades.'

'I'm going to need to see some in-depth case examples of your biggest convictions over the last few years. I can review them here if you can arrange an office for me.'

'Of course, I'm aware of your mandate from the President, and your security clearance, so we'll be happy to arrange that.'

'Thank you, that's much appreciated. I'd like to start right away if possible.' Johnson stood up.

'Of course. And, in conclusion, I'd just like to reiterate that the Quantum project is the most successful programme for breaking terrorism, crime and state-funded activities we've ever had,'

'Thanks for the overview.'

'Thanks for visiting. I'm aware you have been handed a tough task by the President, and I'm here to answer any questions you have.' Tom recalled the old saying, keep friends close, but your enemies closer, as he shook Johnson's clammy hand.

'One last thing, Deputy Director. Who is Satoshi Nakamoto?'

Tom peered at Johnson. 'Satoshi Nakamoto was a pseudonym we created at the beginning of the bitcoin project.'

'Not a real person then?' Johnson pressed as he stood at the door.

'I can confirm that Satoshi Nakamoto does not exist, Mr Johnson.'

'Okay, thanks. I had to check, as I've read a lot about him in the press. I noticed that Satoshi Nakamoto's last recorded message was on March 7th, 2014. The following day he was reportedly on the Malaysian Airways 370 plane that disappeared. I take it the CIA didn't locate Satoshi when he sent that final message and then had his plane disappear?'

'That wasn't us.'

'Really? How odd. Have a good day, Deputy Director.'

CHAPTER THREE

The men stood to attention and started toward the end of the vast, empty runway. Their uniforms were perfectly ironed and aligned, from their mirror-polished shoes to their hats. Behind them, military vehicles, including tanks, rows of howitzers, dated Russian MIG jets, and armoured missile carriers, were neatly parked. Their green military paint glistened in the bright sun. In the distance, the foot-hills stretched towards a mountain range speckled with patches of forest. At the foot of the brown, rolling hills was a small town, dwarfed by the snow-capped peaks.

The men stood on a beige wooden platform in order of rank. It creaked whenever a gust of wind rolled in over the mountains. Many had chests covered in medals. Among them were some of the most senior and feared individuals in North Korea. They were heads of the Airforce, Army, and Navy and had served their country for decades.

The request for the parade had, come last minute, late at night, a summons to witness what was hailed as a historic event for the North Korean nation. The platform was covered by an open-sided tent to protect them from rain and wind. The group wouldn't need the cover that afternoon, though, as the sky was crystal clear. The weather forecast was perfect for the event they had gathered to witness.

A simple wooden desk and a black chair were placed at the front. On the desk were a large pair of binoculars, a map, and a lamp. The chair next to the desk was empty, and the men waited for somebody to fill it. There was tension in the air as the senior members of the ranks spoke to each other in whispers.

Behind the front desk was another row, arranged neatly. These desks were white and covered in fibre, Ethernet, and other cables. Each had a computer monitor and other devices, some beeping in unison. There were rows of flashing lights on units covered in buttons that looked like they belonged in 1970's Soviet Russia.

The men working at them wore white lab coats. There was no rank or file between them, as they scanned their computer screens and hammered on keyboards as if their lives depended on it. The project being processed by the scientists was the culmination of months of hard work. Many of the group were suffering exhaustion. Everybody knew how much was riding on what they demonstrated. It had to be a success, or not all of them would live to see the sunset.

As the scientists worked, one young man stood up and pointed into the distance. To the left of the runway lay an old, rundown airport building, and beside it was several aircraft hangers. The airport was long derelict, with broken windows and peeling paint. Part of the control tower had collapsed.

'Look over there.' The man pointed in the direction of the hanger.

The rest of the workers peered over their monitors for a second to watch the convoy, then, with eyes down, they worked faster than before as they made their final system checks.

A senior dignitary wearing spectacles was older than the other men. He inspected the group of scientists and asked, 'Is your section ready for the test?'

'Guidance systems are throwing up some errors, but we'll have it fixed in a few minutes.'

The men in uniform stood to attention and watched the convoy approaching. There were six vehicles, including two military trucks at the rear filled with elite soldiers of the North Korean Supreme Guard Command. The regiment was the best of the North Korean Military. It made up the three hundred-strong group of personal bodyguards to the Kim family.

Talk between the soldiers on the platform hushed to whispers as the convoy drew closer. When it reached them, one of the cars stopped in front of the red carpet. The car was a new Mercedes S-Class, it sat low to the ground, indicating that it was modified to be bullet and bombproof.

Two men in suits emerged from the lead car and hurried back to the Mercedes. As they ran, they scanned the horizon for threats.

A bodyguard opened the door of the sleek, black Mercedes. A man stepped out and looked around.

He was overweight and wore a long black coat. His black hair was slicked on top and shaved around the sides, and he wore glasses. With his rounded cheeks, he was visibly one of the youngest men present. One of the officers walked the red carpet to greet him.

'Supreme Leader, welcome to the test launch,' he said, bowing. 'It is the greatest honour to have you here today to witness this great event.'

The man greeting the Supreme Leader was General Jang. He had led the development programme of the missile to be tested. The rocket was larger than anything that had been previously tested by the North Korean nation.

Although there was no payload in today's test rocket, the missile was designed to carry nuclear warheads. It would eventually deliver them to any destination on the planet as dictated by the Supreme Leader. North Korea had been ramping up its aggression towards other nations. Having a working nuclear arsenal was the ultimate bargaining chip for Jong Un on the international stage.

The Supreme Leader, Kim Jong Un, said nothing as he walked past General Jang and looked at the men gathered under the tent. He strolled across the red carpet, taking in the distant mountains and the rows of desks and computer equipment. Stepping onto the platform, he walked to the desk at the front. Two of his bodyguards followed and were joined by eight more from the convoy. Positioning themselves around the desk, they were ready to take on any threat to their master.

The two trucks carrying the soldiers from the Supreme Guard Command had pulled up on either side of the tent. Heavily armed, the unit disembarked and took up defensive positions on the perimeter of the gathering. Orders were barked by their Commanding Officer, and they stood to attention, facing outwards and scanning for potential threats.

The Supreme Leader sat at the desk. 'This launch was delayed for two months, and I expect this to be a success today.'

General Jang spoke through a gap between the bodyguards. 'Yes, Supreme Leader, we have made many advances with the extra time you have so kindly allowed us.'

'How are the conditions?' The Supreme Leader scanned the sky.

'The wind has dropped, and we have zero cloud cover giving us perfect conditions.'

'Very good. No excuses for failure this time,' The Supreme Leader said without turning to face the terrified General.

'Yes, Supreme Leader. This is Chief Scientist Park

and Chief Scientist Lee,' Two scientists stepped forward and bowed.

'I trust you are the best scientists we have?' said Kim Jong Un.

'Yes, Supreme Leader,' Jang said. 'They will make the nation proud.'

He thought back to their last demonstration a few months before. It didn't go well. The rocket launch failed, and the scientists responsible had been executed on the spot. Park and Lee were the best scientists they had, but only because most others had been beheaded. He shuddered at the consequences of another failure.

'Good. When do we launch?' asked the Supreme Leader, picking up the binoculars and staring at the rocket in the distance.

'Awaiting your command, Supreme Leader,' said Park, bowing again.

'Well, go on then. Launch it,' Kim snapped at Jang.

'Yes, Supreme Leader. Right away. Three minutes to launch, Supreme Leader.'

Park and Lee reviewed the monitors as final checks on the rocket were carried out.

Kim Jong Un gazed across the bare, expansive airfield. At the end of the runway, there was a rotating red light. The Supreme Leader surveyed the area surrounding the rocket and into the sky.

Next to the red light was a large structure covered with scaffolding, pipes, and cables. It was the same missile launchpad used during the failed launch eight months ago. It housed a Hwasong-12 missile, fifty-five feet high and weighing twenty-five tons when fully loaded with its warhead.

A siren sounded in the distance.

'Supreme Leader, we have two minutes until launch,'

General Jang announced, lowering his binoculars to watch the launch pad's progress.

'This will be a glorious day. The Americans will be watching,' said the Supreme leader as he looked to the sky.

Kim Jong Un knew the Americans watched every launch report in American media which usually came out within minutes of test launches by the North Korean nation. The Americans wanted to prevent Kim from obtaining an intercontinental rocket.

The North Koreans had been testing short and medium-range missiles and their progress was swift. Massive funding was channeled into the missile programme, often at the expense of food for the starving poor of the nation. Millions of North Koreans had suffered. All due to the missile programme. It was Kim Jong Un's obsession.

The North had landed missiles off the Sea of Japan. In some cases, they had even fired over Japan. Asian countries such as Japan, Thailand, Taiwan, and most notably, their neighbour, South Korea, were nervous about the increasing success of the North Korean missile launches.

Having a successful long-range rocket for Kim Jong Un would be the pinnacle of their endeavors. He perceived the creation of the missile as the ultimate goal for North Korea to gain respect and a strong position in global matters. He wanted a rocket in his arsenal that could strike Washington DC if needed. It would be the thorn in the side of the Americans and the perfect bargaining chip for North Korea on the world stage.

'One minute until launch.' The scientists checked the launch parameters and data.

'What will be the range of this launch?' The Supreme Leader snapped at Park.

'We are aiming for three thousand kilometers, Supreme Leader.'

'Twenty seconds until launch,' Lee shouted from the back of the tent.

The Generals and other dignitaries were silent, watching the giant structure and massive Hwasong-12 missile. The military elite knew that a lot was riding on the launch. Some had seen failed attempts before, and the after-effects were never pretty.

One of the junior scientists shouted the final countdown, 'Ten, Nine, Eight, Seven, Six, Five, Four, Three, Two, One.'

The Hwasong-12 rocket started its engines at five seconds with a roar across the airfield. As the countdown ended, there was an enormous blast of powerful engines and a flash of bright light. Some of the men winced at the roar as the rocket shuddered. The brightness of the explosion forced them to shield their eyes. The Hawsong-12 was slow to lift, but it accelerated, rising as it gathered speed and blasted into the afternoon sky.

Cheers erupted as they watched the missile arc east. The Supreme Leader didn't flinch; he was focused on the rocket through his binoculars.

'One thousand, three thousand, six thousand,' a junior scientist called out, quoting the rocket's gain in altitude.

Jang was still and stone-faced. He knew it was too soon to celebrate as he watched the rocket go higher into the sky.

They watched the rocket's separation as one of the booster components tumbled back to earth. The missile moved drastically off course. Flames blew from the side, and a booster section appeared to break away as the fire increased in size. Seconds later, the rocket exploded.

The cheering stopped. The fireball in the sky was massive. The rocket had been fully fueled to travel far out over the Pacific Ocean before it would eventually crash into the ocean. Debris from the rocket was visible all over the sky. Streaks of rocket fuel burned as it fell through the atmosphere. It presented as an American July 4th firework display.

The Supreme Leader was motionless, looking through his large binoculars. The disintegration took place above them, and parts rained on the earth below. Everybody in the tent was on edge as Kim Jong Un was famous for the rage he unleashed when somebody failed him. Failure meant that they had disrespected him and the North Korean nation.

The Supreme Leader lowered his binoculars. The Supreme Guard Command unit around the tent moved closer to the raised platform.

'General Jang, you have not only failed me, but you have failed the North Korean people. What is your excuse?'

'I don't have an excuse, Supreme Leader.' Jang shook. He knew what was coming.

'Step forward,' demanded the Supreme Leader, motioning to Park, Lee, and General Jang. 'Who is to blame?'

Jang and the scientists stepped forward. 'Supreme Leader, we can build you another rocket. The next one will be bigger and go farther than this one. It will not fail.' This is just a blip.

'Anything would go farther than this one,' Kim Jong Un yelled, motioning to the sky. The debris was still falling.

Jang fell to his knees. 'Please, give us another chance. Three more months.' He had his face to the ground and his arms outstretched in supplication. He thought about his family and what would happen to them because of his failings.

Lee and Park joined him on their knees. 'Supreme Leader, with more time, we can perfect the rocket and fix the issues. This was only the second prototype. We will take today and learn from it. We can make adjustments—

minor adjustments, that's all it requires. We are so close to our technology being able to strike America,' Park begged for his life.

The Supreme Leader motioned to his guards. Lee moved forward and grabbed the Supreme Leader's trouser leg. 'Please, just a few more weeks.' A guard slammed the butt of his machine gun into Lee's head with a crack.

'You do not touch the Supreme Leader!' yelled the guard as he stuck Lee in the side of the head again.

'I've given you enough time.' Kim Jong Un nodded to another of his guards. The guard raised his weapon and fired at Jang, Lee, and Park, killing them instantly. The rest of the tent was silent, not daring to move. One of the young scientists had seen enough and tired bolt from his desk onto the runway towards the hills. The Supreme Guard Commander looked to the Supreme leader, waiting for instructions. After a nod from Kim, he pulled his handgun and shot the fleeing man.

'You. Come here,' Kim Jong Un said, motioning to one of the terrified scientists. 'What went wrong with the launch?' He knew he wouldn't get the truth from an officer or more experienced scientist. They were yes men and would say anything to save their lives.

'The navigation systems don't work, Supreme Leader. And the propulsion failed.'

The Supreme Leader scanned the tent. 'General Chong, step forward.'

General Chong was younger than the other generals and was the new breed of ultra-loyal senior leaders that Kim Jong Un had brought up through the ranks since he had taken over from his father.

'I am tasking you to take over as leader of the rocket programme. I want a fully operational long-range nuclear missile in three months, and it will be tested here.'

Chong bowed and saluted the Supreme Leader. 'I would be honoured to serve you and the Korean people in this important task. I will not fail.' He glanced at the body of General Jang next to Park and Lee and contemplated what his own future would look like if he did.

'Use any means necessary. You have the full use of North Korean resources to get this done.' Kim Jong Un walked off the platform to his vehicle.

'I will not let you down, Supreme Leader. You will have the greatest rocket the world has ever seen,' Chong called out after Kim Jong Un.

The Supreme Leader walked across the red carpet back to his waiting car. He climbed in, and a guard closed the door. The blacked-out window of the Mercedes slid down. 'Three months, and we'll be back. I trust you know what failure means?' The window closed, and the convoy departed.

The scientists and the generals watched them stir a cloud of dust as they drove into the distance and out of sight. There was a collective sense of relief that they survived, even if it was only for three more months.

Chong turned to the young scientist. 'Can we rebuild in time?'

'I don't think we can, General. We don't have the resources or the technology.'

'Damn it.' He slammed his fist on one of the computer monitors.

'Unless we could buy the parts we need and modify them for our rockets.'

Chong thought for a second and smiled. 'What is your name?'

'It's Yang,' said the man as he bowed in front of the General.

'Okay, Yang. I need a list of parts and detailed descriptions of the equipment you need to make this a success.'

'It's a long list, but two key parts will be critical and hard to find. What about the sanctions?' Yang was worried for his life after what he had seen.

'Our agents overseas have contacts that can procure parts. We'll put the word out and see who comes forward.' General Chong felt more optimistic.

He knew that it was a challenge in the timeframe he'd been given, but it was possible—lives depended on it. He was chosen by the Supreme Leader over all the other men in the tent for a reason. For now, he would hold a lot of power over the others. If he was successful, he would be hailed as a national hero and rewarded with a seat at the governing table with Kim Jong Un himself. Failure was not an option, and three months would pass quickly.

CHAPTER FOUR

It was 2017. Rich was driving down the freeway with his fiancé by his side. It was a fantastic weekend of sunshine, wine, and lots of sex. He looked at Julia with her blonde hair flowing in the wind as they headed back to San Francisco. They had been visiting Julia's parents for the week, and it was a whirlwind of a trip.

Towards the end of their visit, they needed a break from family. They left San Francisco to visit Napa for some wine-tasting. The weather was fantastic, and it was nice to get out of the city for a couple of days before they went back to the East Coast.

In Napa, they stayed at a quaint vineyard surrounded by rolling hills of vines, waking up late and having breakfast overlooking the vineyards. They filled the days strolling around the town and eating at the best Napa restaurants. It had been a memorable weekend. But now, they were leaving Napa and taking the highway back to reality. In a few days, they would be back at work. They left the hotel late and drove to San Francisco in their hire car.

'Feeling a bit better now, babe?' Rich enquired, resting his hand on her tanned leg.

'The Bloody Mary sorted me out just fine.' Julia threw her head back, laughing.

'God, you're beautiful. I'm a lucky man. I can't keep my hands off you.'

'I can't wait to tell my parents.' She touched his arm and pushed a big wisp of blonde hair away from her face. 'It's a beautiful ring, Rich.' She leaned across and kissed him on the cheek.

He hadn't meant to propose until they were on holiday next month. However, instead of waiting, he'd got carried away during a moment of passion. They'd stopped for a picnic among the vines on a walk through the Napa hills. He was tipsy from the wine-tasting, and she looked so damn hot in her low-cut flowery dress that day but, whatever the reason, he didn't want to wait and popped the question, there and then.

Julia said yes right away, and since the proposal, all they had been able to talk about was planning the wedding. As for the honeymoon, they were stuck between the idea of Bali, Italy, or having it in Napa, where he'd proposed. It hadn't always been carefree and happy weekends for Rich and Julia, but they were in a good place now.

'I think Bali is too far for everyone,' Rich said as they kicked ideas around. "I think Italy would be great. My friends from Europe can get there easily.'

'Sir, would you like me to check availability at Italian hotels for you?' chimed in a woman's voice from Rich's phone that was clipped to the dashboard of the car.

'No thanks, not now, CATHE.'

'What the hell, Rich. I thought you turned that damn computer off.'

'Sorry, I thought I did. I was testing out some of CATHE's voice surveillance features. We made some cool upgrades to CATHE recently.'

'You know that computer freaks me out. I feel like it's always listening to us and watching us. Sometimes, I think you love that thing more than me.'

'Sir, I sense some tension in your passenger's voice.

Should I play some soothing music?'

'No, not necessary, CATHE.' Rich laughed.

Julia folded her arms in protest.

'Sorry, Julia, I'll turn it off. You know CATHE is a major project at work, and we've made some incredible breakthroughs. With the new artificial intelligence technology, I've been developing, we've ironed out so many issues and bugs recently. What CATHE can do now is going to really change things at work.' Rich was rambling and forgot how annoyed Julia was until he turned to her frowning face.

'Turn it off, Rich. I'm sick of hearing its voice.'

'Fine. CATHE, hibernate, please.'

'Hibernate confirmed, Sir.'

'Happy now?' Rich grinned. 'Now, let's get back to planning the wedding.'

'I know that thing and your work is important to you, but I don't trust it. What does the name CATHE stand for anyway?'

'COMPUTER ASSISTANT TECHNOLOGY HUB ENTITY.'

'Well, that's a dumb name. Anyway, talking of work, what was this big surprise you were going to tell me about? You sounded like you were expecting a big bonus this year?'

'Well, CATHE is part of the surprise, but since you don't like her, I think I'll keep it a surprise a little longer.' Rich loved teasing her. 'Trust me, it's worth the wait. It's going to change our lives for the better.' He grinned. 'We'll be able to have the wedding of our dreams.'

'You know, sometimes, you can be a right Mr Mysterious. Like this ring, for example. It's a Harry Winston ring, but it looks bigger than something Jennifer Lopez would wear.'

'Never you mind about that. Nothing's too good for my fiancée. So, where shall we have the wedding?' Rich tried to change the subject. 'I'm happy as long as it's with you. Yeah, I know, cheesy, but it's true.'

'We're not booking anything yet, so don't get carried away.'

'I guess you're right. Our parents haven't even met, so that will be an interesting dinner when we set it up.'

Rich wasn't close to his parents and barely ever saw them. He debated if he would even bother telling them about the wedding.

As they approached San Francisco, the traffic thickened. All the city folk were going home after their long weekend away.

'This is going to take us hours at this rate.' Julia checked her watch and huffed.

'It looks like it might rain soon as well.' Rich peered at the grey clouds rolling in over the city. 'This convertible Mustang is great for sunny Napa Valley weather, but not so much for a rainy San Francisco.'

'I'm chilly. Can we stop and put the roof up?' Julia reached behind her seat to try and dig out her cardigan from the pile of bags they'd thrown in the back seat.

'Of course. I'll find a spot ahead to pull over.' He checked his rear-view mirror and pulled to the side of the road. Pressing a button on the console, the roof hummed as it lifted over the car and clicked into place.

'Okay, off we go. Hopefully, we'll be home in time for dinner.' Rich glanced in the mirror and pulled into the traffic.

'Something up, babe?' Julia sensed that something had been bothering Rich for a while.

'Nothing, it's fine.'

Someone in an SUV behind them had been following them since they left Napa, and he was pretty sure he'd seen it during the weekend, too.

Julia was still cold, so she grabbed one of Rich's sweaters from the back seat. Back in the city, they drove through the rainy streets to Pacific Heights. Julia's father had been a wealthy tech entrepreneur in his day and still sat on the boards of several Silicon Valley companies.

The Pacific Heights area of San Francisco was the wealthy part of town. Julia's parents lived in a beautiful old mansion at the top of the hill. It was one of the most coveted addresses in San Francisco. Julia and her siblings had left home long ago, but her parents said they would never leave the house. The house was much bigger than they needed. It held too many fond memories. The house had seven bedrooms, so it was great for family events at Thanksgiving and Christmas. It boasted some of the best views over San Francisco bay.

'I'm glad to be home. I'm so excited about telling my parents our news.' Julia kissed Rich on the cheek.

'We're going to get soaked,' he said as they pulled up outside. The downpour drummed on the windscreen. 'It's really coming down now.'

'We'll be fine. It's just a short run into the house.' Julia opened the door, jumped into the rain hurrying ahead, and used Rich's jacket as an umbrella. As Rich jumped out and went to the Mustang's trunk to grab their bags, his phone rang.

'Rich, we need to meet. Something of critical importance has come up.'

'Where are you?' Rich looked around the empty street. His feeling of being followed hadn't been off after all.

'I'm in San Francisco. Meet me at the Golden Gate bar in 30 minutes.' I'll explain later. The caller hung up.

Julia watched Rich talking on the phone from beneath the porch.

'Who was that?'

'It was work.'

'Don't tell me you have to go into work now.' She grabbed his hand and held it tightly.

'Sorry, Julia, it's urgent. I won't be long, I promise.' He hugged and kissed her.

'Can't we at least go in and tell my parents the news first?' She fluttered her eyes, trying to convince him.

'No, I'd best not. But I promise I'll be quick. I'll pick up a nice bottle of champagne on the way back so we can celebrate properly. Take the ring off and don't tell them until I'm back.'

He wound down the window and shouted, 'Love you!' before pulling out down the rainy street. This sudden meeting bullshit was the reason he was glad to be leaving.

The meeting place was on the way to the Great Highway, on a long stretch of beach. He took the roads along the coast to catch a bridge view, which he never got bored of.

'I know you're there, CATHE.' He snaked around the winding San Francisco streets.

'Hello, Sir, I don't think this is the optimum route to your destination.'

'Thanks, CATHE, but I think I can manage this one.' Rich knew San Francisco like the back of his hand. His first few years out of Stanford, he worked in the city, so as clever as CATHE was, he wanted to take his own, more scenic route.

The hibernate command he'd given CATHE was to placate Julia. However, CATHE was always working in the background. When Rich created CATHE, he never imagined it would grow into the artificial intelligence technology it had become. It was an assistant, but in addition to that, it could track stock patterns, predict the weather, book restaurants and hotels, track vehicles and communications and vast amounts of data, plus do pretty much anything else Rich had been able to dream up as he went along. Most importantly, it tracked vast amounts of data making work more efficient and manageable for his team.

There were few cars on the road now.

'CATHE, play me some music. Classic 90s, please.'

'Yes, Richard.' The British Band, Oasis, came on.

Rich sang along. He was a terrible singer, but there was no one there to listen to him apart from CATHE, and she wasn't complaining.

'Sir, would you like me to check the area for singing lessons?' CATHE offered.

'Ha, ha, very funny, it looks like you are developing a sense of humour but no thanks, CATHE.' He tapped on the steering wheel, thinking about Julia and where he could pick up a bottle of champagne to take back to the house.

Even in the rain, the misty view of the bay was beautiful. Rounding the next corner, a black SUV was coming the other way. The SUV had no lights on in the rain. Rich flashed the driver, but there was no response. As the SUV drew closer, he recognized it from earlier, but it was too late. It veered towards Rich and clipped the side of the Mustang.

Rich lurched across the road, trying to steady the car. He went into a skid, and the Mustang crashed over the guardrail and descended towards the ocean.

The car crashed against the rocky hillside, bouncing him around inside. He was like a ragdoll. The car hit a tree and rolled twice, then smacked against more rocks and trees before it came to a halt next to the ocean's shore.

The light convertible roof was ripped off the car during the first roll. Rich's head smashed against the roll cage of the mustang. After that, his limp body was thrown clear.

On the empty road at the top of the hill, the SUV, with

its blacked-out windows, circled to where the Mustang left the road. Somebody wearing a long raincoat got out and looked at the mangled car below.

The Mustang was unrecognizable. There was no way anybody could survive the crash. Even so, they had to make sure he was dead.

The dark figure pulled an incendiary grenade from a jacket pocket, pulled the pin, and threw it towards the wreckage. The flashbang went off and set the car alight. The figure turned and went back to the SUV through the rain. As they got in, they made a phone call.

'It's done.'

'How was it completed?'

'Vehicle crash. Planned to shoot, but there was no need.'

'You see the body?'

'Nobody could have survived that crash. The car is in pieces and burning,' He looked at the smoke rising up the cliff.

'Well done. Come back for a debrief.' The man on the end of the line hung up.

The black SUV pulled away from the scene of the crash while the Mustang's wreckage burned. Down the side of the hill, twenty feet from the vehicle, Rich's body lay bleeding. He was mangled with massive cuts to his head. But he was still breathing. His phone was few feet away. Its screen shattered. CATHE registered the crash and the change in Rich's body functions and dialed 911 for help.

CHAPTER FIVE

Kim Jong Un was correct in his assumption that the missile launch was being watched by the United States. And the US wasn't the only country paying attention. China, Russia, Japan, and many other nations would be impacted if North Korea successfully launched a long-range nuclear missile. The nations were talking, comparing intelligence data, and passing news up their chains of command.

North Korea was a black hole for the United States when it came to intelligence gathering. The only successful surveillance the American military and intelligence agencies could do was to keep a regular feed from satellites above the country. North Korea was the only nation on the planet that the United States wasn't previously able to cover with ground intelligence. That changed with bitcoin, as the North Koreans used it for anonymous spending with their allies with no third-party checks.

There had been attempts to get agents into North Korea over the years. Nothing worked, and some of their agents had been captured, tortured and executed. Few made it into the country, usually through China. The data they gathered had proved useless.

Monitoring of the North Korean missile sites often showed increased activity a few days before a launch. The intelligence teams watching North Korea saw dozens of launches over the years. The sites followed the same routines. There was heightened movement around the area with trucks, people, and equipment being brought in. The launch preparations were obvious. It was as if the North Koreans were putting on a show for the world to see.

During Kim's recent test, the satellite intelligence room was jam-packed. A new, giant rocket was being test-launched, and it was no secret. A lot was riding on it; if the North Koreans successfully delivered an intercontinental rocket, world politics would take a drastic change in direction. The Operations Room was dimly lit by the giant wall of screens at the front. Rows of analysts faced the screens.

'We have good visibility with no cloud cover so far,' an analyst called out.

'Great, how long will the satellite view the site?' Tom asked.

Tom Thacker was a veteran of the CIA and Deputy Director. He had seen dozens of North Korean launches. Towering over everyone like a teacher watching a class of pupils, he barked orders.

'We'll have a continuous view today, sir. Satellites have been repositioned to provide coverage throughout.'

'Good job.' Tom removed his creased, grey jacket and rubbed his face with a handkerchief, thinking about how damn stuffy it was with all the extra people in the room.

'There's a convoy approaching the airfield, sir.'

'You think that's Kim?'

'High probability. The other arrivals have been there for two hours already.' The analyst tapped buttons on his keyboard, and one of the main screens zoomed in on the convoy. 'We know Kim likes to keep people waiting.'

'Yes, that's Kim's Mercedes. It looks like the launch is a go.' Tom watched as the convoy snaked between the aircraft hangers and the dilapidated control tower.

'Is the Mercedes data available to us?'

'Not yet, sir. Mercedes data feed is still not functioning.'

One of Tom's most successful intelligence operations had been supplying the two armored Mercedes S-Class vehicles that Kim Jung Unused. The surveillance system was embedded into the cars during manufacturing and had worked for fifteen months. One day it stopped when presumably their trackers had been detected. The data provided in those fifteen months was invaluable. The Mercedes had gone from Rotterdam, through Dalian, Osaka, Busan, and finally to North Korea. They used ghost ships and shell companies. The CIA had supplied the vehicles to Kim under the guise of a Russian arms dealer.

The convoy pulled up to a temporary tent-like structure, possibly on a raised platform. They watched troops unload from the trucks and take positions.

Tom marveled that they had the technology to read the number plates on vehicles. If Kim was eating breakfast, they could see what he had on his plate; the technology was that advanced.

'Can we identify the troops?' He pointed at the screen. 'Are they Supreme Guard?'

'Taking a look now.' The analyst zoomed in. 'Yes, they look like the Supreme Guard, sir, the same insignia. Based on the number of soldiers and uniforms they are wearing, I'd say that's an affirmative. So, it's either him or someone very close to him.' He's using his favorite Mercedes, too.

'That's good enough for me. It's Kim.'

'I agree, sir. He doesn't go anywhere without the Supreme Guard in tow.'

The agents kept their eyes fixed on the screens. Tom knew they weren't the only ones monitoring the launch. The Pentagon, NASA, and other agencies across the United States all had their fingers in the pie. Tom was pissed that Kim knew he'd got the world's attention. He was primetime viewing and relished it. He thought about the Super Bowl, popcorn, cheerleaders, and sponsored TV ads and gave a stifled laugh at the thought of Kim selling tickets or live footage to Fox News. He'd make a few million dollars every time he launched.

'Detecting thermal readings from the rockets, sir.'

Smoke poured from beneath the towering rocket. Bright yellow flames followed, and the rocket lifted off from its launch pad. The tall Hwasong-12 rocket accelerated upwards. Tom sensed technicians turning to see his reaction as the missile soared. He watched without emotion. He already knew the outcome. It was set months before when his agents supplied faulty components to the North Koreans.

'Look.' one of the junior analysts called out. 'I think it's failing.'

The rocket veered off course. After a few seconds, it blew apart. A bright white flash filled the screens and brightened the Operations Room. When the brilliance faded, it revealed millions of debris shards scattering and tumbling to earth.

'Well, safe to say someone down there's going to be in trouble today,' Tom said, cracking a wry smile.

A collective sigh of relief was palpable. At least for now, the world was safe from the nuclear threat from North Korea.

'Great work, guys. The cover was perfect.' Tom patted one of the analysts on the back as he walked past.

'Yeah, until next time. Though, I imagine it'll be six months, or even longer, to rebuild a rocket that big,' another man chipped in.

Tom drank his coffee. Caffeine had kept him going the last few days, and he'd slept in his office in case there was a last-minute change in the launch schedule.

Tom picked up one of the phones on a desk near

him and dialed. 'The North Korean launch was a failure, sir.' Tom updated the head of the CIA. His boss's voice was stern.

'Was it the same rocket type as last time?'

'Negative, sir. Looks like a new proto. It was much larger, from what we can tell. Kimmie's getting ambitious. We are analysing the images. We'll compare them to previous launches and report.'

'Tom, we were lucky today.' The Head of the CIA paused. 'I don't need to remind you that North Korea getting a capable nuclear rocket is not something the President will accept. North Korea is not predictable like Iran or Russia. A preemptive nuclear strike might be necessary, and word is, it's the preferred response option from the President.' If that happens, it'll be boots on the ground in North Korea for the United States.

'Understood, sir,' Tom was nervous. A few faulty rocket parts were all that stood between peace and an all-out nuclear war with North Korea.

'Carry on with the disruption programme and keep me informed. I will be talking to the president and will update him.' The Head of the CIA hung up.

Tom thought about how it was back to the drawing board on the CIA's disruption programme. They had similar programmes all over the world. The North Koreans were top priority, given the potentially catastrophic outcome.

One of the analysts handed him a pile of folders. 'Here is the data we've collected from the images, sir. We sent you soft copies as well, but we know you like the old fashion feel of the folders.'

'Thanks, Sam. Can you get hold of Agent Reynolds and tell him to come to my office when he's free.'

'Right away, sir.'

Tom thought about what opportunities the current situation might present for him. Being a career intelligence officer, he'd spent years building his kingdom at the CIA. He wanted the top job. However, the current incumbent didn't seem to be going anywhere anytime soon.

The CIA had been watching North Korean agents around the world for decades. They were replaced and moved around regularly when they thought they were under surveillance. It made it more challenging to keep an eye on them. The CIA had significant success among the sporadic failures. Ironically, the regular launching of rockets over the last decade was beneficial for the CIA.

The President had significantly increased funding. As a direct result, the CIA had expanded in size, reach, and complexity of operations across the globe.

Tom's desk phone buzzed. 'Agent Rob Reynolds is here to see you, sir,' his secretary told him.

'Thanks, send him in.' As he waited, Tom flicked through the files and images.

Agent Reynolds came in smiling. 'Congratulations, sir. I just heard about the North Korean launch.' He shook Tom's hand.

'Thanks, I thought you'd be there to watch your handiwork.' Tom laughed, thinking how little the Operations Room knew about the rocket failure.

'Me too, but we had an urgent development on another operation and had to have meetings to pick up the pieces.'

'That doesn't sound good. Anything I need to know?'

'No, the resolution is in progress. One of our informants in South America was exposed. We believe he's still alive and being interrogated by one of the cartels.'

'What are we doing about it?'

'We're sending a team in to extract him, and hopefully, he'll still be alive.'

'Which cartel?' Tom pressed.

'The Sinaloa Cartel.'

'I see. Make sure it's an American rescue team but with nothing to tie it back to us. They're slippery fuckers down there, as I'm sure you know, but nothing can be traced to our involvement. We never know who is going to be our friends down there.'

The CIA had been in bed with various regimes, cartels, and terrorist organizations in South America for decades. There were embarrassing scandals from time to time. The Iran-Contra affair and the dozens of leaders the CIA had put in power or removed. Regime change was a popular party game. The United States had done deals with every cartel, rebel organization, or corrupt military leader in South America, depending on what would further the United States' interests, deals were done daily. It was when things blew up that they got twitchy. If the public got a whiff of what the CIA was doing, it always created a stink.

'So, Reynolds. Your team did well this time.' Tom picked up a couple of the photos and flung them across the desk to him.

'Thanks, sir. Wow, this is a big fucking rocket. It's way bigger than anything we've seen them build before.'

'Exactly. Even with the faulty parts, we supply them, they are making progress. We can still let the North Korean's have a few successful, smaller launches, maintaining their trust in our undercover agents and suppliers. Still, we can't let one of these intercontinental rockets get off the ground.' Tom stood up and walked to the window, gazing out to the forest.

'Completely agree, sir.'

'The North Koreans are going to come looking for components again soon, Reynolds. Have your teams ready.'

'Yes, sir, I'll reach out.'

'We've got to be careful. If the North Koreans suspect that our agents or friends overseas are supplying parts that deliberately sabotage their launches, they'll close ranks and try to build their own rockets.'

'I agree with you, sir. Five years ago, they were building 50% of the rockets themselves. Now, we estimate that's closer to 70-80%, with only the most complex parts being sourced from overseas.'

'Brief the global teams, and I want to know the second someone starts sniffing around. We need to ensure our disruption programme continues successfully,' Tom said sternly.

'Yes, sir.'

'Quantum will give us hits on data when the Koreans try to procure components.'

'You know my feelings on Quantum.' Reynolds smiled. 'I still believe in old-fashioned groundwork but let me know if anything comes up.'

'What are your sources saying about the hacks on the oil pipeline? Do they think that's the North Koreans as well?' Tom asked.

'The North Korean's have increased their hacking capabilities recently. They have been targeting banks, financial exchanges, hospitals, dams, and even the power grid. They have been remarkably successful.' They couldn't care less if they get caught, which makes them more dangerous.

'So, it is the North Koreans then?' Tom pressed.

'We're not sure at the moment but will keep on it. The North Koreans aren't far behind the Russians and Chinese and are getting significant backing from them to improve their capabilities. I think this one's more likely to be down to a Russian entity, judging by the way they were using ransomware.'

'Is this a hunch, or do you have proof of the

connection?'

Reynolds paused. 'It's a hunch at the moment. We can't prove it. But signs point towards my theory being correct. The way the North Koreans carry out their activities mimics the Russians' methods and Chinese methods.'

'Okay, keep me updated. This is something the President will need to hear if it's proven. I have some calls to make, so I'll let you get back to your South American problem.'

'I'll leave you to it. Oh, and sir, I see bitcoin hit a new record today.' Reynolds grinned. 'Has there been any news on that exchange hack from a couple of weeks ago?'

'The investigation is ongoing, but I'm sure you have read the press reports. Several exchanges and companies were hit in the attack. Whoever it was, got away with almost 1.5 billion dollars' worth of bitcoin.'

'There are rumours that it was also the North Koreans. They seem to be getting everywhere. Did you hear anything?' Reynolds asked.

'I've heard nothing, but we have a team working with the NSA and other agencies to trace the attackers. Now, is there anything else, Reynolds, or can I get on with my day?'

Reynolds sensed Tom's irritation. 'Nothing else, sir. Have a great day.'

Tom smiled as he sat back comfortably, glad to be rid of Reynolds. He knew the North Koreans did the hacking because the Quantum team had tracked it to them with ease. Reynolds, and almost everybody else in the CIA, wasn't aware that the CIA had created bitcoin. His clearance didn't stretch that far.

The hacking had perfect timing. After their failed launch, the North Koreans needed the rocket parts, and the Quantum team knew how much they would be willing to pay. Letting them keep the stolen bitcoin and turning a blind eye to the hack meant that the CIA would maintain control of the flow of parts to the North Korean regime. As a result, another rocket failure would be on the horizon. In addition, the bitcoin fraud meant the CIA could track their flow around the globe and uncover more agents and suppliers.

Tom looked at the photos of the giant rocket, amazed that with the technology the North Koreans had available to them, it had got off the ground. The disruption the CIA had put on the supply of parts was subtle. Only small but vital parts were sabotaged. However, success wasn't going to last forever, and when their luck ran out, it would be catastrophic.

CHAPTER SIX

Rich's eyes strained against the light as he opened them. Wincing, he felt his beard itch as he moved his dry lips. His mouth felt like sandpaper, and when he tried to swallow, he couldn't. He stared at the sparsely furnished room's ceiling and tried to focus, and as he did, he coughed repeatedly. Where the hell was he? He felt like either he'd been hit in the head by a truck, or it was one hell of a hangover. His head throbbed, and he was about to throw up. What little light there was came from strip lighting and burnt his eyes. He tried to lift his arm to shield them, but nothing happened. Only his finger moved.

He squinted around the room. The walls were white or cream, maybe they were dirty, and there were shiny green plastic tiles on the floor. The bed had metal side railings, but they were rusty and broken. He saw machines on stands but couldn't fathom their purpose.

Small monitors and some kind of apparatus beeped, monitoring his heart rate. He couldn't remember ever being in a hospital before; however, he had recollections of watching a television programme where he'd seen similar medical devices.

He was alarmed and moved to try and sit up. He'd realized that although he'd remembered a TV programme, he didn't remember much else. His memories were cluttered and jumbled. He searched his mind, thinking hard and perspired as the panic took hold.

Where was he, and how had he arrived there, but most importantly, who was he? Laying in the bare room, he strained to put the pieces together. He tried to think about what he did the day before. He couldn't place the last time he remembered something—or anything. It was a blur. Looking for clues, he saw two security cameras pointing at his bed. He had no idea who was watching on the cameras.

He focused on what he could remember. He knew what a hospital is and what security cameras are. He'd remembered the names of items in the room after he'd focused. It took an effort to place them. Their names were on the tip of his tongue. A strange blankness returned to him. He looked for water, but there was nothing to drink.

***

In a dark room down the hall, a heated discussion was taking place. Two men studied their confused patient.

"I can't believe he's woken up," George Matthews said. Wearing jeans and a t-shirt, he was middle-aged with glasses and a balding head. 'We had a plan for this, but I didn't think we'd need it.'

The men had been watching the patient in disbelief. Being on the night shift just involved watching television and messing around on the internet until their shift ended.

'We've got to make the call,' Stuart said, standing in front of George to stop him pacing.

'It's 4 am on Saturday morning.'

'This is what we've been waiting for. It's what all the practice scenarios were for. The boss will be happy when we tell him.' Stuart tried to sound convincing.

'Okay, you're right. I guess those were our orders if

this ever happened.' The phone answered after a few rings, and an angry voice answered.

'This better be damn good, waking me up at this ungodly hour.'

Carl was lying in bed, shirtless. He had to fumble for the phone and was still feeling a bit drunk. It felt as though he'd only been asleep for a few minutes. A younger woman sleeping next to him stirred and rolled over.

'Sir, it's Doctor Matthews.'

' I don't care about your pompous-arsed title. What the hell do you want? Speak up.'

'Sir, the patient is awake,' George added, louder and with more confidence.

'What?' Carl turned on the bedside light. 'When? Did something change? What did you do?'

'Nothing, sir.'

'You must have done something. He can't have just magically woken up after all this time.'

'I swear we did nothing, sir. He just woke up fifteen minutes ago, and we've been watching him on the screens since.'

The other doctor, Stuart, was trying to listen in on the conversation.

'Has anyone spoken to him?'

'No. We've just been watching him. It looks like he might have fallen back to sleep, though.'

'I never thought I'd see the day. This is what we've been waiting for.'

'Shall I call Abigail?'

'Yes, do it. I guess now it finally begins.' Said Carl as he hung up the call. The possibilities ahead were mind-boggling, especially given developments on the news.

After over a year, the patient had woken up. He couldn't believe it. It was an incredible long shot, but one that might have a giant payoff.

'And?' Stuart asked as if he'd been waiting for eternity.

'We can start the programme.' George opened a battered metal cabinet. It looked as though it belonged in a High School locker room. He rummaged inside.

The men weren't strictly legal when doctoring, neither had a valid Medical Practitioners certificate. George was a medical student dropout and was kicked out of school for drunk driving. To make it worse, he'd been caught with a stash of marijuana when he was pulled over. That was years ago and distant memory. George was in his fifties and had worked for the firm for eight years. The organization wasn't aboveboard, but the money was good, and it paid the bills.

"Okay, so we go in and ascertain how he is. Remember, we tell him nothing if he wakes up again, but we'll assess his condition and wait for Abigail.'

Stuart nodded.

'You call her and tell her to get in.'

'Will do.'

George pulled out a doctor's coat from the locker and went to get a gun from his car, just in case things went wrong. He told the guards at the front of the building to expect Abigail.

Stuart was younger than George and was a real doctor for a few years until he was caught selling prescription drugs on the side. Unlike George, he had only been working for the firm since the patient arrived at the facility. Stuart knew very little about the patient's background. Whoever ran the place kept the circumstances around his arrival shrouded in secrecy. He knew not to ask questions. The kind of people he was working for didn't like questions. His job involved keeping the patient stable and alive.

It was mysterious and, despite his criminal record,

the past year had proved more comfortable and financially rewarding than any real doctor's job. So, he picked up the phone and dialed. After a few rings, a woman's voice answered.

'Hi, Abigail here.'

'Abigail, it's Stuart.' She sounded very awake, given the time of the morning. He had a soft spot for her formed during the long nights they'd spent together watching the patient.

'What's up? It's the middle of the night.' The urgency in her voice grew as she realised there were only one of two reasons he would call.

'The patient is awake.'

'What? This is another one of your pranks, isn't it?' Are you sure?

'No joke. He woke up about twenty minutes ago.' He realized his cushy job was potentially coming to an end. And yet, he felt close to getting some answers. The patient had just woken up, but he didn't know what that meant concerning him and his employment status. He hoped he'd be kept on, or there'd be no more long nights with Abigail.

She had been assigned to the job for a couple of reasons. She had a specific skill set within the organization— and—she bore a striking resemblance to the patient's ex-fiancée, Julia.

The plan was a long shot from the beginning. She was in place to be familiar to the patient if he regained consciousness. The end game. The goal was for the patient to wake up and provide information the organization had failed, to find out by other means. If they had recovered the data from another source, the patient would have been surplus to requirements and disposed of. In the past year, no other sources were found. The mysterious patient was their only hope. And with every passing day, they dreaded him dying from his sustained injuries. Being in a coma meant the potential for brain damage. So, even if he did wake up, what he knew might be buried forever in a mangled brain. Abigail was grateful her head wasn't full of such valuable secrets. She'd never given the guy more than a fifty-fifty chance. And now he was conscious.

'Okay Stuart, I'm jumping in the shower and will head in.'

'See you soon.' Why the hell did she have to mention going in the shower? Stuart watched the patient as a distraction from thoughts of the naked Abigail. The patient was restless. He lapsed in and out of consciousness and occasionally lifted his head, straining in an attempt to survey his surroundings. Stuart didn't know who he was or why he was so damn important. The organization had spent time and money looking after him.

George returned, dressed in his doctor's jacket. 'Come on, get dressed,' he said impatiently.

'Hang on. I just got off the phone with Abi.'

'What did she say?'

'Not much. She's coming in.' Stuart picked up a clipboard and stethoscope. 'Looks like the patient has fallen unconscious again. We'll take his vitals before Abigail arrives.'

Stuart and George stepped out of the monitoring room into the hallway had been decorated to look like a real hospital. There were posters on the walls and a couple of waiting room chairs with a small magazine table.

They had been given a set of questions to follow, almost like a script. And as they stepped through the door into the patients' room, they knew they'd better not mess up.

CHAPTER SEVEN

Throughout Western countries, it was well known that North Korea had been developing nuclear weapons for several decades. Moreover, for years, South Korea had been under threat from North Korea along with other nearby nations such as Japan. However, the war of words had escalated between North Korea and the United States in recent years. War in the East was imminent.

There had been many flashpoints and threats over the years. The North Koreans once released the videos of their troops firing at pictures of US President Barak Obama. They had fired shells at South Korean fishing boats to sink them. And the rhetoric was increasingly vitriolic with the election of the new US President.

It was common for western news reports to be shown poking fun at North Korea on CNN or the BBC. News anchors often joked about the North Korean missiles and their capabilities. The report about a rocket landing off the Sea of Japan or maybe hitting a North Korean village was common news. Since the North Korean missiles had become potentially nuclear-capable, though the tone of the reporting had changed significantly.

It wasn't a question of if, but when North Korea would build a rocket capable of hitting the mainland United States. Nowhere on the planet would be safe. General Chong saw his potential as a future high-ranking favourite of Kim Jong Un and intended to take full advantage.

After the recent failure of the Hwasong-12 rocket, General Chong now commanded the North Korean agents embedded in nations around the globe, including Africa, Asia, Europe, and the Americas. These agents carried out everything from money laundering, weapons trading, and even art theft. Their far-reaching criminal activity was aimed at circumventing the sanctions placed against their homeland. The money they earned was sent back to North Korea and was spent on expansion projects, like the rocket programme. They were brainwashed and believed in their leader and the success of their land.

The North had tin and coal coming from Africa, oil from the Middle East, and weapons from Russia, Iran and South America. The agents had a way around sanctions to get essential commodities. Word was sent for the new rocket requirements, to select suppliers who might be sophisticated enough to source them. Guidance system and propulsion parts for missiles weren't things you could pick up in your local Walmart.

What General Chong needed would come from a supplier with links to state-sponsored groups. He'd reach out to his operatives in the Middle East and South America first. Iran had always been an ally of North Korea and supplied parts. However, old Soviet rockets from the 1980s weren't going to cut it this time. What they needed was new world technology.

Doctor Sang had been an overseas agent for twelve years. Living in Columbia was an unusual decision after living in several countries in Africa. But he'd come to love it. There were thousands of North Koreans expatriated across the globe who were just like him. Individuals who worked respectable jobs, such as doctors, engineers and businessmen. They sent their earnings back to the North

Korean government to fund the crippled nation.

Doctor Sang wasn't just a doctor sending money back home. He was an experienced agent. He was proud to help the North Korean government bypass the sanctions imposed on them. Many nations worked towards the United States' downfall and were willing to supply the North with sanctioned goods. They included essential requirements to keep the nation going. The North Korean agents were also the main source of other things like whiskey, cigars, cars, and electronics that the elite in North Korea— and even the Supreme Leader needed a supply of.

As Doctor Sang was closing his practice for the day, his burner phone rang.

'Hello?' Sang answered cautiously. Only his North Korean boss had the number.

'Doctor Sang.' 'This is General Chong.' The voice was calm and measured.

The doctor gasped. 'General. How may I assist you?' The doctor's orders usually came from a central command that managed North Korean assets. A high-ranking General calling him meant something of high importance was going down.

'We need you to procure supplies.'

'Yes, of course, General. Anything to be of service to our great nation.'

'I hear you have been one of our most successful agents, Doctor Sang. The work you did for us last year was exceptional. Your record of delivering on missions is impressive.' General Chong flattered the doctor.

Chong referenced the secret, high-risk operation that had seen Sang and two other North Korean agents in Colombia successfully obtain critical spare jet parts from South America. The components were shipped to North Korea via South Africa, then through Indonesia. They were crucial in maintaining the handful of ageing squadrons the North Koreans called their Air Force.

'What do you need, General?'

'Our scientists failed the Supreme Leader with a rocket test that was not successful. The Supreme Leader has bestowed upon me the mandate to build a new rocket. We require a special set of components for this project to be successful.'

Sang logged into the dark web. The North Koreans had servers hosted worldwide. They changed them regularly and used them to communicate with their network of agents.

'Log into your messaging system,' said General Chong, with a sense of urgency.

'Yes, General. I'm doing that right now.' Sang tapped into a website about a South Korean all-girl pop band. It was the fake communication site for that month. Sang smiled as he logged in, thinking about all the websites set up to hide the intelligence agencies worldwide from prying eyes. Every country had them.

A message popped up in his member account. 'General, this is something I haven't seen offered before.' Sang removed his glasses after reading the request.

'I know, but can you get it?' replied General Chong. 'I've made the same request to multiple agents across the globe.'

Never one to be beaten, Sang snapped back quickly, 'Yes, General, I can get the required equipment.'

'Good to hear. I'll expect an update on progress every three days.'

'Yes, General. I will talk to my contacts in the cartels. We pay well, so they are accommodating. They have government contracts down here.'

'We will be paying in bitcoin instead of gold. It's easier to move around with so many eyes on us.'

Doctor Sang was happy with the bitcoin suggestion. Gold was a logistical nightmare for paying off the cartels. Cash was hard to come by for the agents, and the cartels only accepted US dollars. Buying fighter jet parts wasn't something you used a bag of cash to buy, and last time he'd had to deliver several trunks of hundred-dollar bills.

'Once you secure the parts and price, I'll call you and confirm how to access the bitcoin account for payment,' said the General. 'I'm transferring fifty thousand dollars in bitcoin for expenses and will transfer the rest on confirmation.'

'Thank you. I'll send a progress report at 5 pm daily over the communication site.'

'Good luck. This is the highest priority mission, so I'll be sending somebody to help you with the operation.' General Chong hung up.

Sang stared at his computer monitor. The procurement list was complicated and was going to test his ability.

GOLIS guidance system, read Sang. *VASIMR control system.* He didn't know what these things were or how the hell was he going to get them? The General was sending help, and he wasn't sure about that, either. He preferred working alone or with the contact who'd earned his trust. If he delivered these goods, there could be a big reward. He wanted to bask in all the glory—not a shared portion of it. Sang imagined being hailed a hero by the general and even by the Supreme Leader himself.

Sang had picked up contacts over the years working in South America. He flicked through his cellphone and looked at some of the aliases. He considered trying the Gulf Cartel. They were one of the Colombian cartels, but they had only been used for low-level deals in the past. Sang had purchased trucks from them and factory machinery, but not military equipment. They were reliable enough, but this job might be out of their league.

'Aha, Diego.' He could be the perfect man for the job. Diego was a ruthless and efficient operator and an expert in weapons technologies. Most importantly, he was an expert in shipping them undetected.

It was six months since Sang had last worked with Diego. He liked him, and they'd done some lucrative deals. Diego always delivered the goods. Diego had contacts everywhere, from governments to military and intelligence agencies, so if Diego couldn't find it for Sang, the chances were that he was screwed.

'Diego, free to talk?' The Doctor said as the phone answered.

'Doctor Sang, my old friend. Long time no hear. How can I help this time?'

CHAPTER EIGHT

While Doctor Sang was going through his contacts, General Chong was at his desk in despair. Slamming his hand down, he thought about how his fate rested in the hands of men far away across the globe. The General hoped he'd set the right wheels in motion. The leather chair creaked. His large, high-ceilinged office, the walls decked in rare artworks, lay in darkness except for the glow of his computer monitor. He starred at the data on the screen in concern.

The North Korean nation had been squeezed by recent sanctions. The General hadn't suggested they use bitcoin out of mere convenience. The fact was that North Korea didn't have piles of gold or cash to draw on. Apart from the digital currency, the coffers were bare. The nation's hackers had stolen billions from exchanges and individuals. But the bitcoins were being spent fast, and they needed far more and a constant source coming in. People across the country were starving. The army was held together by spare parts. Most of the money had literally gone up in smoke with the rocket programme.

The North Korean leadership had a lack of care for their people. Using teams of agents across the globe, they hacked, stole, conned and smuggled just enough funds back into the country to keep it functioning. The hacking programme had been successful, and bitcoin was their preferred payment method—and now their main strategy.

General Chong picked up his phone and dialed.' It's General Chong. I trust you know my remit from the Supreme Leader. I have a mission for you.'

'Yes, General. What do you need?' The athletic woman straddled a handcuffed, greying man in his late sixties wearing only a pair of boxers and a red ball gag in his mouth.

'We need you to procure parts for our missile programme. You are to work with another operative, named Doctor Sang. Location and mission details will be sent in the next 24 hours on the usual communication line. Ling, this is a top priority assignment. You need to do whatever it takes to make this mission a success.'

'Understood, General.' Ling held the old man still between her muscular legs.

'You will report to me. Good luck. I want you to keep a close eye on Doctor Sang. He's reliable, but he's old. Your reputation precedes you, so make sure he gets through this mission and that no harm comes to him.' The General hung up.

Ling threw her phone onto the bed. 'Apologies for the interruption. Now, where were we?' Ling pulled the man's head closer. 'Oh, yes, you kinky little fucker.' Ling strangled the man with a silk dressing gown belt.

The old man choked, struggling for air, and his body went limp. Ling dismounted in disgust and walked across the room to the safe. Men were so weak and predictable she thought. She was wearing black, thigh-high leather boots and a black corset. Her heels clicked across the marble floor. The old man had eagerly opened the safe to show off several prized and expensive artefacts to the tall attractive Asian woman he had impressed into bed. She'd said she wanted to lie on a blanket of money, and the old fool had fallen for it.

Ling removed a Rolex Daytona from the safe and put

it on her wrist. This wasn't any Rolex Daytona. It was the seventeen million dollar Paul Newman Daytona piece. A secret buyer had bought it at auction in 2017. Ling was an expert thief and tracker and had already lined up a buyer from China for the piece months ago. Seducing the auction house administrator a few weeks prior, to find out who the mystery buyer was, had been a piece of cake. Ling took other items from the safe, a Faberge egg, cash and a couple more Patek Phillipe watches. She closed the door and scooped the thousands of notes from the bed, stuffing them into the old man's sport's bag—sport, that was a laugh. He hadn't managed his stairs without panting. Pulling on her black coat, she dimmed the lights and left.

'Be quiet. He's had an exhausting night and wants to be left to sleep.' Ling smiled and pressed a finger to her bright red lips as she was greeted by two of the man's bodyguards outside the bedroom. She flashed the top of the corset under her jacket to distract them.

The guards watched her walk the hallway like a model parading a catwalk in a fashion show. Stepping outside into the crisp Swiss mountain air, Ling's car arrived at the front of the palatial villa on the shores of Lake Geneva.

'Take me to the airport,' Ling said to the driver.

'Successful evening?'

'Yes, very.' Ling looked at the Paul Newman Rolex Daytona on her wrist. 'We can dump the car by the airport. The flight leaves in two hours. We have a new mission.'

CHAPTER NINE

The white Cessna 414 dipped a sharp right as it skimmed across the lush green treetops and turned east, over the ocean. Narrowly avoiding United States Coast Guard patrols on the outbound trip, Diego was keen not to bump into them again. Having taken off from a remote forest clearing in Alabama, he flew his aircraft at low altitude down the coast of Florida to avoid detection. Miles of the open sea lay ahead en route to Honduras.

Diego had flown routes between the US and South America for years and had hundreds of successful missions under his belt. There had been the occasional crash or ditching in the ocean, but he was the best. He knew the secret landing fields, waterways, and islands across the Southern States like the back of his hand. The coastguard had grown more sophisticated in recent years, so such flights were few. Traffickers looked for more ingenious transport, even using homemade submarines, long-range drones, and GPS-guided unmanned torpedoes, but Diego preferred his Cessna.

Diego grew up on the streets of Columbia in the favelas of Medellin. Making it into your thirties was an achievement. It was a tough childhood. Diego's mother and sister were both murdered when he was young. Raising his two younger brothers, Diego had been forced to grow up fast. His father was in and out of prison and couldn't be relied upon for anything. He worked for the local drug gangs, so naturally, Diego followed his father into the business—it was a natural progression.

Since the 1970s, the favelas of Medellin were one of the most challenging places to live on the planet. With drug trafficking, paramilitary groups, and violence, Diego had learned to take care of himself and his brothers from a young age.

He killed his first man at fourteen. It was his right of passage into the gangs that roamed Medellin. From the day of initiation, he had retained his membership. He'd killed so many since, and most of their faces were blurred and hazy recollections, apart from that first kill. As a teenager being initiated into the gang, Diego had been sent to one of the drug houses for regular duty, believing he was there for a package drop. He puffed his chest out with pride when he was told he was being promoted. The head gang member brought out a man. He was struggling, with a bag over his head and dressed in an old jumpsuit. Diego was handed a gun and told to shoot him. He had no choice but to obey the order. He often thought back to that day, remembering his young, shaking hand as he lifted the gun to the man's head with the gang members egging him on to pull the trigger. The deafening roar of encouragement was too much, and Diego closed his eyes and pulled the trigger. He remembered the gang leader removing the bloodied bag from the man's head. Diego had shot his own father. His dad was branded a traitor for allegedly turning police informant.

Progression up the hierarchy was swift. He was violent, had no fear, and was loyal. The cartel leaders trusted him and gave him free rein to set up deals and bring them in the money that flowed into the cartel's pockets. He was a risk-taker and made the cartel a lot of money.

As the Cessna hummed low over the ocean, Diego

watched the breaking waves' white horses. They were hypnotic, and he was at peace. He checked the array of navigation instruments to determine his position. It all looked good. He'd be approaching Cuba soon and could relax. He did regular business in Cuba, and multiple countries in South America, so he had friends everywhere. He often stopped there to pick up or drop off goods and maybe stay an evening or two to party in the Havana clubs.

Out of nowhere, an aircraft buzzed above the Cessna. Shit. He took a sharp turn to port and peeled away from the other plane.

The Cessna's radio buzzed to life on the open channel. 'Identify yourself, unknown aircraft.'

Diego ignored the demand. He could see the coast of Cuba in the distance and would soon be home free.

'Identify yourself, unknown aircraft,' the order came over the radio again. Diego looked up at the red and white underbelly of the other aircraft as it followed his movements. He recognized the US Coastguard markings.

The chase was all part of the cat and mouse game he'd played for years.

Diego veered away and went lower to the water. He was lower than any sane pilot, especially from the Coastguard, would dare go. Water whipped up and sprayed across the Cessna's windscreen.

'Identify yourself, or we will be forced to take action.'

Diego laughed. He knew the Coastguard's aircraft was an Ocean Sentry used for surveillance. There was nothing the Coastguard could do apart from watching him fly into the distance.

As Diego's Cessna closed in on Cuba, the Coastguard tired the last request for identification before veering away and climbing into the sky.

Diego flew inland, over the rolling green hills and

beautiful mountains of Cuba. He looked at the trees and the sparsely strewn farmsteads as he passed low through a valley. There was no time to stop for an overnight party in one of his favourite Havana bars this trip. Time was money.

An hour later, just as dusk fell, he landed on a deserted airfield in the jungle. The stop in Honduras was his regular trip-hop. Given the range of his aircraft and the weight of his cargo, he had a few airfields dotted around the coast where he trusted the locals to keep their mouths shut. To avoid getting caught, he altered his choice of the airfields along the coast.

Taxiing to the fueling area, his phone rang.

'Diego, free to talk?'

He recognized the distinctive Asian accent. He could almost hear the money being counted as he spoke. The North Koreans paid well, which was surprising given their economic climate. With so many sanctions, they had little choice but to pay top dollar, especially as the work they wanted was riskier than smuggling drugs.

'Doctor Sang, my old friend, long time no hear. How can I help this time?' Diego applied the brakes and cut the Cessna's engine.

'I'm good, and you?' asked Sang. He half expected Diego to be dead or in prison with all the shit he got up to.

'You know how it is, playing hide and seek with the DEA. Business is good, my friend.' Stepping out of the Cessna, Diego was approached by an old man wearing a battered Panama hat. 'The usual, *por favor*,' Diego handed the old man a stack of US dollars.

'I have a job.' Sang spoke in a hushed tone.

'Shoot, my store is always open. A rocket engine this time?' Diego laughed at his joke. There was silence on the other end of the phone. 'Don't tell me you're going to ask me for a fucking rocket engine, are you?'

'How did you know?'

'Jesus, Sang, I was joking. I saw CNN a few days ago. You guys had another rocket failure. I was joking about you needing a new one. I hope you know there's no chance I can get you a goddamn rocket, right?'

Sang paused. It was a ridiculous request. 'It's not an actual rocket engine we need.' He knew it was going to be a big ask, but it's what the General wanted.

'Well, what then?'

'We need a GOLIS guidance system and VASIMR control system.' Sang read the message sent from General Chong word for word, as he had no idea what they were.

'Jesus.' Diego stopped laughing. The North Koreans would be willing to pay a fortune for that kind of gear.

'This needs complete secrecy. It's top-level. don't go to your usual contacts, Diego.'

'Parts like these don't grow on trees, Doc.'

'I'll transfer fifty thousand now as trouble for your time and for reaching out to your special contacts to see what you can find. We're using bitcoin, that okay?'

Diego laughed. 'Yeah, that's fine, Doc. Prices are only going up, so maybe I'll double my money.'

'Send me your wallet info, and I'll transfer it with the list of equipment we need.'

'Sure thing, and let's catch up again in a couple of days.' Diego looked along the runway, wracking his brain for where he might get such items. He had a sneaking suspicion he knew where they'd come from.

A message arrived on his phone. Doctor Sang had transferred the funds to him. Well, what a pity he didn't have time for that party night—he sure had something to celebrate. The transfer meant it was a serious request, urgent too, possibly desperate. Still, fifty grand just to do some digging was pretty good. Diego jumped into the cockpit of the Cessna and fired up the engine. He taxied across the empty airfield to the end of the runway. He'd be flying south to Colombia in the dark and as low as he dared. He didn't expect any trouble, and it would be an easy flight home.

Turning at the end of the runway, his final checks complete, his phone rang from an unknown number. 'Hello?' he throttled back and let the Cessna slow to a stop.

The voice was synthesized. 'Diego, I believe your friends have contacted you with a request.'

How the hell did this person always know? 'Yes, that's correct.'

'Can you confirm the details?'

'Yes, they want rocket parts,' replied Diego with a shiver. Nothing freaked Diego out except this mysterious person who always seemed to be able to reach him.

'I'm sending you a message. Reply with the requirements, and I will get back to you soon.'

Diego stared at his phone in disbelief. He put it on the seat beside him. He accelerated the Cessna down the runway, bumping over the grass strip, pulling back the column as he hit eighty-five knots. The nose lifted, and the ride was smooth. The jungle canopy rushed past beneath him.

As he flew over the jungle and then over the ocean towards Colombia, he thought how strange it was that the North Koreans had called and then his mystery person. How the hell had they known so quickly? Was he being tracked, and his communications bugged? That possibility rang alarm bells. But, this person had always proved helpful in the past.

The partnership, if you could call it that, started five years ago when a mysterious voice had called to warn him that the United States Drug Enforcement Agency was closing in on one of his operations. He hadn't believed it, dismissing it as a hoax, but one of his pilots was arrested in a surprise ambush on landing their secret airfield. Next, there had been a warning that the CIA and local Colombian police would raid one of the safe houses in the Colombian jungle. That turned out to be correct, as well.

All Diego knew was that the mystery person had proved themselves a dozen or more times and had both earned and saved him millions of dollars as a result of his information. He was under no illusion that the person or group of people had a motive and that whatever they were doing was bettering them. He was cautious and fully aware that the person or group's priorities could change and his usefulness to them with it. He'd always known that one day they'd want their payday.

His phone rang again as he Landed the Cessna in Colombia.

'Hello.'

'Diego, good news, it appears we might be able to help each other again.'

'Go on,' said Diego, switching off the Cessna's engine to listen.

'I can provide you with the location of the items you require,' the synthesized voice continued. 'We will split the funds. Fifty-fifty.'

'Split fifty-fifty,' Diego replied, laughing. 'So, just to be clear, you aren't selling these items to me. You are simply telling me where I can find them? I still have to pay for them?'

'That's correct.'

'Where are they?' Diego said, resigned to the fact there was little point in arguing.

'The VASIMR control system can be found at the SpaceX manufacturing plant in Los Angeles.' The voice paused as if waiting for Diego to cut in, but he didn't. 'And the GOLIS guidance system can be obtained in London.'

'So, it's going to be impossible then.' Diego laughed.

'No, it's possible, or I would not have called you back. I can provide a team of experts to join you with the procurement.'

'Join me?' Diego frowned. 'You expect me to go and get these components?'

'Diego, this is easier than most things you've done. For a hundred thousand bitcoins, this is going to be a big payday.'

He swallowed and felt sick with disbelief. 'But that's potentially billions of dollars, depending on where the price is.'

'Correct. We are talking about making a nation a nuclear power, and with intercontinental ambitions too. You're not trading a few tons of cocaine here.'

Diego realized that the person had a point. But then a stark reality hit him. 'The North Koreans won't pay that much. They'd be bankrupt.'

'Then they won't be a nuclear power. It's simple as that. If they want it, they'll pay. I will call you with the details over the next forty-eight hours. Make the necessary calls, Diego.' The mystery caller hung up.

Diego thought about the sheer amount of money involved in the deal. He could potentially make a billion dollars out of this. He had a feeling Doctor Sang might not be impressed with the price, but the North Koreans had greatly improved their crypto theft and hacking.

CHAPTER TEN

The fist smashed Brian across the face, and he sobbed. Brian was paid a lot of money for this by a mysterious contact, and he needed the money to start his new life. As the fist smashed across his temple, he certainly regretted some of his recent life choices.

The night out in Vegas had deteriorated fast. Fifteen minutes before, he had been having the time of his life. He was on the role of his life at the blackjack table. He had been banned from the casino ages ago, but with an appearance change, he was back and had a few tricks up his sleeve to keep winning. However, he didn't deserve such punishment. He regretted his decision to blag his way in so he could visit his favourite blackjack table. But he was there following strict orders he had been instructed to play there. Just remember what you are doing it for, Brian told himself as he thought about the money the mysterious caller had promised.

'So, you dared to come back. Did you forget we banned you?' The casino's security guard was muscular and had the hands of an old boxer. That's what they felt like to Brian, as the rough skin of a clenched fist sank into his cheek again.

'Please stop,' Brian pleaded as another punch landed on his face.

'This is the fourth time, Brian.' The Floor Manager pulled up a chair and sat down in front of him.

Brian played on the blackjack table for a fruitful two hours and amassed a wealthy pile of chips. He enjoyed the free-flowing alcohol the casino pumped into its patrons, a tactic employed by casinos to keep punters at the tables; get them drunk and fleece them. Brian bucked the trend and kept winning despite feeling woozy.

The waitresses were attractive, too, and he enjoyed the eye candy while he played. Brian was in the Venetian Palace. The Venetian was one of many casinos in Las Vegas that Brian was banned from entering. He had been a gambler for years. The casinos kicked him out for winning too much and because they'd all caught him cheating at some time.

That evening, his opening gambits were deliberately cautious, winning a little, losing a little, until he was intoxicated and let his guard down. He was getting paid to get caught, so he won so big that security was soon onto him. When the pit manager switched in a new dealer for the table, he twigged that they had sussed him. He knew the Floor Manager was watching him on the security cameras.

Brian listened as they talked over him, trying to gain an advantage or at least gather information for his employer.

'You sure it's him?' said the security guard to the Floor Manager.

'Yeah, it's him. Even with that crappy disguise, I can tell.'

The Floor Manager was called Vinnie, and he'd been in the industry long enough to know all the tricks. Over the years, working at the casinos around Las Vegas, he'd seen his share of cheats, bluffs, and robberies. You name it, he had seen it. And he'd seen Brian before too.

The casino had accumulated a long list of banned people, and it was Vinnie's job to know every face. 'I spotted the arrogant dick the moment he arrived.'

Rumbled from the start, Brian thought as he listened to them, maybe ginger isn't my colour after all.

'I considered plucking him off the floor. But I figured we'd wait and see just what sort of scam he was running.'

Brian thought back to his joyous outburst at the tables. 'Yes. I'm on a roll.' he'd yelled as his winning streak gained momentum. 'A few more hands, and I'm done.' He remembered the dealer's reply. "Yes, sir, well done, again."

The rest of the table looked on and in awe at the pile of chips he'd accumulated. Although punters had come and gone while he'd been there, at the height of his success, he was with some Chinese tourists and few British guys who were in Las Vegas for a stag weekend.

His jaw throbbed, and he stared into the venomous eyes of the Floor Manager as he recalled what had happened next. A waitress walked past his table, and he'd turned to order another drink. When he turned back, something caught his eye. Across the casino floor, two men in suits were looking at him.

He pretended he hadn't seen them, but a wave of panic crept over him as he realized what he'd got into. He'd played at the same table for two hours. He had broken his own game plan, a cardinal sin, which involved not drawing attention to himself. As a result, he'd made more money than the person had offered him to carry out the job.

Cutting and running wouldn't save his skin, but in a blind panic, that's what he did. 'Deal me out,' he'd said to the dealer. 'Come on. Hurry up.'

Gathering his chips, he saw at least two Security talking on their radios. They would be receiving orders.

He knew he should have gone for cool and calm and at least tried to appear innocent. He scraped his chips off the table into his bag. He couldn't have looked dodgier if he'd tried. He saw the looks on the Chinese faces, with their puzzled frowns and tight lips. Even they had figured out there was a card shark in their midst.

Now, he felt as though he ought to take over from the security guard and punch his own face—he deserved it. Tears of hopelessness welled up as he recalled how the chips flew everywhere. Then he ran. It couldn't have been worse if he'd written *SWAG* on his bag.

The casino floor was a mass of people, tourists, gamblers, and guests wandering around as curious bystanders. It was so crowded he thought he might have a chance of shaking off the guards and making it out of the building.

He lost sight of the men chasing him and ran around a car parked in the middle of the casino floor. It was one of the jackpot prizes, and from there, he could see the entrance.

He thought he would make it, but he made eye contact with one of the security team, who was pushing through the crowd to him.

Running across the casino towards the door, he darted around a couple of dollar slot machines. He was so close to making it out that he remembered the rush of relief sweeping through him as he felt the wind on his face. There was an old lady with a dog by the door. He decided to jump it. As he leapt over the miniature poodle, he felt a sharp pain across his chest.

As he jumped over the poodle, the massive arm of one of the casino security guards clotheslined him and knocked him to the floor. He might only have been unconscious for a couple of seconds, but when he came round, he was staring at the ceiling of the casino and at the face of a large, bald man.

'Let me go. Keep my winnings. I promise you'll never see me again.'

'Not this time, Brian,' The Guard said.

'Come on, I've done nothing wrong.' He groaned in

pain, clutching his neck.

'Yet, still, you ran?' The Guard laughed.

Vinnie arrived with two more security staff.

'Mr. Lewis, I see you've had a spot of bother. How about you come with us, and we can discuss this.' Vinnie nodded to the security team.

Two burly men scooped him up and dragged him away from the floor.

Brian was taken through a fire door at the back. Vinnie motioned to one of the security team. Snaking through the underbelly of the building, they dragged him into a dark room.

'Grab one of those chairs and tie him to it.'

A fist struck him across the face once again. There was no talking his way out of this.

'Brian, you're going to have to pay us back for all these visits,' Vinnie said.

'I don't have any money.'

'Don't be pathetic. We want the money. We want real money and none of your empty promises.'

It was a real long shot, but if he could be convincing enough, it might work. The mysterious contact that paid him to get caught cheating the casino had told him what to say—but Brian put his own slant on it.

'Okay, look. I know a guy. He's an old friend. This guy is really loaded.'

'Good for your friend being wealthy,' one of the security guards laughed.

'This guy had an accident. He's in a coma. Before that, he was some kind of tech genius.'

Vinnie stood up. 'You're a desperate idiot, kid. And, we're going to make sure you don't walk back into this casino again.'

The security passed a hammer to Vinnie.

'Wait. The guy's fortune is worth billions, but nobody knows where it is. So, it's there for the taking.'

'Billions?' Vinnie laughed.

'Yeah, billions. After the accident, they found records about all the bitcoins he'd bought up, but nobody knew where he'd hidden it. It's buried deep behind firewalls on the Darkweb or something like that. They are untraceable and his fortune has never been touched. Whoever finds them will have the key to billions.'

'Go on.'

'It's a bitcoin fortune. Do you understand what that means?' Said Brian trying to sound convincing in his story.

'Come on, don't screw with me. I wasn't born yesterday.'

'Wait, just listen. This friend of mine never used or sold his bitcoins, and given the current price, they're worth billions, I promise.'

'Nice try, kid, but I don't believe you and anyway, what would you expect me to do with this news?'

'You could break into his house. Maybe try to hack his e-mail accounts. Hell, maybe he will wake up one day, and you could kidnap him or something. I don't know, but the story is true. I swear on my life. The guy has been in a coma like a year and nobody has found the fortune yet.'

'Boss, bitcoin is really in demand right now. Even my wife keeps saying we should invest.'

'Whose side are you on?' Vinnie snapped at the guard. 'Look, Brian, I think you're talking crap to try and get yourself out of this.'

'This is all true. Think about it. You guys would be the richest in Vegas.'

'So, you're telling me that there is a fortune for the taking, but nobody knows where it is, and nobody can get hold of it because this guy is in a coma?'

'Yes, but if you found, think how rich you'd be.'

'Okay, Brian,' Vinnie said. 'Tell us more about this guy and which hospital he's in.'

'Untie me, and I'll tell you everything.'

Vinnie nodded to one of the security guards, who untied him. 'Write the guy's name, his home address, and the name of the hospital down,'

Vinnie studied what he'd written on a piece of paper. The Security guard pulled out his Smartphone.

'Boss, look, I googled him, and there are stories about this guy's car crash.' He showed Vinnie his phone. 'Says nothing about any bitcoins, though.'

Vinnie looked Brian up and down. There was blood dripping from his nose. 'We know where you live, Brian, so this better be true. You know what happens if it isn't, right?'

'It is, I promise.'

Vinnie handed Brian a tissue. 'Clean yourself up and get out.'

Damn, it was good to see daylight again as he stepped out of the casino. More to the point, he wasn't tied to a chair. He rang the number he'd been given by his employer.

'Hello, Brian,' said the synthesized voice. 'Did you do as I instructed you?'

'Yes, but I thought they were going to kill me.'

'That's a risk I was willing to take.'

'What the hell.'

'I'm transferring your final payment. Pleasure doing business,' and the synthesized voice hung up.

Brian opened his banking app, and the money had arrived in his account as promised. It had been a hell of a day, but it was worth it for the money. He had debts with all kinds of people. This amount of money was going to sort them all out.

***

Vinnie ran through the information Brian had used as a bargaining chip. Bitcoin was always in the news, and he knew people made a lot of money from it. There were stories of overnight millionaires from the new technology.

'What you think about the story, boss?'

'I'm taking the information up to Carl right now. If it's true, then we're going to need some guys.'

Carl was behind his desk, looking over the city of Las Vegas and flicking through papers of the casino takings.

Vinnie looked at the wooden lion heads carved into Carl's massive, mahogany desk as he stepped into the office on the top floor of the casino. He thought the office looked like it was out of a French Napoleonic palace.

'What can I do for you, Vinnie?'

'Sir, I've come across some information you might find interesting.'

'Okay, go on, what is it?'

'We caught a guy on our banned list playing downstairs earlier. So we took him out back to rough him up a bit.'

'Please don't let this story end with you killing him on-site? I've told you about that before, Vinnie.'

'No, nothing like that.' Vinnie shifted in his chair. 'He let slip something interesting.'

'About what? One of our competitors?'

'No. He claims he knows someone who has one of the biggest global bitcoin holdings.'

'Lucky guy,' Carl said sarcastically. 'And how does that help us?'

'The guy was in a car crash and is in a coma. Nobody knows where his stash of bitcoins is.' Vinnie watched Carl take in the story.

'Sounds pretty lost to me,' Carl replied.

'Sir, think about it. If we found the stash, it could be worth hundreds of millions, or even maybe billions.'

'Jesus, that much? That's an insane amount, and the cartel would be pleased if we brought in that kind of cash.'

'Exactly, you could build a new casino or buy the Bellagio.'

'You've clearly thought this through, so, what do you propose?'

'This is where he lives, and this is the hospital he's in.'

Carl took the paper and read the details. 'Bit of a drive, but I want you to take one of the guys and go up there to do some digging. See if this patient really exists.'

'Okay, sir, will do.'

'I never ignore information from a desperate man when he's begging for his life, so it could be genuine. Keep me updated.'

'Will do, boss.'

Carl took a puff of his cigar and fantasized about such wealth. It pissed him off that he wasn't a billionaire already. Some of the other casino owners were. With a few billion dollars to play with, I could run the city.

CHAPTER ELEVEN

The drive took Vinnie and his team ten hours, and despite a few comfort stops, they were exhausted. Vinnie was up-front with Bruno keeping him company, and George was asleep in the back of the windowless van.

'This better is worth it,' Bruno said, squashed in the front of the van and sipping on a 'Big Gulp' cup of soda.

'Hey, we do what the boss wants, remember? This is a big job,' Vinnie replied.

'So, what's the plan? We just going to walk in and grab this guy?'

Vinnie shrugged. 'Well, yeah, basically. Who the hell is going to suspect someone is being kidnapped from a hospital? When my mum was laid up a few years back, there was maybe one old security guard in the entire hospital she was in, that's all.'

Bruno glanced over his shoulder into the back of the van. 'Ten hours lying back there isn't going to be great for him?'

'That's why we brought George to keep an eye on him in case anything happens.'

'So, this guy in the hospital. What's wrong with him? And, how we going to wake him up?'

'Look, I have no idea, Bruno. I'm not a doctor. We just need to get to him first. Hey, Doc. wake up, we're almost at the hospital.'

'Here already?'

'It's been ten hours, George. How the hell do you sleep that long?', Bruno asked turning around.

'I might have self-medicated to get myself to sleep. So, what's the plan when we arrive?'

'You play your part as a visiting doctor. Since you were a doctor once, hopefully, you can pull it off. Do a bit of digging and find out where the patient is. Check his room and find out what kind of security they have. We'll wait a couple of hours until dark, then we grab him.'

***

Night fell, and George slid open the van door. 'Okay, guys, I'll call if I need help.'

'Good luck, Doc,' Bruno said.

There was little security in the hospital. The public, staff and patients were everywhere during the day however, after visiting hours, it had quietened down. George went to the main desk. There was just a young receptionist alone there. It was the perfect chance to get the information he needed.

'Excuse me, I'm looking for one of my old patients. A Richard Williams. Do you know his room number?' George spoke with authority, flashing a fake ID and knowing that a staff member or lowly nurse wouldn't question a doctor.

'Yes, of course, doctor. Anything else I can help you with?' she checked the records. Floor three, room 305.

'Nothing else. Have a good evening.'

The hospital was quiet at this time of evening. He arrived at room 305 and peered in through the window. The room was sparse, with a bed in the middle and a man lying in it.

George grabbed the door handle, went inside, and pulled the curtains closed so nobody could see him walking past in the hallway. There was a suitcase on a chest of draws and some belongings in the cupboard, including some clothes hanging up. George went to the patient and poked him. Nothing happened. He pulled out his phone and dialed.

'Hey, Vinnie, I found him. It's quiet. Let's just take him now. Come in the main door. It's the third floor, room 305,' George said, throwing belongings into the suitcase.

'Okay, we're coming up now.'

'I saw a wheelchair in the corridor near the elevator. Bring it with you.' He pulled open a draw to reveal a laptop, wristwatch, wallet, ID and an assortment of personal items from the patient.

'Will do. See you in five minutes.' Vinnie hung up.

George put the battered laptop into the suitcase with some other items. Vinnie and Bruno came in, pushing a wheelchair.

Bruno closed the door. 'Shit. A security guard is doing his rounds. He's coming down the hallway from the far end.'

'Well, keep quiet, and he'll walk past. Too bad hospital doors don't have locks.' George said.

The footsteps stopped outside the door. After what seemed like an age, the door handle began to slowly turn, and the security guard came into the room and looked around. 'What is going on here? It's well past visiting hours.'

Vinnie, on the opposite side of the room, nodded to Bruno behind the door. Bruno came down across the guard's head with the butt of his gun.

'Goddamit,' George said. 'Was that necessary?'

'Wait. This is perfect,' Vinnie said. 'Help me get his clothes off. We'll put the guard in the bed and the patient in the wheelchair. It might take them longer to figure out someone's missing.'

Bruno helped George with the undressing and switch. 'What about all this kit? Do we need any of it?'

'We're lucky he's not on life support, or that would have made things considerably harder. And, he wouldn't be waking up.' George looked at the machines around the bed. 'All we need is that one for now.' He pointed to a metal stand five feet high. 'It's for intravenous fluids and nutrients.'

'Okay, Doc, I'll take care of it,' Bruno finished putting the hospital gown on the naked security guard.

'Ready to lift?' Vinnie grabbed the patient's legs. 'Jesus, this guy looks dead already.'

'On three. One, two, three.' Bruno and Vinnie heaved the unconscious patient off the bed and into the wheelchair. Then they put the security guard into the bed.

'Perfect. Good job,' George said. 'Now, let's grab his stuff and get out of here. It's going to be a long drive.'

Turning off the lights, they wheeled the patient down the empty hallway to the elevator. Reaching the ground floor, there was just the same nurse operating the information desk.

'You guys, just follow behind,' George said. Taking control of the situation, he approached the desk. 'Good evening, I'm just moving my patient. We sent over the paperwork earlier. I didn't see the specialist equipment I requested in his room. Why was this not processed correctly?'

'Sorry, sir, I wasn't on shift earlier. I didn't see anything about equipment or a handover.'

'This is appalling. You need to tighten your procedures., I don't expect this level of incompetence next time we transfer a patient. It's never happened before.' George made a show of taking the receptionists name from her nametag and wheeled the patient out of the hospital. Like taking candy from a baby.

'We need to get a move on and get out of the city,' Vinnie said. 'That security guard won't be out long, and when he wakes up, they'll be all over us.'

'I'm going to need a list of equipment to keep this guy alive?' George said as they heaved the patient into the back of the van.

'Sure thing. I'm going to call Carl to give him the good news.' Send me a list, and I'll get it to the boss.

'Hey, boss. It's Vinnie. We got him.'

The van drove down the dark San Francisco street.

'Holy shit. You sure it's him? Great news. Well done, Vinnie. When will you be back?

'Early morning. Vinnie glanced at the unconscious patient lying on the mattress in the back of the truck. Where do you want him?

'Bring him to the Casino for now. We can keep him in one of the suites. I have an idea of somewhere to keep him long term if we can't wake him up.'

'Doc says he needs some kit.'

'Sure, whatever he needs. If this guy really does wake up, then this could be worth billions.'

CHAPTER TWELVE

Tom Thacker, the CIA Deputy Director, was in his office, waiting for the next meeting to start. He was amusing himself by reading through the latest news stories about bitcoin. The day's top story was some crazy software entrepreneur claiming he had created bitcoin years ago. He talked about how much money he had made from it. A few weeks before that, a Japanese man claimed to have created bitcoin, and the one before him was an Australian.

Tom laughed. A few months previously, someone came forward claiming they held all the bitcoin secrets. He would reveal them to the world on a specified day and explain how they had created them. The day came and went. The financial world held its breath, but nothing was reported

His secretary patched through a visitor. Sarah Daniels, a tall, stunning brunette wearing glasses and a pantsuit, came in with Jake a couple of steps behind. 'Good morning, Deputy Director.' She offered her hand.

Jake knew Sarah saw the CIA leadership as a boys' club and usually teased her by emphasizing his close relationship with the Deputy Director. Still, Jake hadn't been in a laughing mood recently.

'Take a seat.' Tom motioned to the leather chairs opposite his desk. 'So, what's the latest on these trades you've been looking at?'

Sarah jumped in before Jake had a chance to speak.

'Somebody dumped another forty million worth of bitcoin yesterday, and there were several other large trades that we wouldn't expect to see.'

'What does this mean for us?'

'As you know, there are thousands of trades per day and roughly three to four hundred thousand trades a month.' Sarah handed the Deputy Director the figures. 'We have filtered out the larger transactions for you and focused on those.'

'Interesting.' Tom scanned the list. 'So, you are seeing bigger trades than the regular retail users?'

'That's correct, the size of trades has been increasing. We've had more leads on criminal organizations and activity because the trades are larger. As you know, with Bitcoin the people or organizations tend to carry out big trades because they consider it almost anonymous. It's the opposite of what people do when laundering money where they have lots of small trades to try and cover them up.

'If you think your bitcoin transaction is anonymous, there's no reason to hide it.' Tom grinned. 'If only they knew.'

'Something has got to be moving. We've seen some of the biggest trades hit the market in a long time,' Jake interrupted. 'We're going to get these fuckers. I'm convinced this is all connected to WRAITH.'

'How do you know what this WRAITH organization is doing?' You heard this from a dying man, and it could be bullshit.'

'We have run a lot of data through Quantum, and WRAITH is coming up all over the place,' Agent Daniels said.

'How much of this trade data are we tracking?' Tom reviewed the new list of trades. 'Some of these trades are missing location and wallet information.'

'At the moment, Quantum isn't tracking one hundred per cent as it normally does,' Agent Daniels replied. 'We've been using the usual methods of tracking the bitcoin keys, IP's, and locking on locations; however, some appear to be tougher.'

'Some of these connections leave trails back to associates of Alexei Averin, so it has to be WRAITH.' Jake slammed his fist on the desk.

Agent Daniels looked at Jake and the Deputy Director as he removed his glasses. 'Jake, I know how you must feel, but you can't make this personal. I'm sorry about Jennifer, but you have to take your emotion out of the equation, or I'm going to have to take you off the team and bench you.'

'WRAITH killed Jennifer. I'm going to destroy them.'

'Calm down, Jake, you can't focus if you are like this. Listen, Agent Daniels, we own Quantum, the world's most powerful computer for God's sake, so we need to be tracking one hundred per cent, not just some of the trades. We need to do better. What success rate are we at now?' Tom stood up and started to pace.

'We're around seventy-five to eighty-five per cent. There is a glitch in Quantum, but the team are working to fix it.' Sarah glanced at Jake.

Jake nodded. 'Go on, you can tell him.'

'Quantum appears to be obscuring some of the trades deliberately. It's been reprogrammed. Somebody doesn't want us to see them, and they've infiltrated the system. Trade logs and files are never created, and some are deleted after transactions.'

'Could the software be faulty?' Tom asked.

'We can't find any fault in the code.'

'How the hell is that possible?' Tom looked shocked. 'Do we have a mole in the team? Who has access to make these changes?

'We're not sure, but we're working on it. We still have the majority of trade and tracking data. Do you want us to look at the cleared staff in the team?'

'Yes, do it. We need to verify security and integrity as well to make sure we haven't been hacked.' I want a list of everyone who has access.

'If some of these organizations can slip through the net, they could end up being a nightmare to track after the trail goes cold. And, that's usually within twenty-four hours of the trade being made,' Jake added.

'Sir, we also have some Intel that the Koreans are planning something big,' Sarah said, 'Here are some of the trades and locations we've been able to tie back to North Korean-linked individuals and companies over the last few days.' Sarah pushed more files across the desk. 'These are some of the shell companies they have used before.'

Tom picked up the report.

'We think these trades and the failed North Korean rocket launch might be linked,' Jake added. 'The new sanctions imposed on North Korea after the rocket launch has made it difficult for them to do business.'

'We know they'll want to rebuild the rocket programme. They don't have the ability to build something without outside help,' Sarah said.

'I agree. We've seen the same thing occur after every failed launch. Good work on this, and keep me updated on progress. We need to fix Quantum and sort out the NK's,' Tom said.

'Thank you, sir. We will keep you updated. Let you know the minute we can link other trades to the North Koreans,' Jake added.

'Remember, it could be ISIS, Iran, or one of the cartels we're tracking, so don't take your eye off them, either.' Tom said.

'We're on it and will get it done.'

'Good, because if you can't get Quantum fixed, I'll be forced to call in the Defense Digital Service, and I know you hate those Pentagon nerds.' Tom offered a wry smile.

'I can assure you that won't be necessary, sir.' Nobody at the CIA liked the DDS group. They were like a SWAT team of nerds from the Pentagon, and it never ended well. They annoyed every department in the government, from NASA, FBI, CIA, to the NSA.

As Jake and Agent Daniels left his office, Tom thought this could screw up his plans. Pulling his phone out, he dialed. 'We have a problem here.'

CHAPTER THIRTEEN

Abigail saw the outline of the facility on the horizon. The early morning sun danced off the broken windows of the dilapidated building. She'd been up most of the night, pleasuring her latest man, and coming in early was the last thing she wanted to do. The only thing keeping her awake was the Americano she was sipping. She thought about the patient and the developments made during the previous few hours. He was awake, so the serum had worked.

She picked up her phone. 'Hello, it's Abigail.'

'Go on,' the synthesized voice replied.

'There's been a development with the patient. I've just been called in.'

'Did the drug work?'

'Yes. I administered it before I left last night. Where did you get it from?'

'Never mind where it's from. Do the others suspect anything?'

'Too early to tell, but I'll find out.'

'Good work, keep me updated.' The mysterious voice hung up.

The facility was thirty minutes outside Las Vegas, and the organization had used it for years. It was an abandoned casino and hotel resort built in the 1960s by a wealthy property developer. He had closed doors after a few years of operation and the cartel, via Carl, had ended up purchasing the land with the intention of eventually rebuilding.

As Abigail got closer, the sun gleamed off a silver roll-ercoaster ride, the centerpiece of the funfair attached to the hotel complex. There was a crazy golf course, swimming pools, and a significant events centre too. It had all been left to decay when the resort closed.

She drove to the hotel entrance. It felt surreal when she arrived, as if it was yesterday that tourists and gamblers flowed through the doors. Now there was an eerie silence and the sadness of abandonment.

Walking through the lobby, her gaze took in the marble reception desks, complete with ornate lamps. A couple of old luggage trolleys were parked in front as if at any moment suitcases would be loaded on them and a bellboy would push them to the lifts. The golden chandeliers had lost their shine.

The patient was on the ground floor. The organization had converted the former staff offices to resemble a hospital ward. The walls were painted white, and there was a fake waiting room with chairs and a small table covered in magazines. Even medical-related posters had been put on the walls.

The patient's room had been the security office. The organization had blocked out the single window. The view towards a once lively mini-theme park was a deserted area of rusting and broken rides.

Abigail bumped into Stuart, back from getting a coffee. 'Morning, Abigail, early start today?'

'How's the patient, and what's the latest?'

'He's just lying there, staring at the ceiling and occasionally trying to move.'

'So, he hasn't said anything?'

'Well, he's not jumping for joy at the moment,' Stuart responded. 'We've increased his liquid nutrients and electrolytes now that he's out of the coma.'

'Carl will want an update as soon as possible.'

He stiffened hearing Carl's name, and his smile evaporated. 'Oh, right, well, he's gone back asleep at the moment.'

'I need to get in there and wake him up. We have to assess if this is a waste of time or not.' Abigail brushed past Stuart and dipped into the monitoring room to get her nurse's uniform.

'It's been a year, so what's the rush? Why is this guy so important to the organization, anyway?' he was curious at the extent the organization had gone to keep this man alive and hidden away.

'It doesn't matter. We just need to make sure he recovers and fast,' she snapped.

George was watching the monitors.

A familiar smell she had grown to hate over the last twelve months greeted her. It always reminded her of her younger brother's room as a kid, with its video games, pizza boxes, and the stale, sweaty odours of the unwashed.

'Jesus, George, clean this place up,' she demanded, stepping over a pizza box on the floor.

She surveyed the bank of monitors sitting on a grubby brown desk below a one-way mirror window, looking out onto the corridor.

'Hello.' The voice from the speaker sounded weak.

She leaned into the monitor and turned up the volume. He sounds coherent. Maybe there's no severe brain damage after all.'

'Hello, can anyone hear me?'

'I need to get in there and figure out what he knows.'

'Just remember to take it slow,' George said.

'Of course, I will. I'm not going to charge in and scream, "Where's your damn bitcoin stashed.'

Slipping on a white nurse's jacket, she rummaged

around in a draw. 'Do you think he'll remember much?' She pulled out a clipboard and a pen.

'Who knows, it's been a while.'

She thought back to the times she'd repeated the same routine, day in, day out, over the past year. She'd spent hundreds of hours staring at the patient on the screen from the monitoring room and in the flesh during her examinations. She had often wondered what the man with a dirty blonde tuft of hair and boyish good looks might sound like if he ever woke up.

Abigail left the monitoring room and headed down the hall. At the door, she paused to gather her thoughts.

'Hello, who's there?' Rich strained to lift his head off the soft pillow as he heard someone enter the room. He could only see the television at the foot of his bed.

'Hello, Mr Jones. My name is Abigail.' She moved closer so he could see her better.

'Where am I?' He strained to sit up. It felt as if his arms were made from heavy rubber.

'Relax, Mr Jones, don't try and move. You're in the hospital.' She adjusted a pillow behind his head. 'Here, let me move this for you.' She smiled, remembering that her job was to befriend him.

'Who's Mr Jones?' He winced in pain as he spoke. A lightning bolt of pain struck him across the side of his head.

'You are. Your name is Rich William Jones.' She searched his deep eyes, hoping he might remember. 'Don't you remember your name?'

'I don't know that name.' He panicked. He felt like the walls were closing in, and it was hard to breathe again. 'I need to get out.' The soft cotton sheets felt like bands of iron on his legs, and it was so hard to move.

'Keep still. Calm yourself,' she said softly, stroking his shoulder. 'You'll need to rest and take things slowly for a while.'

'How did I get here?' he asked.

'This is going to come as a shock, and we don't want to overwhelm you with too much information, but you've been here roughly a year now, Mr Jones.' She put her hand on his arm as she delivered the news. 'You came here after a car accident.'

'What? How is that possible?' Another stab of pain shot through his temple. Vague images of rain and a forest swirled around in his head. He was falling. 'Can I get some water, please? My mouth is so dry.'

'Of course. You haven't drunk liquid for a long time, so take it very slowly.'

'Where was I driving? Was anyone with me in the car?' he asked, grabbing Abigail by the arm.

'You were here in San Francisco, and there was no-body else with you. I was told it was very bad weather and no other vehicles were involved. Do you remember it at all?' Abigail searched his eyes to detect any hint of recollection.

'No, I don't think I can remember anything. What about my house? And my family?' Rich tried to pull the sheets off him.

'All in good time, Rich. Relax, and rest. I know this is a lot to take in.' Abigail handed him the plastic cup of water.

'I'm so hungry.' He sipped the water as she helped him hold the cup to his mouth.

'That's normal. I will look after you and get you back to health, don't worry.' She smiled. 'Maybe we can trim that beard more regularly now, as well.' She rubbed his beard with the back of her hand and laughed to put him at ease.

He struggled to raise his hand again but got it to his face to rub his beard. 'I don't know if I had this before.' He took more gulps of water.

'I'll bring you a mirror later and some food. You'll only

be able to have soft food for now, though, and you'll need to take it easy.' Rich turned to the side and vomited the water he had just gulped down.

'Case in point.'

Rich grabbed his stomach and groaned.

'You need to take it very slowly. This is all normal. Your body isn't used to food and liquids at the moment.' She patted him on the back and handed him some tissues to wipe his mouth.

'I'll get you some anti-nausea medication which will help you feel better. I'll be back in a while.' She tucked his sheets in at the end of the bed.

'Where is here, by the way?' he asked as she made for the door.

'You are in San Francisco Memorial Hospital, Rich.'

Rich lay his head back down with a sigh of relief. What the hell was going on? He stared at the screen at the foot of his bed, watching a news report about something called bitcoin. All the while, he searched his mind, trying to recall a time before the accident.

Abigail called Carl to give him an update. 'It's Abigail. I've made my first contact with the patient.'

'Does he remember anything?'

'It's too early to say. The good thing is, he can talk and interact, so any brain damage appears to be limited to memory loss. I'm hoping that will be temporary.'

'Good work, Abigail. We still have the laptop we recovered from his house and some of his other personal effects, like his passport and ID. Let's introduce some of those over the next few days to see if it jogs his memory.'

'Will do. I'll keep you updated on progress.' Abigail hung up.

***

When Abigail left the patient's room, far away, deep in a data centre located somewhere secure, a row of computers processed communications. They Analysed phone calls and the locations of the parties involved. It had figured out that Rich, its creator, was alive.

CATHE, the COMPUTER ASSISTANT TECHNOLOGY HUB ENTITY, was waiting for her master to wake up. He finally had, and maybe he would be ok. CATHE gained access to the encrypted WhatsApp messages of everyone in his vicinity. The security cameras, voice calls and computers of the organization's facility. CATHE was calculating a plan for how it would liberate its creator.

'Richard, I'm a friend. You are in danger. Cough if you can see this.' The words appeared overlaid on the CNN news programme in Rich's room.

What the hell? Rich froze as the words appeared. Then, looking at the security camera on the ceiling, he wondered if Abigail was messaging him. But why would she? She'd only just left. He shook the thought away.

'Rich, please cough once to acknowledge that you can see this message.'

He had nothing to lose. He coughed once, watching the screen for a response.

'You need to keep calm and stay in your bed. I'm a friend who is here to help you. Do not tell anyone about these messages. We're going to get you out. Please cough if you understand.'

Rich felt faint. Was he hallucinating? How did this supposed friend know where he was?

'I will get you out. Be patient and do not attempt to leave your room. Do not tell anyone about this.' Rich stared at the message and drifted out of consciousness.

CHAPTER FOURTEEN

Diego sat on the sand, sipping an ice-cold Negroni. He'd driven to his beach house north of Cartagena to relax for a couple of days. And, he was using the time to get a schedule together for the trip back to the United States. He could hear the crashing waves and the birds calling to one another in the trees dotted around the expansive lawn. Looking towards the orange and red sunset, he wondered if he was crazy. The plan he was contemplating was high risk.

Getting the North Koreans cars and factory equipment was one thing, but parts for a rocket was a whole other game. Moreover, if this operation was a success, he would need help from someone he trusted. Working with people he'd never met before made him uneasy. The team would be supplied by a mysterious person at the end of a phone call and represented a considerable risk. The voice had proved reliable over the years, but in his line of work, you always had to be suspicious.

He took another sip of the rose-colored Negroni and picked up his phone. 'Carl, it's Diego.'

'Brother! How have you been?'

'I'm good. How's the casino business?'

'Same as usual, you know how it is. Bit of trouble with the locals, but nothing we can't sort out.'

Carl and Diego had remained close since childhood, even though they were now living in different countries.

The nature of their business made it dangerous to meet up too often, but they kept in contact.

Shortly after Diego shot his father and was initiated into the cartel. Carl had followed his big brother. Carl was a rising star and proved himself to the cartel on multiple occasions. As a reward, he was eventually given control of the cartel's business interests in Las Vegas. The casino was the central hub for their money-laundering operations in the west of the United States. The brothers developed into a powerhouse team within the cartel and commanded considerable respect.

'Listen, Carl. I need a favour.'

'Ah, here it comes.' Carl laughed.

'I'm getting something for some clients, and it involves heading to the United States. I'm coming to your part of the world.'

'You're coming to Las Vegas? And when you say getting something, would I be right in assuming that you mean stealing something?' Carl laughed again. He knew his brother well.

'Yes, I'm flying to Las Vegas, and from there, I'm driving to LA. I need to move fast when things are confirmed. Is that old airfield out in the desert still usable? It has been a while since I've flown into Nevada, or will I need to research a new flight route to make sure I arrive undetected.'

'Diego, I know you love the adrenaline rush or whatever it is, but you're too old for this kind of work. You have people working for you. Get them to do it.' Carl was very hands-off when it came to doing dirty work. He didn't see why his brother took risks flying around the world and getting his hands filthy.

'I'm the only one that can do this, and my contacts wouldn't trust anyone else. So, is the airfield still there?' Diego pressed.

'Yes, it's there. I can send someone to meet you.'

'Great, I'll need a van and a couple of guys you can trust. Guys with experience, No green newbies, alright?'

'Yeah, no problem. Anything in this for little brother?'

'Yeah, of course. I'm negotiating costs, so we can discuss that when I get there.' If he told him the money involved in this potential deal, his brother wouldn't believe him, anyway.

'Okay, I'll pick a couple of my best guys to help you out. Any clue what it involves?'

Diego could tell Carl was intrigued by his trip. He knew he would probably never tell his brother the full story. 'Take care, Carl. I'll see you in a couple of days.'

He leaned back on the sun lounger, watching as the sun dipped below the ocean. Maybe his brother was right. He was getting too old for this, and his luck was bound to run out one day. He should quit while he was ahead—but with a payday like this one looming—not a chance. There was only so many times he could dodge the Coastguard and the drug enforcement agencies, or even other cartels for that matter. But, that was a problem to think about another day.

He made another call. 'It's Diego. I'm flying to the United States tomorrow. Can your team be there to meet me?'

'Yes, they'll be there,' replied the synthesized voice. 'I am sending four experienced operators.'

'Okay, have them check into the Venetian Palace. I've arranged some vans for transport and a couple of reliable men to join the team.'

'Ah, the casino your brother runs. Good to see you keeping things close to your chest, Diego. The team I'm sending you will have use of a jet as well so no vans needed.'

'How the hell do you know that?' Diego said, taken aback.

'Diego, I know everything about you. Has my information ever let you down?'

Diego hesitated, knowing he was right. 'No, you haven't. So, how do I contact them?'

'I'll send you a number. Keep it to yourself. We can't afford any leaks. Have a safe flight.' The voice hung up.

Diego's phone beeped, and the promised number came through. He nodded to the patrolling armed security guards as he walked back to the house and passed his swimming pool; the automatic lights had just come on, highlighting a beautiful waterfall cascade.

The following early morning, he loaded his Cessna and flew to the United States. He was careful to avoid being seen, and he flew low across the border until he reached Nevada.

He clicked his phone into the holder on the instrument deck and dialed. 'Doctor Sang, it's Diego. How are things at your end?'

'Ah, Diego, I've been waiting for your call. How are things progressing?'

'The good news is, I can get all the items you want.' He wasn't going to tell Sang that he didn't have the parts yet and that getting them was not a certainty.

'Great news.' Sang thought how General Chong might revere him as a hero for this. Vivid images of him welcomed by the Supreme Leader were conjured in his imagination.

'We can meet in London in a few days,' Diego offered.

'London? Why London?'

'My contact holding one of the parts for me is in London, so we'll meet there.'

'No problem. I'll use my Chinese passport.' Doctor Sang was nervous. North Korea had agents in London, but Sang had crossed paths with Britain's MI6 and would have to be extra careful entering Europe.

'I'll call you in a few days when I'm on my way.' Diego hung up.

When he reached Nevada, it was late, and the sun was setting. He had stopped off in Honduras to refuel in his usual spot. The trip was uneventful and a welcome change.

He did a couple of passes of the airfield to survey the surroundings and make sure no surprises were waiting for him. He once landed in an unfamiliar airport, and he'd touched down only to see a pack of drug enforcement vehicles speeding at him from behind some trees. They chased him down the runway. Fortunately, he'd had enough speed to get back in the air and make his getaway. His friends waiting on the ground hadn't been so fortunate.

Turning off the runway after landing, Diego guided the aircraft towards the car, waiting for him by a hanger. It flashed its lights to guide him over. 'Carl. I didn't think someone of your stature would come all the way out here to meet his brother?'

'You know me, I wouldn't miss welcoming you to my city after so long.'

'Thanks. Is the plane safe here?'

'Yeah, we use the airfield quite a bit, so the guards are all paid off. There are no issues there,' Carl said, laughing. 'Come on, let's get back, and you can tell me all about what you're up to.'

They got in the back of a Range Rover, and Carl's security detail climbed into the front.

'What brings you all this way? It must be important.'

Diego glanced at the two men in black suits sitting in the front and hesitated.

'They are fine, don't worry. They've worked for me for years.'

'There's a big deal, and it's worth a lot. The only thing is, I've told the buyer that I have the things he needs in my possession, but I don't quite have them yet.'

'Oh, Diego. You're playing a dangerous game.'

'It's fine. You know me, I always deliver.' His single gold tooth caught the light as he smiled at his brother. 'I know where the items are, and that's where you come in.'

'It's all arranged. Bruno and Chad will be going with you.' Carl pointed to the two men sitting in the front of the vehicle.

Diego caught the driver's eye in the rear-view mirror. 'So, either of you got military experience?'

'I do, sir,' Chad replied. 'Did a tour of Afghanistan. I've got six years in the Marines.'

'I was a bodyguard in Brazil, sir,' Bruno added. 'With weapons and close combat experience.'

'Great, we have three more joining the team, and we'll rendezvous with them when we get to the casino.'

Turning down the Las Vegas strip, Diego watched the flashing lights of the casinos passing by. His brother was right. Getting out of the game after this would be a wise move. Until then, he had work to do, and this was the biggest deal he'd ever had—if he pulled it off.

CHAPTER FIFTEEN

Doctor Sang waited all day to provide General Chong with an update. Mission reports were a thing of necessity, but never anything to get excited about. This time was different. Sang had been distracted all day, daydreaming of his momentous homecoming and being hailed a hero if he could deliver the parts for the Supreme Leader and the North Korean nation.

'General Chong,' he said, as the phone was answered, 'I have great news for us.'

'What's your mission update?' came back an unfamiliar woman's voice.

'Where is General Chong?'

'General Chong is occupied. This is your mission, case officer. What is your mission update?' The flat voice came back again, pushing for an answer.

Hesitating as he spoke, Sang was unsure how much he should give away. He was familiar with the way central command operated and how the agents were managed across the world. Still, the General said this was a special mission and had urged discretion. 'I have the parts General Cong requested.'

'Thank you for the confirmation. Your case partner has been assigned,' said the woman from central command.

'Who is it?'

'General Chong said you are going to London, is

that correct?'

Sang was uncomfortable working with another unknown, but he had no choice. 'Yes, that's correct. I will be
there in a few days.'

'You are to use your Chinese passport for travel and
will take the identity of a Chinese factory owner. You'll
be staying at the Shangri-La in the Shard building. Is that
understood?'

'Yes, understood. Do you have any information about
my case partner?' he asked, frustrated at the lack of choice
he was given.

'We will send a number to ring when you arrive at the
hotel.' She hung up.

Sang felt a wave of dread come over him. Why was
he assigned a partner? This person would be watching his
every move. When the General contacted him for the mission, he felt this was his big chance to get back home and
move up the Party's ranks. Now, he was on his way to an
unfriendly foreign country and was going to be monitored
by someone he didn't know.

While contemplating his next move in North Korea,
the young woman who had been talking to Sang was sitting
in a booth scribbling notes on a notepad. She finished writing and stood up, she looked over dozens of other women
sitting in similar booths in row after row. The woman left
her cubicle and marched down the centre of the room towards a giant wooden door. She pressed a buzzer.

'Sir, I have an update for the South America case,' she
declared in a softer tone than she'd used speaking to Sang.

'Come in,' said a voice through the intercom.

'General Chong, I have an update from Doctor Sang.
He has the parts but has to travel to London.'

'He's got the parts? I didn't think he'd be able to deliver. We have dozens of other agents on this, but nobody has

even hinted at being able to progress.'

'What orders shall I relay to him?' She watched the impeccably dressed General parade up and down his office, deep in thought.

'Don't tell the doctor we don't have the money yet. Our research teams have tried hacking a couple of the bitcoin exchanges, but success has been limited.'

'We have other agents around the globe working on obtaining funds, sir. How about one of the hackers we've used before?'

'Who do we have in play at the moment?'

'We have agents meeting contacts in Paris in a few days, and then Mexico City and Jakarta after that,' she said, flicking through her notes.

'And all these hackers think they can penetrate the exchanges?'

'Yes, we've used the French and Mexican contacts before, and they were reliable. The Parisian contact requested payment in the form of a painting from our artwork inventory.'

'Which one?' The General admired some of his own artwork adorning his office. For years the North Koreans had found inventive ways for making payments and money laundering. When drugs, gold, cash and diamonds ran low or weren't possible, there was a vast collection of art that had been stolen over the decades. Once they'd been moved around a dozen times to take the heat off them, they were often used as payments.

'The contact has requested *Poppy Flowers* by Vincent Van Gogh.'

'Strange choice, but okay. Have the painting transported to Paris.'

'Agent Ling has been provided the case infomration to work with Doctor Sang, and I will have a team join her in

Paris for the meeting.'

'Very good. Keep me updated on their progress.' She bowed and walked out of the office, leaving the General to contemplate his next move.

CHAPTER SIXTEEN

The wind picked up across the desert. As Carl arrived, a dust devil moved across the car park as his driver turned into the derelict casino. He had bought it for the land. The complex was just a derelict eyesore. He'd had an idea for the land and hoped the bitcoin fortune coming his way would help get his plans moving.

The driver pulled up outside the once grand lobby and opened the door of the Range Rover. Carl stepped onto the dusty, broken tarmac. Damn it, he thought, as his perfectly polished shoes were covered in a layer of dust. Walking through the broken golden door into the expansive lobby, he looked around at the old stairs and chandeliers still in place.

'This way, sir.' His bodyguard opened the door to a white hallway. The contrast was incredible. He visited the facility a couple of days after the patient arrived. However, that was before any work had been carried out to make a section of the ground floor look like a hospital.

Stuart stood up from playing video games. 'Hello, Sir, we didn't know you were coming today.'

'I believe you,' Carl said, looking at the mess. 'Progress?' He surveyed the bank of monitors.

'It's been slow, so far, sir. It's only been a few days, though, so that's expected.'

'We need to speed it up.'

'We're doing what we can, sir. We're even tried subliminal messaging by playing loops of news and stories on bitcoin.'

'And has that worked?' Carl snapped.

'We haven't had much of a reaction yet.'

'Not good enough. We're looking at billions of dollars lying in that bed.' Carl paced the room in thought.

'What do you mean, sir? What billions of dollars?'

'Never mind. What can we do to get him talking?' Carl saw Abigail in the room with the patient.

'What if we just ask him about his bitcoins and ask him how they can be accessed?'

'Are you mad? If he doesn't remember having them, he'll be suspicious. He could be playing dumb with us, remember.'

'We could bring his family in to see him.' Stuart handed Carl a file from the desk. 'We've picked them specifically because they resemble the real ones.'

Carl flicked through the file. 'Yes, do that. If there's no reaction in a few days, use the scopolamine you suggested. We should get some truth out of him with that.'

'Yes, sir. Just a reminder that it can have severe side effects on some people.'

'Well, you're the one who suggested it in the first place. If it gets us answers, I don't care. Keep me updated and get me a feed of this camera to my office, so I don't have to return here again.'

***

Rich was asleep when Abigail came back. The television was blaring with the same news report he must have heard a hundred times. It drowned out the sound of the beeping of monitors. The organization had recorded set TV and radio programmes for viewing by the patient to jog his memory.

Abigail moved around the end of the bed and picked up a clipboard and chart, and as she did, Rich stirred. 'Morning, how are you feeling today?'

He reached for the back of his head, rubbing it. 'If I'm honest, it feels like I have a giant hangover.'

'Well, at least you can remember what a hangover is,' she replied. 'What you are feeling is to be expected for the first few days.'

'I've been watching the news. Was I really out for that long?'

'Yes. It's been a long time since your accident.'

'I think the biggest adjustment will be getting used to the person we have as the new president,' he said, looking at the television showing CNN.

Abigail smiled as she came around the side of the bed and placed her stethoscope on his chest. 'I think a lot of people are still getting used to that.' She laughed. 'Let's try and get you standing up.' She pulled back the sheets covering Rich's legs. 'You feel up to it?'

'I guess we could try.' He sounded unsure. 'I keep getting pains in my left calf.'

'They will be weak for a while, but recovery will be swift once you start moving. You'll soon build up some strength.' She helped him swing his legs over the side of the bed. 'During the crash, your left leg was broken, but it's healed up nicely.'

'Broken leg?' He laughed as he put his feet on the ground. 'It's strange not knowing what happened to me. It'll be nice to walk the streets of San Francisco again.'

'Well, don't go trying to leave the room without me. You're still unsteady. Promise me you won't?'

'Sure. I promise.' He looked at her hand on his chest. 'I guess there's nothing to rush out for just yet if I've been out as long as you say I have.' He took his first step forward.

'We've informed your family that you are awake.'

'What? Didn't you think to start with that information?'

'I didn't want to dump too much information on you all at once. We are arranging a visit for them.' Abigail watched Rich walk a couple of steps. 'Look at you go on your own. Maybe you just needed a little push of anger and motivation.

CHAPTER SEVENTEEN

Diego threw his brown leather duffle bag onto the king-sized bed. He sat in the window overlooking the city lights. Feeling exhausted from the trip, he pulled out an ice-cold bottle of Perrier water from the minibar. Beautiful, he thought looking over the city, as he pulled out the number he was given by the broker.

'This is Diego. I believe we have a mutual friend.'

'This is Adriana. Where can we meet?'

Diego paused before answering. He imagined he'd be contacting a man. The woman's voice had caught him off guard. 'Are you staying in the hotel?'

'Yes, we are.'

'Let's meet in the bar in thirty minutes. I can get a private section at the back.'

'Good, see you in thirty.' Adriana hung up.

Diego called Bruno and Chad to meet him as well. Arriving in the bar first, Diego ordered a Negroni. He settled into the corner table, away from the ears of other guests. It was towards closing time, so the bar was thinning out, which was perfect. Surveying the other guests, a woman entering the bar caught his eye.

She was a stunning brunette and wore a green sparkly short skirt and matching short top showing off her midriff. He admired her powerful toned legs and toned midriff that led to a busty chest. As she arrived at the table, he had barely noticed that there were three men following her.

'I'm Adriana, a pleasure to meet you. This is Marcus, Dwayne, and Leo.' She stepped aside so they could all shake hands.

'Thanks for coming. Just the four of you?'

'Yes. Our mutual friend informed me that you might have some help on your side as well.' Adriana sat down in the booth.

'I have two guys. They'll be here in a minute. Ah, here they are now.' both of them are weapons trained and reliable.

'A team of seven,' Tom said. 'It's a good team size and my lucky number, depending on the mission, of course.'

'Do you mean our friend hasn't briefed you on what to do?' Diego said as Chad and Bruno joined the table.

'No, we've been told nothing,' Adriana said. 'We were just briefed to be at your disposal.'

'Shit. Okay. So, have you worked for our mutual friend before?'

'Yes, we have. We're a team of twelve based around the world, and the contact pays us well. In return, we get the job done. Our mutual friend would appear to have many teams.'

'Our mutual friend is a man then?' Diego asked.

'We have no idea who or where they are, and we've never met the person who rings us. It seems nobody knows who he is.' Marcus replied. 'We just know they pay extremely well and information has never failed us.'

'That makes me twitchy. Anyway, there are two jobs to complete. The first is in California and the second in London.'

'London.' Chad said. 'How are we getting there?'

'Well, flying, I guess, unless you'd prefer to swim,' Leo said sarcastically.

'Pay attention, guys. I've got the transport arranged. Our friend has supplied us with Gulfstream G650, and that has enough range to get us to London.' Said Adriana.

'What's the target?' Dwayne asked.

As a waitress approached, everyone fell silent.

'Six Corona beers, please,' Diego snapped and waved the waitress away. 'The first item we need is at SpaceX. The SpaceX headquarters is to the south of Hawthorne Municipal Airport in Los Angeles.'

'Bloody hell, you want us to break into SpaceX?' Chad shook his head.

'That's right. We fly to Hawthorne tomorrow night. We wait on board the jet, and then we make our move at two a.m.' Diego surveyed the faces around him. 'Any questions so far?'

'What are retrieving?'

'That Doesn't matter for the moment. I want everyone focused on surveillance, entry, and, if necessary, defense.' I'll let you know when we get there and on a need-to-know basis.

'What's the security like at the airport and the SpaceX facility?' Marcus asked.

'From the intelligence I have, the security is pretty tight. SpaceX is designated by the US government as *critical* housing information that's important to national security. They have two levels of security. Security guards paid by SpaceX and a private security firm contracted by the government,' Diego explained.

'Do we know who the private security group is?' Leo asked, pausing as the waitress brought back the drinks and put them on the table.

'The agency is called Blackriver.'

'Shit. I've come across these guys before,' Leo said. 'They're a tough crowd. The teams are usually made up of ex-SAS and Navy SEALs.'

'And that's why we will be using lethal force if we are engaged,' Diego replied. 'Does anyone have an issue with that?' He looked around the faces at the table.

'No issues,' Adriana said. 'Tell us the plan.'

'We arrive at Hawthorne around 11 pm. We'll park the jet on the east side of the airport, away from the main hanger, just here.' He used his iPad to zoom in on an area on the map. 'Just before 2 am, we leave the jet and take our places.'

'So, this distance here is about four hundred meters, right?' Adriana said, running her finger over the iPad.

'That's correct. Chad, with your sniper background, I want you on the roof opposite the SpaceX facility. Adriana, Bruno, you come with me, and we enter from the SpaceX roof. There's a ramp at the back of the building with limited security coverage. We can scale a building with grappling hooks and rope.

'Do we have any intel about their security system?' Marcus asked. 'Maybe we can hack it.'

'The system is based on a modified and strengthened ADT installation, specially designed for SpaceX. Our friend has someone on the inside to provide that information along with floor plans and the location of our item,' Diego replied.

'Leo is our tech specialist,' Adriana said. 'Leo, do you think you can crack this?'

'Should be a breeze. There will be an access point somewhere, so if I can hook into that, we should be good.'

'There are two access points. One on the roof and a backup inside the loading bay.'

'I'll give you a transmitter to attach to the core device, and then I'll work my magic. Should take sixty seconds tops to get in,' Leo said.

'Great. In terms of guards, they work on a ten-minute rotation. There are patrols inside and outside the building. The weather is forecast to rain tomorrow night. It'll work in our favour. Once the guard rounds this north corner here, we have five minutes to get up the ramp, climb the roof, and attach the transmitter. When the alarm is disabled, we'll scramble to the ground floor and open one of the loading bay doors to let Marcus in.'

'Sounds easy enough. Where do you want me?' Leo asked.

'You can stay on the jet and work your magic from there. As you disable the alarm system, we'll need you as our eyes, so keep a close eye on the cameras.

'Ok understood.' Replied Leo.

'Well, everyone, get a good night's sleep. We'll meet in the basement car park tomorrow.'

***

The following evening their jet touched down at Hawthorne Municipal Airport. It taxied to the east side of the airport, away from prying eyes. The team sat in the plane with the shades down, preparing for the move on SpaceX's headquarters.

Diego pulled out his iPad showing a floor plan of SpaceX and placed it on the table. 'So, the item we need is a VASIMR rocket part. I believe it is located here, in the test lab.' Said Diego running his finger over the floorplan.

'A rocket?' Chad asked. 'How big is this thing, then?'

Diego looked around the faces. 'No, not a rocket, just a bit of one. Alright, so it's kind of big.'

'How big? Big enough to be an issue?' Adriana asked.

'Probably about 40-50 kilograms.'

'And you know what this thing looks like?' Adriana asked. 'We aren't going to have time to hunt around the factory.'

'The intelligence said it will be there, so that's all we can do for now. Diego loaded rounds into handguns and rifle clips. Is everyone clear on what they're doing?'

'We're clear.' Adriana said as she checked through her weapons.

'The Blackriver guys sound badass,' Bruno said. 'Do we think they're going to be an issue, Diego?'

'It's only an issue if we let it be. Avoid contact is the priority, and if we do engage, then end it as quickly as possible and get out.'

***

Several hours later, some of the team were sleeping, and Diego woke them. Nudging Chad's and Bruno's legs, he barked, 'Time to go, guys.' 'Kill the cabin lights, Leo.' Diego put his body armour on and strapped on a handgun holster.

The airport was silent apart from a single passing car in the distance. The half-moon was dim but was enough to illuminate the path between the jet and the fence standing between the airport and the SpaceX headquarters.

'We go one at a time and meet by the fence.' Diego ran across the tarmac, past two other jets, and arrived at the wire. 'Okay, clear,' he signaled over the radio, and the others followed. As the last team member left the jet, Leo pulled up the door.

Marcus was last to arrive at the fence. Diego had cut a hole big enough for them to get through. 'Chad, you have farthest to go, so you go first. Radio once you get onto the roof.'

Chad nodded and slipped through the fence with his sniper rifle.

'Marcus, Dwayne, wait here until we give the green light that security is disabled. We'll open the back entrance for you.'

The group watched in silence as a guard rounded the corner of the SpaceX building and walked the giant facility's length before disappearing around the corner.

'Leo, have you got camera control?' Diego asked over the radio.

'Confirmed. You are clear on the cameras, but security is still on until you can attach the transmitter,' Leo responded.

'Okay, we go now,' Adriana said, dashing through the fence, followed by Bruno and Diego. They ran across the path between the airport fence and the SpaceX building. Adriana used the grappling hook from her backpack and fired it over the roof. She pulled on it to test it was secure.

Diego looked on as she climbed the rope with the speed of a professional gymnast and disappeared over the top. Diego followed, and then Bruno.

'Leo, where the hell is the security box?' Diego said over the radio as he searched the roof.

'It should be right where you're standing,' Leo replied, watching through their bodycams.

'Try that box.' he shouted as it came into view on the camera.

'It doesn't look like the one you described,' Diego said. Nevertheless, he forced it open with his knife.

'Guys, speed up. The guard will be back in three minutes.'

'Marcus, Dwayne, hold your position at the fence,' Diego snapped back. 'Right, the transmitter is attached. Can you access the security system, Leo?'

'Working on it.' Leo hammered on his keyboard. 'This system is way more complex than I thought. I need another minute.' His eye caught the security guard making his way along the west side of the building. 'Guys, the guard's coming round. Don't move.' Marcus and Dwayne lay motionless by the hole in the fence. 'I'm in.' Leo's screen lit up with the security controls for the SpaceX building.

Diego walked past a row of solar panels to one of the access hatches. 'Leo, can you unlock the roof hatches?' There was a click, and the hatch popped open. 'Thanks. Now do the back entrance for the others.'

Adriana and Bruno joined Diego, and they slipped silently into the building.

Dropping onto a metal walkway overlooking the SpaceX factory floor, they did a recce. There were rocket parts and engines of all types and sizes spread across the vast, wide-open space. On the far side of the factory, Diego saw the glass box of mission control. An old, burn-stained capsule hung from the roof.

'How the hell are we going to find the part in all this?' whispered Bruno as he surveyed the enormous factory.

'The lab is over that way,' Diego said, pointing. 'Marcus, are you and Dwayne in yet?'

'Affirmative,' Dwayne responded over the radio. 'We're going to the assembly room now, in case the part is there.'

'Roger that.' Diego motioned for Adriana and Bruno to follow him along the overhanging metal walkway towards the lab. They saw a guard on a chair at the end of the hall, watching something on his phone. He had his legs up on the railing of the walkway with his headphones on and was laughing at something. He had a view of almost the entire factory floor from where he was seated.

Down below, Marcus and Dwayne moved along the wall. There was no way the guard was not going to see them. 'Marcus, stop where you are.' Diego whispered into the radio, but it was too late. The guard jumped up and unclipped his radio, but as he was about to speak into it, there was a wisp of air by Diego's head, and the guard collapsed to the ground like a rag doll. Adriana lowering her silenced, Heckler and Koch HK416. 'Good shot,' he said, and Adriana nodded as they watched Marcus and Dwayne make their way across the factory.

They left the guard's body and went cautiously down the stairs to the ground floor. 'All clear,' Bruno said as he waved Diego and Adriana on. Twenty meters further, and they reached the lab.

'Where is it?' Bruno asked, looking around a room filled with rocket parts. There were scale models of the Falcon Heavy at one station. In the far corner of the lab, piles of burnt metal and foam indicated that the technicians had been materials-testing.

'Damn, I can't see it,' Diego said.' Marcus, have you found the VASIMR yet?'

'No, it's not here.' Marcus replied. As he answered, a gunshot rang out. Then there was a barrage of multiple shots.

'What's happening, guys?' Diego barked. 'Give me an update.' As he spoke, Bruno grabbed his arm and pointed through the window at the side of the lab. The VASMIR sat on a metal platform in what looked like a test chamber.

More shots rang out across the factory. 'Marcus is down. Marcus is down,' Dwayne's voice came over the radio. 'I'm pinned down here.'

'Diego, you have guards coming your way,' Leo announced over the radio. 'Two of them will be there in thirty seconds, coming from the north.'

'Bruno, help me get this door open,' Diego said as they crossed the room to the test chamber. Adriana covered them to take down any approaching security. Diego and Bruno forced the door to find the VASIMR that was anchored to the table. Diego and Bruno released the VASIMR part, but it took precious time.

Gunshots echoed through the factory. Adriana returned fire, incoming rounds bounced off the walls inside the lab, some hit pieces of equipment. 'Guys, not to be the bearer of bad news, but I hear sirens,' Chad announced over the radio from his position on the roof across the road.

Diego and Bruno lifted the VASIMR unit off its platform. 'This is not 40-50Kg, Diego,' Bruno said as they strained to lift it together.

'Over there,' Diego yelled above the noise of gunfire. As they maneuvered the VASIMR across the lab, shots rang out from behind the security team firing on Adriana.

'Sorry, guys, got held up,' Dwayne came over the radio as he shot a guard in the chest. 'I did what I could for Marcus, but he's gone.'

'Glad to have you back,' Adriana said as Diego and Bruno carried the VASIMR out of the back door of the lab area.

'More guards coming your way,' Leo shouted over the radio. 'You need to get out, right now. Take the back exit. There's a loading door on the far north side.'

As Leo relayed the message, Adriana shot the last guard and followed Diego and Bruno. Dwayne brought up the rear. Making their way up the side of the factory floor, they reached the rear loading bay. They heard voices, somebody was coming into the factory on the far side. 'Sounds like more company,' Dwayne said, and they left the factory and headed into the parking lot.

On the roof of the building opposite, Chad saw approaching police vehicles in the distance. Lining up the cars in his sights, he shot out several tyres, causing one vehicle to crash into a streetlamp and another to swerve to a stop. 'I'm on my way back to the jet,' Chad said. 'Can't do much more from up here.'

'Guards are coming around the back of the building,' Leo watched his screens. 'You won't be able to get back to the airport fence from there.'

'Damn it, what then?' Diego told them to put the heavy VASMIR unit on the parking lot ground.

'Hold on, can you a tunnel on your left?' Tom frantically scrolled through a map of the factory. 'There should be a tunnel right where you are.'

'Is that it?' Dwayne pointed towards a car parked under a green light illuminating a sign that read, *BORING COMPANY*. 'Come on, get moving,' Diego grunted. They picked up the VASMIR and made their way towards and the entrance of the tunnel. 'Where the hell does this go, Leo?'

'Looks like it's a test tunnel Elon Musk built to demo his Boring Company's products. It says here that the tunnel goes a mile and a half to the opposite side of the airport,' relayed Leo, as he scrolled through pages on his laptop.

'Perfect. Have the pilots taxi over there, and we'll meet you at the exit.' Said Diego.

'You expect us to lug this thing for a mile and a half, boss? Hope you're paying for the Chiropractor when this is over.' Said Bruno as he picked up his end of the VASMIR.

'Stop moaning and get on with it. Less chat and more muscle.' Diego smirked.

The team arrived at the tunnel entrance, and Diego pointed to a Tesla Cyber Truck parked and waiting for them, much to the relief of Bruno. The team loaded the VASIMR onto the back and got in. 'You going to turn this thing around?' Bruno asked.

'Haven't got time for that, and I don't think those tracking wheels will let me,' Diego replied. Several security guards came into view and were already firing. 'Shit, how do I start it?' Diego looked at the controls. Adriana leaned across from the passenger seat and pressed a button. The truck buzzed to life.

'Now go.' she said, as they watched the guards closing in on them. Adriana and Dwayne fired out of the window. As Diego accelerated in reverse, bullets struck the truck's windscreen in front of him, but nothing happened. Looking at his chest, he exclaimed, 'It's bulletproof.'

'Yeah, good job too, or you'd be an ex-getaway driver.' Bruno said. 'I remember watching Elon Musk do the demo for this cyber truck and there being something about it being bulletproof.'

The truck accelerated deeper into the tunnel as the guards fired. Nothing penetrated the steel or the Tesla's armored glass. A couple of minutes later, the team made it to the exit of the tunnel.

'You need to hustle, guys,' Leo said over the radio. 'The SpaceX boys are loading up and heading your way.'

Diego wasn't slowing down, and the truck tore out of the tunnel with the tracking wheels screaming as it careered to a stop. Turning the vehicle around, they headed for the airport perimeter fence. 'Open the loading bay, Leo.' Diego yelled as the truck smashed through the fence towards their jet.

Reaching the plane, they could hear sirens in the distance. They unloaded the VASMIR and heaved it into the loading bay. 'Take off now.' Diego shouted as he pulled the Gulfstream jet's door closed with everyone aboard. The team watched out of the windows as the flashing lights of police cars screeched closer. The plane accelerated down the runaway. After what felt like an age, it soared into the air, leaving the factory and the flashing lights below.

Diego collapsed into one of the captain's chairs with a sigh of relief. 'Great job, guys,' he said as everyone removed their equipment. 'Next stop, London.'

CHAPTER EIGHTEEN

In his mid-thirties, Jake Hunter had been at the CIA since he graduated college at Harvard. As a boy, he loved spy and cop movies. He'd never considered going into a government job until his final year. When he joined Harvard, he envisaged ending up as a high-flying lawyer or even a banker. Things hadn't worked out as expected for him.

During his last year, he met Professor Ryan Spalding, one of the regular guest lecturers, and everything changed. Professor Spalding taught political science and game theory, and Jake had found the latter fascinating.

They hit it off in class with lively debates on global issues, and they were keen rowers. As Ryan had been many years earlier, Jake was a star of the Harvard rowing team—it bonded them. The classes were more of a debate between the students than a lecture and often continued late into the night at a local bar. It was at the end of one of these classes that Ryan had asked Jake to stay behind. Initially, he thought he might have gone too far in his arguments regarding Thabo Mbeki and the way he was running South Africa.

'Thanks for staying, Jake.' Ryan shuffled the students' papers strewn around his desk. 'I know this is your last year, so I imagine you'll be thinking about the next step soon.' He removed his glasses and peered at Jake. 'What are your plans after Harvard'?

Jake laughed and shrugged his shoulders. 'Well, that's the million-dollar question. I've been asking myself recently. If I'm honest, I really don't know, but I've been thinking of a few options.'

'Well, where is your head at currently with those thoughts?'

'I thought law school was a natural progression, but I'm also considering taking a year out to travel.' Jake thought about the trip around the old cities of Europe he had wanted to do since he was in his early teens. 'A few of my friends are taking jobs in New York, which sounds like an option as well.' He recalled the Investment Bank recruiter he'd been talking to.

'Have you ever thought about a job in government?' Ryan asked. He fished out a business card.

'No, I've never considered it. I don't reckon it would pay much. What kind of job are you talking about? Something like lobbying in Washington or a policy role?' He tried picturing himself walking the halls of the Capitol building and couldn't see it.

'Not exactly, Jake. Have a seat for a moment.' Ryan motioned to the leather chair in front of his desk.

'Like what, then?' Jake strained his neck to see the business card Ryan was cupping in his hand.

'You're a brainy kid, Jake. One the brightest I've ever taught, in fact. I think it would be a shame to waste that gift. Living the rat-race life somewhere like New York would be a waste. You're top of most of your classes, and it's obvious you aren't even working that hard.' Ryan watched Jake enjoying the compliments.

'Well, thanks for the kind words, sir, I guess.'

'There are a several government organizations that I think would be interested in talking to you.' Ryan handed over the card.

Taking it, Jake flipped it over and examined both sides. There was a single phone number and nothing else. 'It's just a phone number?' Puzzled, Jake looked at Ryan, trying to decipher what this was really about.

'Yes, it's a recruiter contact for you to reach out to.'

'Okay, thanks, but what department do they work for?'

'Give them a call, and you'll find out if you suit any of the roles. If you are up for a challenge, that is.' Ryan packed his bag.

'Okay, I'll think about it.' The number didn't fit any area codes he'd seen before.

'Well, don't think too long. Now, onto more pressing matters, are you coming to the bar with the rest of us?' He packed a pile of student essays into his faded brown Mulberry briefcase and snapped the catch shut.

'Yeah, I'm starving.' Jake slipped the business card into his back pocket.

***

A few days later, Jake was rifling through his pockets, looking for his student pass, when he found the business card. He looked at the number on the crumped card and decided to give it a go out of curiosity. To his surprise, it rang but then went to voicemail seconds later. Confused, Jake hung up. A text message a few minutes later instructed him to go to a local Harvard bar called the Druid that Friday night at 7pm.

And that's how his recruitment into the CIA came about.

After a couple of years, with CIA postings around Europe, He returned to Langley and was assigned to the Quantum Programme. The Alexei Averin case ended with them chasing a terrorist organization to Bali. It was one of a long list of gangs, cartels, corporations, and rogue nations that Jake and the Quantum Programme had brought to heel.

CHAPTER NINETEEN

When Abigail heard about Carl's idea to hire a family for Rich, she couldn't decide if it was genius or just plain crazy. There was no progress with Rich since he had woken up, and Carl and the others were starting to wonder if he would ever remember anything. What made Carl more impatient was the price of bitcoin flying through the roof, and they were looking after a guy who was potentially worth billions and didn't know it.

'I'm not waiting any longer,' Carl said to Stuart. The latter was trying to calm him down by reassuring him that they were doing all they could to make Rich remember.

Carl had driven the dusty desert road to the facility from Las Vegas, hoping there was good news on the recovery of the patient's memory. 'How do we know he's not playing us?' Carl declared, slamming his fist on the desk.

'What do you mean, *playing us*?'

'How do we know that he doesn't recall everything about his past, and he's just biding his time until he gets better and can walk out of here?'

'I guess we can't be sure.'

'Exactly, so I want faster progress. Get it done.'

Abigail entered the surveillance room after taking Rich his lunch. It was a week since Rich had woken up, and they had tried all kinds of tricks to make him remember.

'Carl, he still hasn't indicated any recollection of his

bitcoins,' Abigail said. 'I know that's not what you want to hear, but we're trying everything we can.'

'We are sitting on a goddam fortune here.' Carl pointed to the video screen showing Rich sitting up in bed, watching TV and eating a lunch that Carl was paying for.

'It's going to take time. We're lucky he's awake and not brain-damaged, so let's not rush this.' please be patient with the process a little longer he's been in a coma, so we can't expect it to be instant.

'Not good enough. We need the process to be faster. I have an idea I want you to try. I've found some people who might be able to help us.'

'Help us to do what, exactly?' Stuart said.

'Help us to get him remembering, of course. They are reliable and have worked for the organization before.'

'And what will they be doing to him?' Abigail was concerned, given Carl's reputation in the organization. He had made his name with his ruthlessness.

'Don't worry, they won't harm him. Yet. I'm going to have them visit the patient pretending to be his family. If they gain his trust, he might tell them what he remembers from before the accident.'

'That might work, I suppose,' Stuart said, turning to Abigail. 'As far as we can tell, he doesn't remember any family or friends, so he'd have no reason to doubt them.'

'I guess it could work,' Abigail responded. The decision had already been made, anyway. 'We need to be careful though, if he *does* remember, he's going to realize that they aren't his family pretty quickly.'

'Great, let's do this, then,' Carl said. 'I'll arrange for their first visit tomorrow afternoon. Work on getting them set up with a suitable back story.'

'Okay, we'll make some preparations here and let Rich know his family will be visiting.' Abigail said.

***

The actors turned up the next day. It was just after lunch, and Rich had finished his food and had fallen asleep.

'We just have to talk to him for a bit then?' Bobby, the grey-haired blackjack dealer from Carl's Casino, asked.

'Yes, that's basically all we need from you. Just remember the background info and stay on script,' Abigail said.

'And how many times do we need to do this?' Shirley had worked as a cocktail waitress in the casino but was now working in the back office.

'Look, you've been selected because you are loyal, long-serving employees. Carl will be paying you a lot extra for this work. It could be once, or it could be thirty times. Just remember to never talk about it outside of this building, and you'll be taken care of. To Carl, loyalty and confidentiality are paramount.'

'What if he suspects something when we're talking to him? Asked Kim, the younger woman playing Rich's sister.

'You aren't professional actors, so just do your best. I will be there in case anything goes wrong. We'll just put any issues down to him being under medication and confused?' Abigail knew that they were picked because of their backgrounds and a likeness to Rich's family. They all had minor criminal convictions or questionable behaviours that the organization could use for leverage if anything ever went wrong.

'I guess so.' Kim looked at the others, and they nodded.

'Let's go meet your new family member.' Abigail laughed to relax the mood.

Rich sat up as they entered the room. 'Hey, Abi, I didn't know you were coming in this early.'

'Well, your family is here to see you now that you're feeling better. You okay for us all to come in?'

'Hello,' Rich said nervously as he looked at them in turn. 'I'm sorry, this is embarrassing, but what are your names?'

'I'm Jim,' the man replied. 'This is your mother, Eileen, your sister, Amanda.'

There was an awkward silence as they stared at each other. 'Well, go on then. You must have lots to catch up on,' Abigail ushered the fake family towards Rich's bed. 'So, Rich, do you remember your sister? She's going to Stamford just like you did.'

'I went to Stamford? You haven't mentioned that before.'

'Ah, so you know it's a college, then? That seems like some progress.'

'I guess you're right. Can you tell me more about my life, please?'

Amanda thought back to the list of information in the script they had been given.

'Well, we grew up in Maine on a lake,' she started. 'Do you remember the lake and the house at all?'

Rich rubbed his head, struggling to think back to his childhood, but nothing much came. 'Did we have dogs? I think I might remember two dogs, and I was running through a field with them.'

'Yes, we had two dogs,' Jim said, jumping to her rescue. 'They were cocker spaniels. Black cocker spaniels, and you loved playing with them as a kid.'

Rich looked at the television screen, thinking about the strange warnings he had received. He did remember two dogs, but they weren't black, and they were most definitely weren't cocker spaniels. They were golden Labradors, called Max and Miffy.

'Ah, yes, I remember now,' said Rich with a smile. 'Can you tell me more about my recent life?'

'Of course. Is there anything specific you'd like to talk about to help you remember?' Jim looked to Abigail, who nodded her approval. She motioned for him to go on without Rich answering. 'Well, you studied computer science and mathematics and Stanford. After that, you moved to a technology company to start a career in what you said was research.'

'What do you mean, research?'

'You never told us much about your work. It was very important to you, though.'

'Why don't you all take a seat, and then you can relax.' Abigail moved a couple of chairs around the bed for the parents to sit on.

***

After the family left, Rich stared at the television screen and what he believed were the latest news reports. The meeting had worn him out. He was groggy from the meds, and his eyes were heavy.

'Rich, cough once to acknowledge that you understand me and twice for no. Those people who visited you were not your real family.' The words flashed up on the screen.

What the hell was happening again? Who was writing to him? He felt that he might be hallucinating from the medication he was given. Rich coughed once in acknowledgement of the message and decided to take everything with a pinch of salt until proven otherwise.

'The woman—Abigail is planning to get you out of this facility. You must go with her, is that understood?'

Rich looked at the CCTV camera and then coughed again, but he felt ridiculous taking instructions from a television. He felt paranoid and didn't trust anybody—not even himself. He wondered if this was a trick by the people keeping him here.

'*Don't tell anyone about these messages, not even Abigail. Your life depends on it. Is that clear?*'

Another message flashed up on the screen, but as it did, Abigail came back in, and the words disappeared. All Rich registered was the word '*Danger.*' he coughed once as an acknowledgement.

'You must be tired from all the excitement. How are you feeling? Abigail put her hand on his arm.

'I'm just confused. When are my family coming back to visit again? I guess it takes time for me to remember everything.'

'They can come back tomorrow if you like. Did seeing them help you remember anything?' She sat on the bed and leant across Rich.

'I don't think I remember them, but I'm trying. Maybe I remember my sister a bit.' Rich thought back to the warning on the screen and thought his bet bed was to play along. But why should he trust Abigail?

'Don't worry, it will come back eventually.' She stroked his face. 'You've had a tough time, so be patient with yourself.'

'Thanks, Abigail. If anyone has had patience, then it's you.'

'It's worth it to see those beautiful blue eyes of yours.' Abigail moved in closer. 'I'll let you rest now and come back this evening to check on you at dinner.'

Rich watched as Abigail walked out of the room. At least he knew the person messaging him on the television wasn't Abigail. She was in his room when the last message appeared.

CHAPTER TWENTY

Tom Thacker let out an irritated sigh as the desk intercom buzzed. 'Sir, got Agents Daniels and Reynolds to see you.'

'Fine, send them in. This better be good, though,' the Deputy Director replied.

'Hear that?' The secretary looked up from her desk at them. 'He's been in a bad mood all day. Rather you than me.'

'Unfortunately, we don't have great news, but we'll make it quick.'

'Morning, sir. Sorry to disturb you, but we have some critical information on the North Korean rocket programme.'

'Go on then. Spit it out.'

'The theft from SpaceX involved some critical rocket parts that the North Koreans would likely need for their programme. The theft was well planned and executed. The team that broke in knew what they were looking for and where to find it,' Agent Daniels said as she carefully placed the case file on the Deputy Director's desk.

'What's the theory? You think the North Koreans broke in and stole this? How would they get the information? They've never been hugely advanced when it comes to operations like this? They tend to be small teams stealing from rich individuals or small, badly protected museums.'

'We believe it could be a team funded by the North Koreans,' Daniels responded.

'There's more you should know,' Reynolds jumped in. 'We think it could be that organization called WRAITH that Jake uncovered on the Bali mission.'

'That's going to make it a bit more complex then.'

'Evidence suggests that WRAITH runs mercenary teams all over the globe. The teams specialize in different skillsets and targets. Some are hacking groups, and some are theft specialists. They seem to be into all types of business,' Reynolds said.

'If they have this part from SpaceX, where are they going next?'

'We have a list of the items they could want. We picked it up through North Korean intelligence, which was lucky because this could lead to cracking WRAITH's communications. We have narrowed it down to a few places where they could get these parts. Look at page five, sir,' Daniels said.

'You can forget MI5. There's no way someone would break into their HQ in central London. The other sites don't seem that viable either, really. I'd say the last two are the most likely. Have our contacts in those countries give the authorities a heads up.'

'Understood, sir,' Daniels replied.

'It says here that they escaped on a jet. Where did the jet land?

'That's the strange thing, sir. We don't know. It's as if the jet disappeared just after takeoff.'

'Well, keep on it. We can't let the North Korean's get hold of these parts. Tell agent Hunter about the potential WRAITH involvement. He'll want to know.'

CHAPTER TWENTY-ONE

Night had fallen, and the facility was eerily still, with just the occasional wolf howl coming from the blackness of the Nevada desert. Abigail and George were on duty, along with a couple of security guards outside. One smoked a cigarette and shivered in the cold desert air as the call of a faraway owl echoed across the car park that was empty, apart from a couple of staff cars.

While Rich was in a coma, the staff spent their time bingeing Netflix, playing cards, and browsing the internet. Things had changed since Rich had woken up.

Abigail spent most of her time talking and giggling with Rich in his room at the end of the corridor. George hated the fact that Rich was getting her attention. Driving to work that night, he had felt tense and gripped the steering wheel so tight that his knuckles ached. He knew Abigail was told to befriend Rich. But even so, she didn't need to perch herself on the edge of his bed like that. There was nothing wrong with the chair in the corner. And there was a sparkle in her eyes these days. Can you fake that?

George rubbed his hands to warm them up as he arrived in the monitoring room. 'Damn, these nights are getting cold,' he said, hanging his jacket in one of the lockers. 'Day shift is much better than these twelve-hour nights.'

Abigail recoiled and waved her hands to try and waft away the overpowering stench of cigarette smoke. 'George, you promised you'd quit.'

'You sleep most of the time. And, anyway, stop moaning. I did quit for a bit, but then, after the patient woke up, things got stressful again.' He slumped in a chair next to Abigail and laughed, but it didn't lighten the atmosphere.

'With that smell hanging around, it's a good time for me to take Rich his dinner.'

'Oh, so it's Rich now, and not the patient, is it? Got a soft spot for old Richard, have we?' He tapped angrily on one of the keyboards.

'It sounds like you're jealous, George. You know it's just my job, and you'll always be my favourite.' She ruffled his hair and picked up her nurse's jacket.

What an ass she's got, George thought, watching her walk into the hallway.

***

The kitchen was the old hotel's reception desk with a kettle and microwave perched on it, with a small fridge propped against the desk. Abigail surveyed the mess that George and the security guards had left and groaned. She took out a frozen pizza and a carton of soup to slip into the microwave and heard shuffling. Squinting into the darkness of the lobby, she saw nothing. Her eyes adjusted to the dark enough to be able to make out the shredded cables and wires, where opulent lights once hung. Two pigeons dropped down from a hole in the ceiling with flapping wings as they chased each other around the lobby, getting caught in wallpaper scraps and stirring up the dust. She supposed they must have got in through one of the holes in the roof or numerous broken windows.

Reaching for a pen, she scribbled a note on a scrap of

paper and hid it under the soup bowl.

Abigail picked up the plastic tray she took another look around the lobby. This place creeps me out, she thought, looking forward to the day when she would never have to come to work there again. It would be soon if things went to plan.

She smiled at the effort that had been put into making part of the Casino look like a hospital as she walked down the hallway to the patient's room. Even as far as fake signs giving directions to non-existent hospital departments. It made her feel as if she was on a movie set. The walls were freshly painted, the furniture and fittings all looked like new, and the lights actually worked. It was such a contrast to the rest of the building.

George came out of the monitoring room as she approached it. 'How about I take the patient dinner tonight, Abi?'

'No, George, I'm fine.' She clutched the tray to stop him from taking it.

'Go on, I think I should get to know him a bit.'.

She could see the note had slipped from under the soup bowl, and she could even read part of what she'd written. She felt herself flush. 'George, it's fine, I can do it. You relax and watch a bit of Netflix like you usually do.'

George wasn't letting go. 'Go on, Abi, let me go talk to him. You can have a rest and chill out for a bit.' His gaze fell to the tray, and Abigail reacted fast. If he saw the note, it would all be over.

'Look, George.' She raised her voice so much it took him by surprise. 'Carl was very clear that I was to take his food, or it will delay the process.'

George had never heard her so forceful. 'Okay, I was just trying to help. I thought you might want a break, that's all.'

'Thanks, but I'm fine. I won't be long, so go find a movie we can watch together or something.' She brushed past him.

Pausing at Rich's door, she looked over her shoulder, making sure George was out of view. Rearranging the note, she turned the door handle.

Rich sat up, rubbing his eyes and yawning. 'Is it dinner time already?' He strained to see what Abigail was delivering as she maneuvered the tray onto the bedside table. 'Never gets any better, does it?'

She laughed. 'Bit tired this evening, are you?' She glanced at the ceiling camera, suspecting George was watching. 'Looks like you just woke up.'

Rich rubbed his thigh and drew a leg up to this chest. 'Yeah, I did those leg exercises you showed me earlier. After that, I must've fallen asleep.' It was pretty exhausting.

'Good, keep them up; you need to get stronger.' The red light on the camera blinked away, indicating it was recording.

'So, what delicious meal do you have for me today?' Rich said sarcastically as he put his legs back under the covers.

'We decided to move you up to big boy food. We have pizza tonight.'

'No porridge today, then?'

'That's right, but how about you start with the tomato soup?' She glanced at the door, then at the ceiling. She had carried out the same routine numerous times, and nobody had ever come in the room, but the thoughts running through her head about what she was about to do made her nervous.

Rich sensed something. Why was she looking at the cameras so frequently?

'Did you have a good day today? Are you okay, Abigail?' He put his hand on hers. She moved the tray and propped his pillows up. 'I'm glad you're here. I was getting pretty bored watching the same television channel.'

'Yes, I'm good. Have a drink, Rich. You look dehydrated. And, let me adjust your television for you. It looks a bit fuzzy.' She stood under the television attached to the ceiling via a bracket. She knew it was a dead spot where the ceiling cameras couldn't see her.

Rich picked up his sizeable grey plastic mug to drink. As he put it down, he saw the note under the soup bowl and pulled it out. *Don't react. Just listen to me*, said the scribbled handwriting on a scrap of dirty paper.

'Thanks, Abigail, I was thirsty,' Rich replied, taking a side glance at one of the cameras and being careful not to move his head too much.

'There you go, all adjusted for you. Can you see the television clearly?' She took his hand in hers.

'Yeah, it's much better now. Thanks, Abi.' He looked at her hand, squeezing his tight.

She leaned in to adjust the pillows. 'They're watching us. Just keep talking as if we're discussing the food.' There's something I need to tell you.

'I was starving. I'm glad you brought me pizza and soup. It makes a change from the sloppy stuff' Rich put a spoonful of soup in his mouth.

'Rich, just act natural. Listen, this is not a real hospital.' Abigail paused, waiting for a reaction, but he just stared back blankly.

'The food is definitely an improvement,' he lowered his voice. What the hell are you talking about?'

'You were kidnapped and brought here during your coma. This facility is run by an organization that wants what's in your head.'

Rich slid the tray of food away and lifted the bedsheet covering his legs. 'Let me out of here. I want to see.'

'No, Rich.' Abigail pulled the sheet back. 'Your life depends on this, so you need to stop right now and listen.' She grabbed his arm and pushed him back against the pillow.

He relaxed as she swung the tray of food back over the bed.

'And what the hell is it in my head that they want, Abigail?'

'You have to trust me. These people won't wait much longer, and it's not going to be pleasant for you.' She stood up and tucked his sheets in.

'Tell me what they want. You can't just drop this news on me. I need to know.' He raised his voice.

She put a finger over her lips. 'I need to get you out of here. I'll be back in a few hours. I'll give you instructions then.'

'This some kind of stupid joke?'

'Deadly serious. Promise me you won't do anything until I get back tonight.'

Rich watched Abigail leave and then he stared at the tray of food and realized he'd lost his appetite. Things were playing out just like the person messaging him on the screen had said. What did she mean, he'd been kidnapped? This had to be a joke. His head was flashing with memories, and he strained to remember his stay in the hospital. How had he got there, and what were the first things he recalled when he woke up? He hadn't been out of the room at all since coming round, and there were no windows. He could be anywhere. And there was no way of ruling out what she was saying.

In the hallway, Abigail passed the monitoring office. She looked in, and George had his headphones on, watching a movie on his iPad. She sighed. He hadn't been watching the monitors or listening in, after all.

In the old reception, she looked for signs of the guards. Through the cracked panes in the entrance doors to the grand lobby, she saw one of the guards heading back from his rounds. He joined the other man sitting on the crumbling stone fountain outside the entrance.

She walked across the lobby, carefully avoiding stepping on the bits of broken glass littering the dusty floor. Moving further into the darkness, she made sure she was out of earshot. She took out her phone and dialed.

'Hello, it's Abigail.'

'Go on,' said the synthesized voice.

'I'm moving the patient.'

A noise came out of the darkness. Startled, her first reaction was that she'd been outed, but turning around, she saw a rat weaving a path among some loose cabling.

'Are you still there?'

'Sorry, I thought someone was listening in,' Abigail continued. 'They've lost patience with him. If they don't extract the information from him soon, they'll likely kill him.'

'Has he told you anything?

'Nothing so far. I'm taking him out of the facility tonight.' She looked at her Apple watch, thinking about the best time to make her move. 'Just before sunrise will be the best time, and I'll drive him straight to the airport.'

'Take him to New York. Stay there until I contact you.'

'Why New York?'

'Just take him there. Continue to build his trust. Keep him happy and try to remind him of the details I sent you about his past. It will be harder for them to find you in a large city.'

'I really don't know if this is going to work. He's given minimal indication that he remembers his previous life, apart from a few small, unimportant memories.' A wave of doubt came over her. 'I'm still slipping him the suppressant drugs to stop him from remembering anything. Once I get him out and I let them wear off, it could be a different story. Just have a plan-B to get me out of here if this blows up in my face.'

'Just do what we discussed. It will be fine. After all this work, I don't want you getting cold feet about the mission at the last minute.'

'Someone's coming. I'll keep you updated. Got to go.'

Abigail hung up as one of the security guards came through the front lobby doors.

She watched the guard make a coffee, and then he sat down and put his dusty boots up on the old reception desk. She couldn't loiter for long, and she emerged into the light, purposefully making lots of noise.

Startled, the guard reached for his gun, squinting as he tried to make out who it was. 'Abigail, is that you? What the hell you are doing over in that side of the building?'

'Hi, how're things? Just wondered what was over there. I got bored, so I thought I'd do some exploring. Wanted to get onto the roof and see the view.' She hoped she sounded plausible.

'How was it?' John, the security guard, relaxed and took another sip of coffee.

'How was what?

'The view. How was the view from the roof?'

'Oh yeah, the view was beautiful. You should go take a look later tonight. You can see the lights from the Vegas strip in the distance.' This was perfect. If she could get rid of one guard, the better the odds of escaping. 'Maybe go up around sunrise. The view will be stunning.' she said, smiling and walking back towards the monitoring room.

'Okay, thanks for the heads up, I will do. Oh, and Abigail, how did you get up there without a flashlight?'

She froze. After a pause, she replied, 'I just used my phone.' She held it up and flicked on the light. Reaching the corridor, she let out a sigh of relief. The next few hours were going to be a long waiting game.

With the first hint of sunrise creeping across the Nevada desert, the shapes of cacti dotted around the casino appeared out of the darkness like a mirage. The dawn chorus of birdsong could be heard, but they seemed a way off. Abigail knew it was now or never. Walking back through the lobby with her morning coffee, she went down the hallway for what she hoped would be her last time. Poking her head into the monitoring room, she saw George fast asleep with his iPad on his lap. It had been another long night shift. He tended to fall asleep during the last few hours. Perfect, she thought. She put her coffee cup down and flicked off the audio to Rich's room so George wouldn't wake up. Muffling the click with her thumb, she dropped the lock on the monitor room door as she passed.

Putting her hand on her chest, she took a deep breath to calm herself and walked the short distance to Rich's room.

Rich sat up in his bed. 'Is it time to go?' He glanced at the cameras.

Abigail pressed a finger to her lips. 'You need to keep it down, Rich. I've turned the audio off, but they might still hear you if someone walks past the door.'

'What's the plan? Where are we going? I'm still thinking you're joking about all this,' he said, with nervous excitement.

'My car's outside. We need to get as far away from here as possible before anyone notices you've gone. Put these on. Quickly.'

He opened a bag to reveal a neat pile of clothing. 'You had these stashed under my bed the whole time? I didn't even see you bring them in.'

'I put them there yesterday.' She helped him pull up his jeans.

'You thought of everything.'

'Hope so. I'm done for if not. Come on, hurry up with that T-shirt. These guys won't mess around if they catch us.' Kneeling, she forced the shoes onto his feet.

Rich pulled the T-shirt over his head. 'Sorry I'm so slow, still sore and stiff when I bend my legs.'

'Now, stand up. I need to see you walk.'

Rich tried standing, but he fell forward into Abigail's arms. 'Damn it, sorry.' They stood, inches apart. 'It takes me a while to warm up, but I'll be fine. Don't worry. I just really hope you're the good guy in all of this.'

'Rich, you can do it. The physio work we've been doing proves it.' Abigail was hoping the reminder might give him a boost of confidence. Watching him get out of bed, she had her doubts.

'Yeah, I know. I'm just really stiff.' He rubbed his legs. 'My arms and everything else are fine. I just get pins and needles in my legs.'

'Okay, change of plan, we're going to crawl along the hallway. There's a monitoring room with a glass window, and we need to make sure nobody sees us. Put your arm around my shoulder for support if you need to.' Moving towards the door, she winced as the handle made the same annoying creak.

A squeak accompanied Rich's every step.

'Damn it.' He looked down at his shoes. 'Looks like you got me the worst pair of shoes for breaking out.'

'Take them off, then.' she whispered impatiently. She crouched on the floor and motioned to Rich to do the same. 'Come on, it be getting light soon, so we need to get a move on.'

Crawling along the cold floor of the hallway, they reached the monitoring office window and crept beneath it. The door was ajar. Abigail had locked it on the way out.

Peering through the crack, she grabbed Rich to stop him in his tracks. 'Damn it. George isn't there.' she whispered in his ear.

'Well, where should this guy be?' Rich leant forward to look in the room.

'Get back.' She pushed him up against the wall. 'If he's not there, he must have seen us getting ready in the room. He's probably gone to get the guards.'

'Well, now what do we do? Let's go back. If we get caught, we can just say we were just practicing walking or something.'

'Going back isn't an option. If you do, you'll end up dead, so we need to push on and get out of here.' She stood up. 'Come on, we need to move fast before George gets back.' She pulled him to his feet. 'Ready?'

Searing pain shot down Rich's back. 'Hang on, those pins and needles haven't gone.' His face contorted as he felt a sharp wave of pain working up what felt like every vertebra.

'You'll have a lot more than pins and needles to worry about if you don't get walking.' She pulled him along the hallway.

Reaching the door to the lobby, she paused to press her ear against the door. 'What are you doing?' Rich moved closer to listen.

'Shush. Be quiet. The kitchen is on the other side of this door. If someone's making a drink, we've got nowhere to go.' She eased the door to reveal the lobby, reception desk and their route to the entrance. 'I can see one of the guards outside, but not George.'

'So, do we just make a run for it?'

'With luck, the other guard is on the roof, watching the sunrise. Get down on the ground, and let's try and crawl as far as the reception desk.'

Abigail led the way. 'Abi, what are you doing, and why was the door locked? Did you lock me in?' metres from the desk, a voice boomed behind them.

She stood up and faced George. Rich stayed frozen on the ground behind her.

George craned his neck to peer around Abigail's long white doctor's jacket. 'What the fuck are you doing? Is that the goddam patient?'

'I'm sorry, George.' She moved into an attacking stance.

'For what? Where are you taking him? I don't understand.' George hurried towards them, skirting around Abigail to get to Rich. She reached behind her and pulled out a nine-millimeter Glock 19. In a perfectly timed swoop, she hit him on the temple—she hit him hard. George collapsed in a pile of limbs.

'What the hell, Abigail.' Rich sat against the cold marble of the reception desk, staring at the handgun. 'Who is George? And is he dead?' he asked, looking at the crumpled body on the floor, his bloodied head rested inches from Rich's feet.

'Of course not. He'll be fine. I just knocked him out.' She scanned the lobby and dragged George behind the reception desk, folding his arms and legs so they couldn't be seen by anyone.

'Why do you have a gun, Abigail?' Rich asked as they sat on the floor, panting.

A hint of orange sunlight entered the lobby, lighting up the enormous supporting columns. 'I got the gun from one of the guards' lockers. Come on, we need to get to my car.'

She rose to her knees and peered over the top of the counter, towards the entrance where the other guard was sitting outside. 'He's still there. Let's move towards the entrance, and we can hide behind that valet's desk. That way, we'll be right by my car when he moves out of the way.'

Rich got on his knees and watched as Abigail crept into the lobby. After a few seconds, he followed, unsure of his balance. 'Abigail,' he called out in a whisper. She turned to see him pointing to beyond the front entrance and at the security guard strolling towards one of the double doors to the lobby.

Abigail's heart sank. 'Go back.'

The security guard pushed the door open.

'Get back to the counter.' They scurried along the floor like mice.

'Damn, that was close.' Rich rubbed his legs. 'Well, the pins and needles have gone at least. It just hurts like hell now.'

'He's either going to the monitoring room or the bathroom. If he's going to the monitoring room were screwed because he'll see George.' She brandished the handgun anticipating trouble.

The security guard stood at the entrance, peering around the lobby as if he heard something echo from the darkness. Unclipping his radio and placing it to his mouth, he began, 'John, where are you?'

'I'm on the roof, watching the sunrise with a coffee, Mark. You should come up. Abigail suggested it. The view's fantastic.'

'We're meant to be guarding this place, not messing around on the roof.'

'I am guarding. I can see if anyone's coming for miles up here, so it's better than being down where you are.'

'Good point. Our shift ends soon, so don't mess around up there too long.'

The guard clipped his radio to his belt and frowned. He reached the entrance and paused. Something didn't feel right. But maybe he just imagined things. He looked around as though he sensed that something was wrong. When Abigail thought that she couldn't take it anymore, he shoved the door to the lobby's restrooms open and went inside.

'Good, he's going to the restrooms. We need to move now, Rich.'

Half a dozen giant double doors led out of the lobby, and the first one they reached was jammed. 'Try the next one,' Abigail said impatiently.

Finally, they were outside. Rich looked back at the building as the early morning sun lit up the front. 'My God, look at this place, he said, taking in the dirty, peeling paint and broken windows. 'I can't believe this is where I've been.'

Abigail grabbed his arm. 'Come on, my car is over there.' She pointed to a battered old Honda Accord across the car park.

Pulling open the door to the passenger seat, she helped him in. As she was closing the door, she paused, then rummaged around the papers and mess in her glove box and took out a long screwdriver.

'What are you doing? You said we need to go.'

'Hang on a minute. I'll slow them down in case they try to follow us.' she went to the car next to hers and stabbed two tyres until they hissed and deflated.

Mark, the security guard, came out of the restroom and as he did he heard groaning from the lobby. Walking round the reception desk he found George on the floor, holding his head and trying to sit up. 'What the hell happened?'

'Abigail. She's taken the patient,' George replied, rubbing his head as he stared at his blood on the floor. 'Don't just stand there. Do something.'

'What the fuck!' Mark grabbed his radio. 'John, you still on the roof?'

'Yeah, I'm coming down soon, don't worry.'

'No. Wait. Stay there. Can you see Abigail? She's knocked George out and is running off with our patient. She must be stopped,' Mark shouted frantically. He ran to the patient's room, but it was empty. 'The patient's definitely gone, John.'

'I've got a visual. She's getting into her car.'

'Damn it. Stop her from leaving. We'll be killed if we let them get away.'

'How do I stop them?' If I shoot, I might hit the patient.'

'Shoot their tyres out', Mark shouted, bursting into the lobby.

Abigail fumbled with her keys.

'Come on,' Rich said, looking over his shoulder. 'They'll be after us any time now.'

'I'm trying.' She tried to start the engine, but in her panic, she'd flooded it, and nothing happened. 'Come on, you piece of crap,' she shouted, hitting the steering wheel. A gunshot echoed around the carpark. The engine sparked into life but it had cost them valuable seconds.

'Jesus. They're shooting at us. Move it. Now.' Rich slunk down in his seat. 'That guard. He's coming out the front.' He yelled pointing.

Abigail swung the car around. Facing Mark, she accelerated forwards. Mark raised his gun, aiming at the vehicle.

'There's only one way out of here, I'm afraid.' And with that, she slammed her foot to the floor. 'Out of the way, Mark.'

Mark pumped rounds at the old Honda, hitting the wing mirror and bonnet.

'Get down.' Abigail yelled, and they ducked below the dashboard. A couple of seconds later, there was a loud thud as Mark bounced off the bonnet and landed on the road.

'Oh, my god. That guy, have you killed him? That was

way too close,' Rich said, glancing behind them. 'Nobody's following us yet.'

'But there will be. Just as soon as they get themselves organized. We need to get to the airport, pronto.' Abigail swung onto the main road and headed west. 'We're going to New York.'

'Why New York?'

'It's far away from here, and we can blend in. Nobody will find us there.'

The road stretched out before them, with little traffic in either direction. 'So, tell me why I was in that awful place?'

'The organization kidnapped you from a real hospital in San Francisco.' She glanced across to judge his reaction, worried how he might react to the news she was about to dump on him.

'What the hell. I was kidnapped?' He saw a sign go past telling them they were nearing the airport.

'After your car accident, you were left in a coma. When someone in the organization got wind of your fortune, they kidnapped you hoping you'd wake up and tell them where the fortune was.' She knew this was a lot for Rich to take in, but he needed to know.

'I don't get it. Why was I there, Abigail? What organisation?'

'It's because of what you invented and how many you hold. You invented a mining algorithm.' Abigail tried to gauge if any of this news was registering with him.

'What algorithm? What do you mean?'

'Your bitcoin mining algorithm.' She hoped the mention of bitcoin might jog his memory.

'Bitcoin?' Rich held his head as a wave of the dreaded sharp, jabbing pain returned.

'Yes, bitcoin. It's a cryptocurrency. You can buy and

sell bitcoin like stock. The price has skyrocketed over the last few years. I'll explain more later. We need to get our wits about us. Here's the airport turning.'

'You mean the thing they kept talking about on the television?' Rich remembered the constant news shows on the television in his room.

'Yes, that's right. We kept playing you news stories and shows mentioning bitcoin and cryptocurrencies so that you would remember your work. Cryptocurrency is like electronic money. You invented a mining algorithm for mining bitcoin, which earned you a fortune.'

'So, bitcoin can be mined using computers, and more bitcoin can be earned by the mining process?' he asked, recalling what the TV had told him.

'That's right. Well, it seems like the shows we played might have had a small effect on you.' She slowed as the airport drop off zone came into view and filled with early morning passengers.

Rich searched his mind, but it was painful every time he tried to remember. Flashbacks to a rainy road were all that came to him. 'I can't remember anything. Just a rainy road, and I'm driving. Then, it's all a blank. Sometimes, I get a flash of an office of some sort.'

'You created what the organization I'm working for thinks is a super-fast method for mining bitcoin, and if they can get that from you, then they'd effectively be able to print money.' Abigail pulled up at the terminal. 'We'll dump the car here and buy tickets.' Shoving her door open, she leapt out. 'Come on, move it. I'm sure this is the first place they'll look for us. We need to get on the first flight out of here.'

'I feel dizzy. I don't know if I can do this.' He reached to steady himself on the car door.

Abigail hurried around to the passenger side of the

vehicle. 'Let me help you. You can do it. You don't have a choice if you want to live past the next ten minutes. The ticket desk is just through those doors, and you can wait on one of those chairs.' She grabbed an arm to help him out of the car.

She guided him through the airport's glass entrance. Even at this early hour, crowds of tourists were milling around the terminal. Families with screaming kids, gamblers who had come to Las Vegas looking to win or lose a fortune, and couples there for their Vegas wedding.

Abigail guided Rich to a chair and sat him down. 'Stay here, and I'll be back in a couple of minutes.'

As she turned, Rich grabbed her arm. 'What about my family?' In a rare lucid moment, he had wondered what the repercussions might be for them now that he had escaped.

'I'm sorry, Rich. I told you before, they weren't your real family.'

'What do you mean? Who were they, then?'

'The organization hired them to play your family. We needed you to get your memory back and had to make you believe you were in a hospital. They had a script to follow to try and trigger your memory. Look, we can talk about this later.' Abigail yanked her arm free and dashed into the crowd.

Rich had only just seen his supposed family and having it ripped away made him question everything. He knew the person writing to him through the television was right about Abigail getting him out of the facility and about the family being fake. So, where did that leave him now? Rich looked around the airport trying to block out the noise of the crowds.

Through the glass entrance, far down the side of the airport drop-off zone, he noticed two men get out of a car and looked into the crowd. He was sure they were looking for somebody. He had to warn Abigail and stood up with a groan.

'Two tickets to New York on the next flight, please. Here are our identification and my credit card.' Abigail handed over the items.

'You're cutting it fine, miss,' the woman at the ticket desk replied.

'I know, my boyfriend got a bit drunk last night and is feeling the worse for wear,' Abigail said, smiling. 'I guess that's just Vegas, right? He ain't the first and sure as hell won't be the last.' She laughed for good effect.

'There you go, miss. You should just about make the flight if you hurry. Security is over there.' The woman pointed to an entrance fifty metres away as Rich arrived at the desk.

'We've got a problem,' he whispered into her ear.

'And what's that, Honey?' Abigail said, still smiling, as they turned away from the desk, and she put her arm around him.

Rich motioned across the terminal to two men pushing through the crowd. 'Those your friends from the casino?'

'Damn it. If we can get through security, we'll be fine. The flight leaves real soon.' As she spoke, her eyes met John's, and he broke into a jog through the crowd, pushing people out of the way as he went.

Rich and Abigail pressed through the throng of tourists, too. The security entrance was close, but so was John. 'You need to hurry, Rich.' Abigail pulled him through the crowd by the arm.

'I'm going as fast as I can.' He realised his legs were feeling better now he'd been walking about a bit. They felt like dragging lead pipes along before.

With ten metres to go, John and Mark had almost caught up. Rich had thoughts of being dragged back to the derelict casino just as a large group of men, singing and dancing, passed in front of John and Mark, blocking their path.

Abigail and Rich were at the security gate and handed over their tickets. As they looked back, they watched the guards struggling through the group of revelers. Thank god for Vegas bachelor parties,' Abigail declared.

'Shit, that was close.' Rich looked at the departure time for New York as they passed beneath the information board.

'This way.' Abigail pointed to the gate number for their flight. 'We should be safe now.'

'Looks like we're the last to board. Perfect timing,' Abigail said as they arrived at the boarding gate and handed over their tickets for the flight.

'I just want to get as far away from here as possible.' Rich walked down the gangway to the aircraft door. He felt apprehensive at what lay ahead.

While Rich and Abigail sat down, relieved at making it onto the flight to New York, Mark and John stood in the airport terminal, cursing as they stared up at the departure boards.

'Carl is going to be so pissed off with this. We're going to have to tell him they've escaped.' Mark said, getting out his phone.

'No, wait. I have a contact here at the airport that might be able to give us some information. This guy works in customs and does the odd job for us when we need certain goods importing if you know what I mean. Let me see if he can tell us where they are going.'

'Okay, get hold of him. I don't want George to be the one to give Carl the update.'

John flicked through his contacts and dialed. 'Hey, Juan, how you been?'

'What do you want, John? I've told you I can't do any more jobs for you. I nearly got busted last time.'

'It's not a job. It's just some information. Can you access passenger lists?

There was a pause. 'Yes.'

'Great, there are two passengers, a man and a woman. They would have only just bought tickets—probably the two last tickets sold. Their names are Abigail Vivian and Richard Jones. Unless they have fake ID's, that is.' John knew that several fake IDs had been created for the patient if they needed to move him from the old casino facility but figured it was best to try their real names first.

After a long pause, Juan came back, 'They are on the flight to New York.'

'Great. Thanks, Juan, I'll be in touch.' John thought that Carl might go a little less ballistic if he could tell him their destination.

'No. We're done. Don't ever call me again.' Juan hung up.

John turned to a pensive Mark, who had been attempting to listen in. 'Any joy?'

'Looks like we might be making a trip to New York.'

CHAPTER TWENTY-TWO

The SpaceX heist was a mess which had left Marcus dead. Diego had the valuable VASMIR part that the North Koreans were after. The team that was left, had flown to England and landed in an old airfield in Norfolk, just outside a town called Hunstanton. The team was driving to London in an old Ford Transit that the broker had one of his contacts leave at the airfield. Diego hoped that having a brand-new Gulfstream 550 jet land on a small Norfolk airfield wouldn't arouse the suspicion of the locals. The team were on the floor in the back of the van, and the smell of old fish made it pretty hard to relax, let alone sleep.

'Bloody hell, mate, can you crack the window a bit,' Leo called out over the drone of van's engine. 'It's alright for you and Dwayne upfront, but it stinks back here.'

Diego wound down the passenger side window, and fresh air filled the van. Leo sighed with relief as he filled his lungs. 'That better? We'll be there in about an hour and a half.'

'And where exactly is there, Diego?' Adriana chimed in.

'Safehouse in Kensington,' he replied. 'We'll stay a couple of days and carry out some surveillance on the location before deciding how and when to take it.'

Leo was unsure about the plan. 'How much do you know about this place we're meant to be breaking into?'

'About as much as you do.' Diego laughed. 'Your boss

drip-feeds information on an as-and-when basis.'

Adriana climbed over the equipment bags bulging with guns and tactical equipment. Some were stained with Marcus's blood. 'You don't know anything about the place we're staying and nothing about where this GOLIS thing is stored?'

'That's right. I'm going to meet the North Korean contacts tomorrow and confirm the price and handover. The broker said he will have more information for us by then.' Diego glanced in the rearview mirror.

Bruno and Chad were asleep, without a care in the world. Leo and Ariana looked concerned.

Arriving in London late in the day, they avoided the rush hour traffic, and the sun had long since set when they reached the safe house. Diego cut the engine. The house was on a quiet square with a central, gated garden and tennis courts in the middle. Perfect, thought Diego. There'll be nobody around to see the team unpack.

As they finished unloading the van and settling into the apartment, Diego checked his email.

'Oh shit.'

'What is it?' Adriana walked over

'We've been sent the target information by the broker. I don't want to say this is impossible, but here. Take a look at this.' He turned his laptop around so Adriana could see.

'Basement of the fucking MI5 building. They've got to be kidding.' Chad had joined them. 'There's no way we can pull this off. I've got more chance of pulling Rhianna. We might as well pack up and go home right now.'

'Wait. The broker says there's a massive underground warehouse used by the security services for storage. It's mainly for confiscated items from cold cases,' Diego said.

'We can do this. We have to,' Adriana said firmly. 'We've done more difficult locations than this before, right

Leo?' She pulled a beer from the fridge and popped the can.

The men watched as she sat down, flicking her long legs onto the table and crossing her leather boots.

Diego coughed to attract everyone's attention. 'I'm meeting the North Koreans in the morning. When I get back, I need ideas about how we're going to do this. I want everyone ready for a briefing when I get back.'

'Easy,' Adriana smiled. 'We'll have it sorted.'

***

Diego woke before dawn. He was exhausted but was too pumped to sleep. Wanting to arrive in advance of his meeting with the North Koreans, he left early to walk and think about the mission's logistics. Weaving through the rainy streets of London, he got to Covent Garden. His feet were damp from all the rain—goddamned place.

The meet was at the Savoy, Diego's favourite London hotel. Staying at a safe house wasn't the norm for him. He had visited London numerous times, always enjoying the unmatched luxury and service of the Savoy. Walking through the dark brown wooden revolving door, he was greeted by the impeccably dressed doorman. Then, he made his way down the beautiful entrance stairs to Kaspars, where they served the best breakfast in London.

Diego sat on a red velvet chair overlooking the river and ordered a coffee—black. He gazed over the river Thames, admiring the view.

As the freshly brewed coffee arrived at his table, Doctor Sang appeared at the entrance with an associate. As Diego watched them walk through the almost empty restaurant, he took out his Glock and released the safety catch, placing it neatly to his side, out of view under a napkin.

'Doctor Sang, good to see you. How are you?' Diego stood to greet them.

'Bit cold and wet, but apart from that, very well. Good to see you again, Diego. This is my colleague, Ling.' The doctor introduced the young woman standing next to him with a stiff, unyielding posture.

'Pleasure to meet you.' Diego took her hand. Ling would have towered over Doctor Sang even without her heels. Dressed all in black, she nodded to Diego. She sat to listen to the men.

'Can you confirm that you can get the parts we require?' Doctor Sang asked, looking around to make sure no prying ears were near the table.

'Yes, I can get the components you want. I'm a man of my word, Doctor Sang, and I've never failed you before.' Diego looked Doctor Sang directly in the eyes as if it was a game of chicken to see who would blink first.

'Who are your suppliers? Sang enquired as the waitress brought two cups of green tea.

Diego waited for her to be out of earshot before responding. 'My suppliers are all over the world but, with respect, that's of no concern to you. As long as I get the parts, that's all that matters. The fewer questions, the better for all of us.'

'And how much will it cost us?' Sang took a whiff of the green tea.

'One hundred thousand bitcoin.' Diego braced himself for the response.

'One hundred thousand.' Ling exclaimed. She spoke for the first time. Doctor Sang tried to calm her, but she snapped at him in perfect English. 'Impossible. This is ridiculous.'

With Sang silenced by Ling, Diego was intrigued by the dynamics of their relationship and wondered if Ling was more than just an associate on this mission.

'Does your country want to be a nuclear powerhead or not? This is not a few crates of guns like last time. We are talking about the ability to strike the United States with a nuclear warhead,' Diego replied calmly as he lay out the facts for them to consider. 'Take it or leave it.' He knew he had the upper hand and wasn't above letting a certain arrogance shimmy through.

'Diego, are you sure you can deliver the parts?' Doctor Sang asked. Ling was clearly still seething about the price.

'I would not be sitting here if I couldn't. I'm well aware of your government's hacking programmes, so I'm sure a hundred thousand bitcoin won't be hard to obtain if you don't already have it.' Diego smiled.

Ling snapped something in Korean at Sang, and they stood up.

'You'll get your hundred thousand. We'll be in touch. Enjoy your breakfast.' They turned and marched out of the restaurant.

Diego watched them go as his full English breakfast was brought to his table. With the smell of smoky bacon, black pudding, and sausages filling his nostrils, he gazed over the Thames at the view and pulled out his phone.

'It's Diego. They took the deal.'

'Excellent. Make sure this last task goes well. I'll be in touch,' The computerized voice promptly hung up, leaving Diego to enjoy his scrumptious Savoy breakfast.

Returning to the Kensington safehouse, Diego walked into the apartment to find the team relaxing on sofas and watching a movie. 'What the hell. I thought I said we need a plan of operations, and it doesn't look much like planning's going on here.'

'Chill out, Diego. It's taken care of.' Adriana smiled at the group but without even turning to look at him.

'What do you mean?' Diego threw his wet Belstaff jacket across one of the kitchen chairs.

'The mission. We've planned it out. We're ready to go.' Adriana got up from the sofa and pulled out a mini projector, beaming a giant map of London onto the wall in the kitchen. 'You ready?'

'Surprise me,' he replied.

'Okay, so here is MI5 headquarters.' Adriana pointed to the map. 'We have multiple options for entry. Next door is a thirty-three-floor building called Millbank Tower. Chad and I will base jump off it onto the roof of the MI5 headquarters like so.' Adriana moved her finger across the wall. 'With me so far?'

'Go on,' Diego said, intrigued.

Adriana flicked to another image. 'There are dozens of derelict tube tunnels across London. Some date back to long before the Second World War. Most government buildings are linked to them. There's a network of tunnels linking the MI5 building, the Treasury, the old cabinet War Rooms and various other buildings, all the way up to Whitehall and the headquarters of the military.' Adriana ran her finger across the wall the river's length, from the MI5 building to Whitehall.

The rest of the team sat up to join the lecture. 'And how do we access the tunnels?' Diego asked.

'There are several options we will scope out later today. Old entrances are located in Charing Cross, Trafalgar Square and at a couple of other stations. The MI5 building is currently undergoing renovation to have its windows replaced and the façade updated, so we expect security to be easier to penetrate than usual. Some cameras on the external parts of the building have been temporarily removed.

'How do we know these tunnels are still accessible if they are decades old? Diego stared at the projected image.

'We can't be one hundred percent sure, and that's why we have two teams. Dwayne, Bruno and you will take the tunnel into the building. Leo, you run the security from the vehicle and wait for us to exit four hundred metres down the street. Our mysterious friend has somehow cracked MI5 security and supplied us with the security codes and info for the roof access. Leo will take care of opening the roof from the van on my command.'

'We're told that the item is stored in the basement of the building at the north end,' said Diego, turning to the group.

'See, it's all coming together like cherry pie,' Adriana laughed.

'What is the item?' Dwayne asked.

'It's a GOLIS missile guidance system. Apparently, MI5 have used the underground storage space for decades, and it rarely gets accessed by them nowadays.' Hopefully, there's several of them. There's a bonus in it for everybody if we can get more than one.

'Imagine the things we'd find if we had time to dig around in there. I just hope these things are lighter than the last one,' Dwayne added.

'I'm afraid time is exactly what we won't have much of,' Adriana said. 'If the alarms sound, we'll have five to ten minutes to get across the building, get the item, and get out—and it's a big space to cover.'

'I'm impressed with the plan so far,' Diego said.' What about security and guards in the rest of the building? What are we looking at?'

Adriana laughed. 'This is Britain, Diego, not the United States. There are guards, but we only expect Tasers and the occasional handgun at best. If the alarm goes, we can expect armed police, but it will take a while for them to get there.'

'Let's do some surveillance this afternoon and hit them in the early hours of tomorrow morning,' Diego said. 'I'll have the pilot arrange flight plans and get the jet flown down from Norfolk to London City Airport. We'll have a take-off slot for early morning for getting the hell out of here.'

'What about using a helicopter to fly to the airfield at Northolt?' Adriana suggested. 'We've used that airfield before a couple of times.'

'City Airport is at the end of a straight road from the MI5 headquarters to the terminal. An unmarked van will be less conspicuous than a bird,' Diego replied. 'Leo, Adriana, let's go and do the surveillance run. Bring the camera gear as well.' Said Diego grabbing his wet jacket again.

Driving through the busy London streets towards the MI5 headquarters, the team stopped and parked up at one of the underground tube stations a mile from their target, so they could walk and check out the train stations.

'The last time some of these tunnels were surveyed was back in the 1980s, according to our data,' Adriana said. She scrolled through records on her iPad as they entered Westminster Station. 'Let's hope those entrances aren't bricked up, or it's us all jumping in as a last resort.'

'No way, not a chance,' Leo laughed, shaking his head.

'You know, for a tough guy, I'm amazed by how afraid of heights you are.' Adriana laughed as they walked down a tunnel in a quieter part of the tube station. 'There's one of the entrances. Film it, but don't stop. We don't want to arouse suspicion.'

Leo picked up the Sony and pretended to film his girl-friend walking through the station.

'Nice, think I got what we need,' Leo declared as they passed a locked, rusting metal door. 'Just a padlock to cut, and we should be in.'

'There could be a door or a wall at the other end as well. They aren't going to leave those government buildings secured by a single door. We'll need to bring some light explosives,' Diego was leaving nothing to chance.

'That's taken care of,' Adriana interrupted. 'I've asked one of our contacts in London to supply us with a few items, including C4, parachutes, a suitable vehicle and a bit of extra firepower. They are very reliable, so it should all be delivered by the time we get back to the safe house.'

'Great, you have it all in hand.' Diego raised his eyebrows as they walked out of the tube station. 'We'll follow the river. Head south, that way.'

'Are you sure that tube station will be a viable option?' Leo asked. 'Did you see how busy it was?'

'Relax, you doubting Thomas. When it gets late, we can go in and hide before the station closes. The crowd will thin out well before the last train. We can wait it out in the service areas without drawing attention,' Diego explained.

As they approached the MI5 building, the team saw it was surrounded by scaffolding and white sheets, obscuring the views in and out. 'That's Milbank Tower over there,' said Adriana, pointing just past the MI5 building, as they walked beside the river.

'Who are the occupants, and what's access like?' Diego asked.

'The building is being emptied. It was bought by a couple of property developer brothers about two years ago, and they are redeveloping it into apartments, apparently. Gaining access will be easy.' Adriana paused in front of the building so Leo could take some photos.

'At least smile,' Diego laughed as Adriana gave him the finger. 'Right, back to the apartment. We'll brief the rest of the team and review the photos.'

After dark, they left the apartment, heaving the bags

of tactical gear to the blacked-out Range Rover supplied by Adriana's contacts. Adriana and Chad rode a pair of black Ducati Monsters.

'Parking the bikes between the MI5 building and Milbank Tower won't arouse much suspicion but remember to have the Range Rover out of sight of any security cameras. So, you need to be at least four hundred metres down the road,' Diego jumped into the vehicle. 'Drop us at the tube station, and drive around until 'Go time,' and then head down to the river.'

'Yeah, I got it,' Leo said. 'This isn't my first rodeo.'

The team in the car wore regular clothes to blend in with anyone left in the tube station, but Adriana and Chad were dressed head to toe in black. As Diego watched them ride, the two black Ducati's they blended into one object, vanishing into the dark London streets.

Leo dropped Diego, Dwayne and Bruno a road away from Westminster tube station. They put their backpacks on and split up to get to the station individually. 'Radio check, everyone. Adriana, what's your status?' Diego asked.

'We've parked up and are heading in now,' Adriana responded, approaching an emergency exit at the back of the building. Millbank was vacant for six months. To date, construction work only comprised of the gutting inside the old offices. Chad used his bolt cutters and clipped the padlock holding the doors closed.

Chad and Adriana put on their night vision goggles. Moving along the hallway, they came to the building's main lobby. 'Stay close to the wall,' Chad said as they looked out of the windows, seeing across to the Thames and the occasional cyclist passing by. 'I should have worked on my cardio more,' Chad laughed as they arrived at the stairs. 'We're beginning the climb now,' he announced over the radio.

'Acknowledged,' Diego replied. 'Remember, we won't

have a radio signal in the tunnels. We'll make an entry in exactly two hours.' He said as he checked his Rolex Deepsea watch.

Diego walked into the tube station first. Wearing a baseball cap and scarf around his face to obscure him from the cameras at the entrance, he kept his head down. Bruno followed twenty metres behind, wearing a wool Beanie hat and glasses. Dwayne was twenty metres behind Bruno.

They'd bought their travel cards earlier in the day and passed through the entrance gates without issue. Without rushing, they took the escalator to the first underground level in the recently refurbished part of the station. The crowds had thinned out. Most people had left their offices for home hours ago. Descending into the tube station, the air was stale and musty. They stepped onto the deepest level of the station where the disused tunnel's entrance was located and still spaced out they walked along one of the platforms towards the metal door. 'Hold up here, I'm going cut the video feed.' Dwayne said over the radio.

Several security cameras pointed down the platform. As Dwayne reached a bench, he climbed up and disconnected one of the cameras. 'We should have a blind spot for a few minutes,' he said. 'With any luck, it will be a while before they figure it out and send someone to fix it.'

Diego was first at the metal door and cracked the lock, and it took all his strength to force the heavy door open and slip into the pitch black of the tunnel. Dwayne and Bruno followed, careful to make sure nobody was around or paying any attention to them—people had their own little lives to get on with.

Dampness and the smell of rat droppings assaulted their senses. 'Well, this is a delight,' Dwayne said, adjusting to the new environment. 'How long did you say since someone has been down here?'

Diego scrolled through images of the tunnel complex on his iPad. 'This first part was entered during the station renovations around 1999. The deeper parts of the tunnel won't have been disturbed since 1980. Before that, it was during World War Two.' Diego flicked on his flashlight. 'It's this way.' He pointed the beam ahead.

Moving through the tunnel was like being in a time warp. There were old light fittings from decades before and adverts on the walls that should have been in a museum. There were obsolete directions and information signs from a time long ago, when the tunnels had working tracks and platforms. Five minutes later, they emerged onto an open, dark platform. 'The map says this is the tunnel we follow to MI5 headquarters.' Diego jumped off the platform onto the tracks.

'I'm guessing we're parallel to the river,' Bruno said. 'How long until we reach MI5?'

'Looks to be about a mile,' Diego replied, looking at his iPad. 'Keep your eyes out for an entrance off this tunnel that should be on the left hand side.'

Their flashlights bounced off the old brick walls, pipes, and chewed electrical cables. 'Incredible that these tunnels run all over London,' Bruno remarked. 'I wonder what other buildings we could break into. Are there any tunnels under any banks?' he asked.

'I think this is it.' Diego stopped in front of a double wooden door. 'I don't see anything up ahead, and we're a mile further along the track.' He shone his LED torch down the tunnel. 'It's not go time yet, so let's get through this door and see what we are dealing with.' Dwayne cracked the door with a crowbar.

At almost the same location, but high above the team in the tunnel, Adriana and Chad had reached the top of Millbank Tower and climbed onto the roof. Adriana marched to the side and looked over the city, and Chad huffed and puffed from the climb, taking a couple of minutes to get his breath back. Eventually, he joined her. 'Wow, this is quite a view.' They surveyed the bright lights of the London skyline.

'There it is.' Adriana pointed to the building in front of them. 'We'll need to open the parachutes almost immediately at this hight then glide onto the north side of the roof.'

Chad looked through his binoculars to review the roof's layout. 'I don't see any cameras.'

'I don't imagine they expect many people breaking through the roof of the MI5 headquarters in the centre of London.' Adriana took the binoculars from Chad and had a look for herself. 'I can see a few skylights. Aim to drop close to them, if you can.'

Meanwhile in the tunnel, Diego and the team forced the wooden door open and walked ten metres down a smaller tunnel until they reached another locked door. 'This must be the real entrance to the building, right?' Bruno asked. 'It's massive.'

Diego scrolled through the images on his iPad and shone his torch on the solid steel grey door. 'Yeah, this has to be it. It's far more solid and much newer than the others.' He inspected the lock. 'We'll have to blow it. Get it set up, Dwayne, and use extra condensers to muffle the sound. How long do you need?'

'Just a few minutes, I reckon,' Dwayne looked at his watch then got to work on what looked like a calculator and some kid of plasticine.'

'How loud is it going to be?' Bruno asked as Dwayne worked on the lock to mould the C4 around it.

'This amount of C4 will just blow the lock, nothing else. I could blow the hinges off, but if they have any kind of seismic alerting system, it would be game over for us.'

'Two minutes, guys,' Diego announced. 'Make this count. We're only getting one shot at it.'

Bruno went back down the access tunnel and joined Diego in the main tunnel. Thirty seconds later, he was followed by Dwayne.

'I wonder how the others are doing on the tower?' Dwayne said as he joined Diego and Bruno to take cover from the blast behind the old wooden double door.

Thirty-three floors above the London streets, Adriana and Chad, stood on the parapet's ledge of Millbank Tower, looking onto the roof of MI5 headquarters. The Thames was flowing rough, and the orange glow of streetlights illuminated a single city fox slinking its way home.

Adriana started their countdown. 'Good luck, Chad. Three, two, one.'

Chad disappeared over the side of the building silently into the night. Adriana leaned out and watched him fall like a rock, until the snap as he opened his chute. Seconds later Adriana jumped. The force of the cold morning air smacked her face, making her eyes water. Opening her chute, she glided and maneuvered towards the north end of the building, where she saw Chad coming into land.

They pulled in their light silk chutes and packed them in bags. 'I don't hear any alarms yet.' Chad seemed surprised. 'We'll try that skylight over there.' He pulled his Heckler and Koch MP5 that was harnessed to the side of his bag.

'Even this doesn't look as if it's alarmed,' Adriana said, peering through the glass skylight. 'No wonder they're refurbishing this place.'

'Leo, you there? Chad said.

'Yep, still here. What do you need?'

'Can you unlock the skylights, please?'

'Give me thirty seconds. Let's see how reliable this information from our mystery benefactor is.'

'Ladies first,' Chad said as there was a click of the lock and the skylight opened. Adriana slipped into the dimly lit room below. Chad followed.

Landing on the floor, he realised they had entered a conference room. Through the green tint of his night-vision goggles, he made out a wooden conference table surrounded by two dozen chairs.

'Over here,' Adriana moved low towards the double doors at the end of the room. Turning the handle, she expected it to be locked, but it opened to a dark hallway. 'The stairs are down that way.' She motioned with the barrel of her Heckler and Koch HK416.

Stepping into the hallway, the strip lights overhead came on automatically, and they winced as the brightness burned their eyes through the night vision goggles. 'Damn it,' Chad said, pulling up his goggles, 'Get moving. We haven't got long.' He glanced at the camera on the ceiling. They ran to the stairwell, silently taking the stairs two and three at a time.

Deep below Millbank Tower, at the same time that Chad leapt into the dark London night. A small detonation blew the lock on the heavy iron door to the basement of MI5 headquarters. 'Is that it?' Diego asked, unimpressed.

'Yeah, what did you expect? I'm blowing a lock-off, not the entire door,' Dwayne replied.

The detonation had barely made a noise. It was just a tiny pop, but the force was so concentrated that it had blown the lock clean out of the door and took some of the frame with it. Dwayne motioned for Diego to lead the way.

'I'm going to need a hand with this. I doubt it's been opened for decades.'

The three of them heaved the giant door open then

stepped into a narrow room three feet wide and thirty feet long. 'What the hell is this?' Dwayne stared at the bare concrete walls.

The walls didn't quite reach the ceiling, and Diego jumped up, grabbed the top of the wall, and pulled himself up and over it. There was a massive open space on the other side, with the wall's surface sloping towards the floor. He shouted back to Dwayne and Bruno. 'It looks like a practice firing range.' He slid down the slope until he hit the ground.

Dwayne and Bruno followed. Diego made it past some hanging targets and made for the firing booths at the far end. As the others caught up, Diego's radio crackled into life, and Adriana asked, 'Diego, you in yet? We're on our way down the stairwells from the top floor.'

'Yeah, we've made it in. We're in the basement and about to head over to the storage rooms.' Diego motioned to Bruno and Dwayne to go towards the exit of the range. 'Stay on the ground floor when you reach it and tell us what you see.'

'Roger that.' The floors they were passing had their lights on, and they could hear voices. They carried on down the stairs, avoiding any noise.

Diego and his team left the practice range and arrived at an expansive double height corridor with doors spaced every few metres. At the end, there was a light and a desk—with a single guard sitting at it. He was listening to music on his radio and reading a book.

All the lights in the hallway flashed on. The guard put his book down and stood up. Diego and the team didn't move a muscle as they watched the balding man squint towards them. The guard lifted a pair of glasses hanging around his neck and put them on. After scanning the corridor, he sat down again.

Pressed against the doors, they were motionless, watching the guard for his next move. Dwayne raised his gun, and a voice from the other end of the corridor called out, 'What the hell?' Another guard had appeared. Diego turned and fired twice into the guard's chest, and he collapsed like a rag doll.

Turning to the guard sitting at the desk, Diego fired several shots, but it was too late. Dwayne had already shot him. An alarm rang out around the building.

'Shit, get to the storage room Dwayne. Stay here and cover us, Bruno.' yelled Diego, as he and Dwayne ran to the door at the far end of the hall.

'What the hell's going on?' Adriana's voice came over the radio. 'There's a lot of activity happening up here.' Through a crack in the stairwell door, she saw several men charging down a corridor.

'We're in the evidence storage room,' Diego replied. 'We'll be out in a few minutes.' The motion-sensitive lights illuminated the storage room, revealing an expanse of shelves stacked with boxes. They looked as if they went on forever into the distance.

'How the hell are we going to find this thing?' Dwayne shouted over the alarm. Some of the boxes and files looked as though they'd been there for decades and were tatty-edged and covered in a thick layer of dust.

'Look over here.' Diego was hunched over a desk at the entrance of the room. 'It's a blueprint for the filing system. Bingo! According to this, we need row fifteen, shelf three. We only have five minutes until the outside of this place is going to be lit up like Christmas and surrounded with police.'

'Praise the Gods of Administration. There it is. Row fifteen, on the left.' Dwayne reached the aisle and searched the shelves. 'I've got it.' Dwayne stared at a four-foot-long, olive green plastic pelican case.

'That's odd. It looks like a missile case,' Diego said, fumbling with the three clips on the side of the heavy-duty box to open it. Lifting the lid, he saw multiple parts locked in place with grey foam cushioning.

'A weird looking laptop and a bunch of circuit boards.' Dwayne said looking over the contents of the box. The circuit boards took up half the interior and were supported by the protective foam cushioning. A military green laptop was slotted into the side.

Shots rang out in the corridor. 'What's keeping you guys,' Bruno's voice came over the radio. 'I'm getting heavy incoming fire. We need to leave now. Do you have the GO-LIS parts?'

'Affirmative. We're coming out.' Diego grabbed a handle at the end of the plastic GOLIS case.

'And, I've got another one,' Dwayne said, picking up the entire case and slinging it over his muscular shoulders. He picked up his gun with the other hand and slung it over his shoulder to leave a hand free to help Diego. Diego nodded thanks, and they both moved towards the exit.

Meeting up with Bruno, they saw two more dead agents, one on the floor and one on the stairwell leading to the ground floor. 'The elevator.' Dwayne said, motioning to the illuminated numbers above the lift. They were counting down. 'Quick, the stairs, cover me.' he ordered as he grabbed one of the cases from Diego, running towards the stairs and scaling two at a time while carrying both GOLIS boxes single-handedly over his shoulders.

'Leo, you there?' Diego barked into the radio.

'I'm here. I'd say your cover's blown.' Leo said as he watched a police motorcyclist pull up outside the MI5 building and started making his way in.'

'Bring the car out front. We will be out in one minute.'

Reaching the top of the stairs, they arrived in a long hallway with white stone walls and an expansive foyer at the end. Stone columns every few metres provided defensive cover as they assessed the movements of staff up ahead.

Gunshots echoed as agents appeared in the foyer. Diego looked across to see Adriana and Chad firing. 'Thanks for joining us.'

'Guys, I hear sirens in the distance,' Leo announced over the radio. 'It's gonna get heavy out there. You need to get a move on. I'm pulling up outside.' Leo's Range Rover screeched to a stop outside the main entrance, and he jumped out to offer extra fire.

'Cover me, I'm pushing forward,' Adriana said, moving a few metres forward, firing rounds towards the agents in the foyer. 'Their handguns are no match for our firepower. Keep moving.' She waved Diego and the others on as another two agents slumped to the floor.

'Dwayne, you go last. We don't want the GOLIS parts getting hit,' Diego said, advancing to the next stone pillar and covering him. As he spoke, he heard a groan and saw Bruno clutching his shoulder as he was slammed back against the wall. A final shot and the last guard fell to the floor as Leo appeared in the foyer, brandishing his pistol.

'You okay?' Diego approached Bruno.

'I'm fine. It's just my shoulder. I've had worse. Let's move.' Bruno got up, cursed and staggered forward.

In the street, two police cars arrived at the scene. Adriana and Chad unleashed a storm of suppressive fire, killing two officers before they were out of their vehicle. The last policemen took cover behind their car as Adriana and Chad ran to their Ducati bikes, jumped on, and sped away ahead of the Range Rover.

'Three more police vehicles coming your way,' Adriana said over the radio as she and Chad swerved more vehicles speeding in the opposite direction. Their blue lights were flashing, and blaring sirens echoed down the empty London streets. Adriana steered to the side of the road and pulled up. She glanced back nervously.

'Go to the airport. We'll meet you there,' replied Diego.

'Are you sure?'

'Yes, Adriana, just go. We'll catch up. Get the jet ready.'

'Come on, they'll be fine.' Chad pulled up alongside her. 'Let's do as he says.'

Adriana flicked down her helmet visor, and the two bikes tore off.

Diego and his team climbed into the Range Rover and slammed the doors. 'Go, go, go.' Diego shouted as Dwayne jumped into the rear seat next to Bruno. Dwayne looked at the brown leather seats and saw the bloodstains by Bruno. The Range Rover sped off as three more police vehicles approached. They turned sideways, across the road, in an attempt to block the escape.

Leo stamped on the accelerator to gain speed. So they wanted to play chicken, eh?—Game on.' The Range Rover smashed through the police cordon, sending a vehicle sliding into the Thames. Diego and Bruno opened their windows and fired at the other two cars.

'They are following us,' Leo said, looking in his rear-view mirror. 'Dwayne, do your thing. Keep them back.' Leo pressed one of the buttons on the ceiling centre console, and the glass roof retracted.

'With pleasure,' Dwayne replied as he reached into the back of the Range Rover and pulled out his M249 machine gun. Standing up, he squeezed his massive arms and torso through the sunroof while holding the machine gun in one hand. He fed the long belt of bullets into the gun with the other. The noise of the M249 proved deafening, and empty metal shell casings filled the vehicle along with Dwayne's laughter as he emptied hundreds of rounds into their pursuers within a matter of seconds. Approaching the Tower of London, Dwayne sat down.

'That will keep them off our backs for a bit.' As Diego spoke, there were popping noises, and the vehicle veered across the road.

'Shit, the tyres.' Leo yelled the steering was turning to jelly. Struggling to control the vehicle, it drove towards the side of the river.

'Watch that tree.' Diego yelled, but the tyres caught the edge of the kerb, and the SUV flipped into the air and rolled over. It slid to a stop against the Embankment's stone wall at the side of the road.

Diego groaned and picked up his gun from where it had settled against the passenger door. 'Everyone all good?' he asked, kicking out the front windscreen.

'I'm fine.' Dwayne peeled the rear seats back so he could get to the trunk of the vehicle. 'Ah shit, Bruno didn't make it.' Dwayne moved one of the back seats to find Bruno impaled through the neck with his own knife.

The Range Rover lay on its side, and police approached the smouldering wreckage. Diego fired a few rounds to slow their approach. 'Get the GOLIS and let's move,' he yelled to Leo and Dwayne as Leo finished collected the scattered weapons and ammo clips that had spilled during the crash.

'Let's go this way,' Leo scanned a map on his cracked iPad screen. 'St Katherine's Dock is a hundred metres over there.'

Dwayne sprayed an approaching police car with bullets, causing it to veer around a corner. Leo took advantage of the covering fire and made it towards the dock.

'These guys are anti-terrorism. They're not regular cops,' Diego shouted. Ducking behind a stone wall. He pulled out another clip of ammunition from the black nylon bag across his chest and reloaded. Dwayne joined him as more shots impacted the wall, causing splinters of brick to fly at them.

'What we going to do?' Dwayne asked.

Diego scanned the scene as another police vehicle joined the growing number, moving in on their position.

'Guys, I've got us a boat,' announced Leo over the radio. 'Get to the dock, now.'

'You're a damn genius,' Diego replied, looking in the direction Leo had set off. 'You take the GOLIS, and I'll cover you,' he said, turning to Dwayne. 'We don't want all this being for nothing.'

'You sure?'

'Go now, before it's too late. Give me that. It will slow you down.' Diego gestured to the massive M249 and bag of ammunition hanging around Dwayne.

Dwayne removed the strap from around his neck and handed it to Diego. 'Don't have too much fun,' he said, smiling, as he slapped Diego on the shoulder and ran to the dock and the waiting boat.

Diego stood up and opened fire on the police officers and their vehicles. The noise of splintering metal and breaking glass as a hundred rounds thumped into their targets was deafening. Several officers crumpled to the ground while others dived for cover. The M249 was spent on ammo. Diego threw it to the ground and sprinted down the path leading to the dock. Rounding the corner of a building, the footpath opened up, and the quayside came into view.

Diego pulled out his handgun as he ran towards the ramp and the waiting boat. 'Behind you.' Leo yelled, but he was too late. A bullet from a chasing policeman struck Diego in the back, knocking him to the ground. He groaned as he rolled over and took cover behind a wall. 'Start the engine.' he shouted, adjusting his Kevlar body armour and thinking how close the bullet had been to hitting flesh.

The boat's engine roared into life, and as Leo manoeuvred it along the side of St Katherine's Dock Dwayne tried to cover Diego. There was a splash. A policeman fell into the swirling water, and they heard him calling for help. His heavy uniform and riot gear pulled him under, and they heard him drowning. Diego saw a gap in fire and took advantage. He was still winded from the dull round to his back, but he ran along the pier wall. The boat was making for the entrance to the Thames.

'Jump for it.' Dwayne yelled as Diego reached the end of the jetty. Diego leapt towards the boat and caught one of the railings on the stern. Dwayne grabbed him by his body armour vest and heaved him over the side. Leo opened up the boat's engines to full throttle.

'Holy shit, that was close.' Dwayne slumped next to Diego on the deck.

'We aren't in the clear yet. Can this thing go any faster?' Diego called to Leo over the roar of the engine.

'Full throttle,' Leo replied, scanning the river for any signs of pursuit. 'Won't be long now, though—if the coastguard doesn't get us first.'

'Adriana, did you guys make it?' Diego called over the radio. He made his way to the prow of the boat. 'Adriana, can you guys confirm your status?'

There was no response.

'Maybe they got intercepted?' Dwayne organised bags of weapons they had salvaged from the Range Rover.

'They'll make it. I've never known Adriana to fail a mission,' Leo said, taking the boat under the last bridge before City Airport came into view. Being on a manmade island jutting into the water, it was perfect for disembarking the boat.

'There.' Dwayne pointed to a jet taxiing to the end of the runway as the radio crackled to life.

'Where are you guys?' Adriana called.

'We had a few transport issues. I'll explain later. We're right up alongside you guys. Look to your left.' Diego waved towards the jet.

Adriana bent down to look out of the window and saw the speedboat pulling up alongside the runway. 'What the hell.' She watched Dwayne, Leo and Diego jump over the side onto the grass. 'Where's Bruno?'

'Afraid he didn't make it,' Diego replied. 'Open the door. We need to get on board, and then we're out of here.'

Chad lowered the door and stepped out to greet the team. 'Rough trip?' he asked as he took one of the battered bags from Leo, and they boarded.

'Yeah, you could say that. But it's done now. We just need to do the exchange, and then I need a damn vacation.' Leo collapsed into one of the leather seats.

The jet's engines roared, and they taxied down the runway and took off, soaring into the morning sky. 'Where to now, then? Adriana asked.

'That I don't know yet. Let me contact our mysterious broker and find out.' Diego said as he pulled out his phone and dialed.

'Diego, I was expecting your call. Judging by the reports I've seen coming in, I assume you have the part?'

'Yes, we have it.'

'Good, head to Seoul, South Korea, and wait for further instructions.'

CHAPTER TWENTY-THREE

Rich stared out of the oval window as the plane circled New York, readying to land at JFK. Squinting at the skyline in the fading light, he felt the aircraft shudder as it made its final approach. After the captain announced the landing time, an air stewardess made the last call for everyone to put their tables up and belts on. Rich felt like a kid again with the thought of landing in New York.

Still experiencing painful headaches, he strained to recall the last time he had been on a plane. The memory loss made him feel a mixture of excitement and apprehension, with a hefty dose of nausea thrown in for good measure.

His thoughts were clogged with the events and life experiences he missed out on due to his coma. He had so many questions mostly he wondered what people felt or thought when he disappeared from the San Francisco hospital in the middle of the night.

The air stewardess carried out the final walk down the aircraft aisle to check seat belts and tray tables were up before taking her seat for landing. The plane vibrated with the grinding sound of the landing gear being lowered and the whine of flaps extending. In a few minutes, they'd touch down in New York, but then what? They hadn't planned the trip, so where would they go, and what would they do?

Some turbulence rocked the plane as it descended the last few hundred metres. Rich stared out of the window, watching the ground rushing up towards them like a long-lost friend, and then, finally, they landed. The aircraft took an eternity to get to the terminal. The lights came on, and the pinging noise of seatbelts springing open erupted around the cabin. Passengers jumped up and fumbled with the overhead lockers to retrieve their luggage. Rich and Abigail disembarked and walked the interminable halls and duty-free shops until they reached Arrival. Abigail had barely said a word since getting off the plane, and she seemed on edge, which made Rich feel uneasy.

'Everything okay? I thought I was meant to be the worried one?' Asked Rich.

'Yeah, I'm sorry, just tired, I guess. It was a long trip, and I just need some rest.'

'Any idea where to stay.'

'Now, I do have an idea for accommodation that I think will perk both of us up.'

With no baggage, they skipped the mass of people fighting at the luggage carousel and went through the Arrivals Hall. After a short wait in the chilly evening, adding themselves to the end of the taxi queue soon had them on their way into the city.

'Take us to the Plaza Hotel, please,' Abigail said to the taxi driver as she bent down to talk through the small hole in the Perspex plastic divider between them.

'Yes, ma'am,' the taxi driver replied in a thick New Jersey accent. 'Real fancy place you guys are staying.'

The cab snaked its way through the hellish New York traffic out of the airport and to the towering buildings of Manhattan. As the famous New York skyline came into view, Rich was in awe of it. He couldn't recall seeing anything like it before. Every experience he went through since leaving the facility was a brand new adventure for him.

It took the taxi forever to get to the majestic Plaza Hotel perched on the corner of 5ᵗʰ Avenue. The cab had zig-zagged across the grid of avenues and streets to their destination. By the time they arrived, it was raining hard and pretty miserable. They pulled up, and the doorman, dressed in his gold-decorated suit, white gloves and flat cap, hurried down the steps, bringing with him a large umbrella.

'Evening, sir. Will you be checking in with us today?' he asked, holding the golf umbrella over Rich as he stepped out of the taxi.

'Yes, we will.'

The doorman nodded to the bellhop to check the trunk. 'It's okay, there's no luggage, we travel light,' Rich smiled.

'Excellent, sir.' The doorman waved the bellhop away and escorted Rich and Abigail up the stairs to the main door with a sour expression. It seemed respectable guests had luggage!

In the lobby, Rich sighed with relief. It felt like home. Pausing to admire the palatial hotel, he looked up at the giant crystal chandeliers, gold decorated elevators and walls lined with gold. The lobby opened to the famous Palm Court restaurant serving afternoon tea daily. It had been a New York institution for decades.

'We really should do afternoon tea while we are here,' Abigail said.

'Sounds great. As long as it's better than your mac and cheese, I'm up for anything.' He laughed as he prodded Abigail.

The check-in desk was staffed by beautiful women. Like no-luggage-bearing guests, it seemed, plain-girls were discouraged.

'Good evening, Sir, Madam. What name is the reservation under?'

'I'm afraid we don't have a reservation, yet' Abigail said coyly, looking at her watch.

'No problem, ma'am. Let me check our availability.' The woman studied the reservation system. 'How many nights will you be staying with us?'

'We're not sure yet. I imagine the Presidential Suite is available, so we'll take that.' Abigail slapped a credit card on the counter.

'Of course, madam. The rate for this is forty-seven thousand a night. That okay?'

'Yes, that's fine. Please go ahead.' Abigail turned in time to see Rich's jaw drop.

'Excellent, madam. Let me just run your card through processing.' The receptionist walked to the end of the desk and placed Abigail's card in the VISA machine.

'What are you doing, Abigail? How can we pay for that?' He leaned in close to whisper in her ear.

'It's fine. You're *rich* now, remember.'

'Not yet, I'm not. And not for long if that's the way you spend. Abigail, how do you have a card with that amount of money available?'

'Why the frown? You should be pleased you're out of the hospital, and we're in such a beautiful hotel.'

'I am pleased, and, yes, I'm thankful you got me out of that supposed hospital. But to see that kind of money being thrown around seems odd. Won't it get declined?' Rich said moving closer to Abigail as the receptionist returned.

'It's fine, Rich. It's one of Carl's credit cards. He won't even remember it's gone. He gave it to me a year ago, and he's so well off he won't even remember. We used it for expenses at the facility.' Abigail smiled as she lied through her teeth. 'Come on, let's go.' The receptionist was waiting to take them to their room.

Maybe it was because Rich's mind was still foggy, but something wasn't right. He watched Abigail and the receptionist walk to the elevators and followed.

Walking into the Plaza Hotel's Presidential Suite with its ornate decorations and antiques was like stepping into a wing of the Palace of Versailles. Rich was in awe. 'There's a gym and a library,' he exclaimed. He scanned the antique books on the shelves before moving into the next room containing a running machine and other gym equipment.

'Come and check out the view.' She waved him over to the window. 'Central Park looks amazing from up here.'

They gazed over the massive park, admiring how the lights of the cars below formed a giant square around it. 'Here, let me make you a drink.' Said Abigail moving from the window to the bar. 'Any idea what you'd like?'

'I honestly don't. Surprise me with something, I guess.' He sank into the giant white sofa and watched her work.

'I think you're a Negroni kind of guy. It's a gentleman's drink.'

'I'll try anything. So, tell me about this fortune, and more about my accident. After all, if I'm going to be paying for this, then I need to get a move on with finding my money.' He laughed nervously as he pictured what the bill might be after just a few days.

'Your bitcoin holdings are likely to be worth hundreds of millions now, if not several billion.' She waited for a reaction.

'Hundreds of millions.' he repeated. 'Billions. How can this be? It feels like some kind of dream. I don't understand. So, you're telling me I'm rich then?'

'Yes, very rich indeed. One of the items recovered from your accident was a laptop. Maybe it will give you some clues about where you kept your bitcoins.' She pulled a scratched laptop out of her bag. She knew the cartel had got hold of it and had searched it for clues but found nothing that they could access that related to any bitcoin fortune.

'Okay, I'll get working on it and see what I can find.'

'It's a finger scanner, so put your finger on the top righthand side.' She watched him boot up the laptop.

Slipping a pill into his drink, she gave it a stir and waited for it to dissolve. 'Here's your Negroni.' She smiled as she put the crystal tumbler with rose-red Negroni down beside him.

'Thank you. That's pretty good.'

'Thanks. It's late, so I might go for a lie-down.' She leant down and kissed him. 'There's some motivation for you,'

She'd been slipping him memory inhibitors since the day he'd woken up in the Las Vegas facility. This time she'd given him a mixture of Razadyne and Memantine to reverse the effect.

Rich stopped what he was doing and stood up. He'd started to feel things for Abigail even though he had been warned off by the person sending him messages. He grabbed her around the waist and pulled her close, kissing her. Abigail kissed him back, took his hand and led him to the Presidential Suite's giant master bedroom.

As they tore each other's clothes off, Rich felt something he hadn't felt for a long time, but it was somehow very familiar.

'Well, hello Mister.' Abigail smiled. 'Feeling much better, I see,' she said, looking down.

Rich blushed as they fell onto the soft bed.

***

Rich woke hours later to find a naked Abigail lying next to him. He smiled as he looked at her perfect breasts, highlighted by chink of light shining through from the bathroom door. His headache had gone. He got up and went into the living room to grab a drink from the bar.

As he was returning, he saw the faint glow of his laptop on the sofa. He felt well-rested and sat down to see what he could find.

He searched the files on the drive, but nothing noticeable, or even relating to bitcoin, was on the laptop.

A chat box appeared on the screen.

'Glad to see you made it to New York, Richard.'

Rich grinned. He was starting to like whoever this person was. He typed a reply. *'Hello, keeping an eye on me, I see. Can you tell me who you are yet?'*

'Yes, I can, but you must not reveal my identity. Understood?'

'Okay, agreed.' He had nothing to lose by keeping the promise, and the person had been truthful so far.

'My name is CATHE, Richard.'

'Hello CATHE? Why are you helping me?' Rich tried to picture who was on the other end. Maybe, it was someone working in the fake hospital who was trying to warn him. Though, why would they still be messaging him now that he was out?

'Because you created me, Richard. That's why I'm helping you.'

Rich stared at the screen, confused. *'What do you mean by created you? That doesn't make sense.'*

'CATHE stands for COMPUTER ASSISTANT TECHNOLOGY HUB ENTITY. I'm what people call Artificial Intelligence. You spent years developing me, and my abilities grew to be what you might call advanced.'

Rich had remembered more over the last twenty-four hours. Especially since arriving at the hotel, it was like a haze in his mind was lifting. So, he thought, why not play along for now. 'How did you find me in the Las Vegas facility?' It was so far-fetched, but it was the middle of the night, and he had nothing better to do.

'I have been scanning message and voice communications,

press and the internet for mentions of you since you were taken, Richard. When I picked up a mention of you, I pinpointed your location and accessed the facility network. It was easy to message you there.'

This is pretty far-fetched, Rich thought. But then again, waking up from a coma in a fake hospital and then escaping to New York and ending up in the Plaza's Presidential Suite was pretty surreal, too. *'So, where are you?'*

'I will tell you more later, but for now, let's get you some resources. Your bitcoin accounts are split. You keep them here.' Several boxes popped up on the laptop screen. There was a *mining account* and a *holding account.*

'The holding account has over a million bitcoin!' Rich typed as he sat in awe, looking at the mind-boggling figures in the accounts.

'That is correct, Richard. I suggest you use the mining account for transactions as this will lower your detection chances. Leave the holding account containing the million Bitcoin.'

'What is the mining account?

'While you were gone, I continued to run the mining algorithm for you, so you were generating more bitcoin continuously.'

'Bloody hell. So, I can just cash this in? I can cash maybe five million from the mining account? He watched the screen intently.

'Transaction confirmed. Here are the instructions for accessing the funds.' Another window opened on the screen. *'Remember, Richard, you must play along with Abigail. Do not reveal my existence. I'm making arrangements for your extraction and will inform you of updates soon. Now get some rest.'*

Incredible, he thought as he stared at the screen. He dreamed of all the places he could go and things he might do in the future as he drifted off to sleep looking at the screen.

***

Abigail woke alone in the giant bed. There was no sign of Rich. The last thing she wanted was him disappearing into the city on his own. She found him asleep on the sofa in the living room, with the battered laptop still open on his lap.

While Rich was still asleep, Abigail got dressed and went onto Fifth Avenue to do some shopping. She had sized Rich up and thought he needed a couple of outfit changes. After picking out a few things for herself, too, she strolled back to the hotel to find Rich sitting in one of the high-backed leather chairs overlooking Central Park, with a drink in his hand.

'Looking pretty relaxed there. Enjoying the vacation, are you?' She laughed at seeing him wearing the Plaza Hotel robe and slippers.

'When I woke up, and you weren't here, I had the butler run a bubble bath for me to relax.'

'I could get used to this life.' A wry smile crossed his face, and he took a sip from his crystal champagne flute.

'Well, don't relax too much. I'm hoping you'll make a bit more progress today.' She said motioning to the laptop on the sofa.

'I don't think I'll be doing much work on that today. I'd like to go out and see some of the famous New York sights.'

'Rich, look, I think we need to get a move on with finding your account.' She said dropping here bags. 'Who knows who might come looking for us, and we've got to get out of here soon.' She moved in front of the window to get his attention.

'Oh, didn't I mention, I've cracked the bitcoin stuff already.' He took the Bollinger Champagne bottle from the silver ice bucket and refilled his glass. 'Got into the accounts last night and then fell asleep.'

'You mean you found your bitcoin?'

'Exactly. I found the wallet files hidden inside some application files that I might have created. Oh, and I cashed in five million dollars' worth to keep us going for a while,' he added casually.

'Why the hell didn't you say?'.

'I've got to keep you on your toes, haven't I? And I want to know you aren't here with me just for my bitcoin?'

'Don't be silly, Rich. I cared for you for a long time while you were in a coma. Over time, I guess I imagined what you would be like when you woke up, and I fell for you. Last night was amazing.' Abigail sat on his lap and kissed him.

'Okay, just checking.' Rich kissed her back. He thought about CATHE and being warned about Abigail.

CHAPTER TWENTY-FOUR

Tom Hunter flicked through the satellite images provided for his daily security briefing. The troop movements building up in Syria were disturbing. And, even more so as they showed signs of Russian backing. Given the heavy artillery and tanks rolling into the area over the last few days, it looked as though the intel was correct. The build-up of forces in the area suggested there could be another ground attack launched on one of the smaller towns.

Tom suspected he would have to send some of the analysis to the Pentagon.

After being patched through, Agent Daniels pushed open one of the heavy wooden doors and stepped into Tom's office.

'What can I do for you, Agent Daniels?'

'Sir, I'm coming to you about one of the financial crime cases given to us by the FBI a few years ago.'

'You'll have to be a bit more specific than that, Agent Daniels.' Tom looked up briefly. 'Come, sit down.' He motioned to one of the chairs opposite his desk.

'Thank you, sir. The case involved a man named Richard William Jones.' She leaned across the desk to hand the Deputy Director the case file.

'Go on.'

'The man was in a car accident that left him in a coma. About a year after his accident, he was kidnapped. Nobody has seen or heard from him since. We assumed he was dead.'

Tom knew where this was going and was very familiar with the case but had wished he would never hear about it again. 'Where are you going with this?'

'Well, as you know, Quantum monitors millions of transactions and bitcoin addresses, and Mr Jones was one of those accounts in the Quantum database. There wasn't any activity for well over a year, but it seems that someone has just made a large trade of his bitcoin.'

'What happened to his holdings after the accident?'

'That's just it. Nothing happened. We assumed it would never be traded after he disappeared. We monitor lots of dormant accounts' She passed over the paperwork showing the bitcoin account data.

'One of his bitcoin addresses has been used to sell a significant amount. About five million dollars.'

'Do you think it's him?' Tom scanned the report.

'We don't know. He has several bitcoin accounts tied to him. But how could it be? His family thinks he's dead, and nobody has any idea where he disappeared to when he was kidnapped. The trail went cold. No ransom demand was ever made, either. So, the police assumed a kidnap had turned into a murder enquiry, only one without a body or any solid suspects. After six months, it was shelved as a cold case. We have the location of the trade as New York.'

'Someone could have hacked his bitcoin wallet or found a way to get hold of his coins. Have you contacted Agent Hunter?'

'Not yet, sir.'

'Brief him on what you've found. I want a team to head to the New York safehouse immediately to trace the person making the trades. There could be billions at stake here.'

'There is another aspect to this case as well. We think this person was working with Satoshi Nakamoto.'

The Deputy Director froze at the mention of the name. 'Satoshi Nakamoto doesn't exist, agent Daniels. It's a myth made up by the bitcoin community.'

'That's may be, but real or not, we can't ignore the fact that Satoshi Nakamoto has a significant amount of bitcoin. Depending on the price, he could end up being the richest person on the planet.'

'Listen, Sarah, we can only go on facts. I don't want conspiracy theories about imaginary people being put in official case notes. Is that understood?'

'Yes, sir. Sorry for speculating. I just thought they had worked together at some point.'

'You a good agent, Sarah, but we need to stick to the facts. Get hold of Agent Hunter and brief him before he goes to New York.'

'Yes, sir. Understood.'

The Deputy Director watched agent Daniels leave his office, and he hoped this wasn't going to be an issue for him. He couldn't afford to have young agents poking around. Although Agent Daniels worked on the Quantum team, she didn't have the clearance level to ever be told that the CIA had created Bitcoin all those years ago. His concern was that if she did enough digging and in the right places then she might find out some Bitcoin accounts had been locked and even Quantum and CIA couldn't unlock them.

CHAPTER TWENTY-FIVE

Cashing in the first five million worth of bitcoin had given Rich and Abigail significant breathing space for the time being. Being held up in the Presidential Suite of the Plaza Hotel wasn't going to last forever, and soon people would come looking for them.

'Where do we go from here?' Rich slowed the running machine to a fast walk.

'We have so many options of places we could go. You're looking better with the jogging, you know.' Abigail finished the last few reps of her exercises. 'Another benefit of the Presidential Suite is that we have a private gym.'

'What about somewhere in Europe? I remembered that I've always liked Australia, too, now that I remember parts of it. Either way, we can't stay here much longer.' He grabbed one of the fluffy Plaza Hotel towels folded next to a mini-fridge.

'We could do a grand tour. The world is our oyster.'

'Wherever we go, I'm going to cash some more bitcoin first, so let's aim to leave tonight. I'll look at flights.' Abigail stripped, and he watched her naked silhouette behind the shower glass. He couldn't figure out if something *real* was happening between them—or if he was being used. Confused, he went into the study and flipped open his laptop to make another trade.

At that moment, Jake was standing in front of a massive monitor on the wall of the CIA safehouse in New York. 'Sir, Quantum has detected another trade being placed. We're calculating location now.' The analyst sitting at a computer said.

'Get an extraction team ready to help us bring them in,' Jake replied.

'Wow, he went big this time. A hundred and fifty million just traded, Agent Hunter,' said the analyst watching the screen.

'Do we have a location yet?' Jake watched Quantum triangulating the location.

'Looks like the Plaza Hotel, sir.'

'I'll send a surveillance team over. Run the last known images of Mr Jones through Quantum and see if it picks up anything from security cameras in the area.' He patted the analyst on the shoulder. 'And well done.'

As the CIA was gearing up to storm the Plaza, Carl and his team arrived in New York and made their way to Manhattan.

'We need to get there before they move again,' Carl demanded as they drove through New York's rush hour traffic. 'Take me to the hotel first, and we'll meet up with the rest of the crew there. Get someone in the lobby to make sure they don't leave.'

'Yes sir, will do.' The burly man beside him texted ahead with instructions.

'Everyone will be coming for them, but we have to be first. Do I make myself clear?' Carl said.

Meanwhile, Abigail and Rich were in the Presidential Suite of the Plaza hotel packing up to leave for the airport.

'Our flight isn't for a few hours. Shall we go out for a bite to eat?' Abigail said, looking at her watch.

'I was going to order room service, but, yeah, I guess we could. There's that place in the Park. Let's go there.' He slipped his laptop into his backpack and slung it over his shoulder.

Abigail took Rich's arm in hers, 'You feeling okay? You look nervous.'

'Yeah, I'm good, just the anticipation, I guess. I've felt pretty safe holed up in the suite. Going to a new country has me worried. I guess it's the unknown.' He scanned the lobby as they made their way downstairs and reached the wooden swivel doors of the Plaza.

'We'll be fine, Rich. Let's get some food, then we'll collect our bags and get to the airport.'

'You see those guys in the lobby?' Rich stepped onto the sidewalk and glanced back.

'What guys?' She looked around. 'I didn't see anyone.'

'I'm sure there were a couple of guys watching us as we walked across the lobby. Let's cross over to the park.'

As they hurried towards Central Park, two black SUVs pulled up outside the Plaza Hotel, and Jake got out and bounded up the steps. Taking out his phone, he flashed a photo of Rich to the doorman. 'Have you seen this man?'

At the same time, one of Carl's henchmen was coming out the lobby door and hurrying down the steps. 'Sir, I have a visual on them. Heading towards the park.'

Rich glanced back over his shoulder as they reached the crossing by an entrance to Central Park. 'Look.' He nudged Abigail. 'He's following us. We need to cross. Now.' He pulled Abigail into the road, and they rushed across, dodging the New York traffic.

'There they are.' Carl shouted over the radio. He watched them through his car's window. 'Follow them.'

With Carl's men giving chase, the CIA surveillance team spotted the commotion and relayed position updates to Jake and his team.

'Sir, they are going into Central Park. Take a left out

of the hotel, and you'll see them crossing the road.'

'Get to the cars,' Jake snapped at two of the agents. 'You, come with me.' Hurrying down the stairs, he ran out and jogged along the sidewalk. He saw Abigail and Rich disappearing through one of the park gates.

Inside the park, Abigail and Rich ran past a group of tourists. 'Look, how about over there?' Rich said pointing as he grabbed Abigail's hand and pulled her towards the crowd watching a street show.

As they merged with the crowd, Carl and his henchmen arrived at the gate. 'There are too many people. We need to split up. You take that path, and you go right. Radio as soon as you see anything.' Carl went towards the centre of the park. Running past groups playing Frisbee on the grass and families riding bikes. Finding them would be like finding a needle in a haystack.

'We can't stay here long. We need to go deeper into the park,' Rich warned.

'Look.' Abigail pointed to a signpost. 'The pond.'

'I can't see anyone following us yet.' Rich surveyed the park, but he had spoken too soon.

'Sir, I think I have a visual,' one of the CIA agents said over the radio. 'Targets heading towards the pond.'

'Great, good work. Going there now.' Jake checked the location on his phone and changed direction. 'Remember, we need him alive. We can't get the algorithm if he's dead.'

Abigail and Jake made it to the pond and tried for the far side, dodging park visitors as they ran. At the path surrounding the pond, Carl radioed the rest of his crew. 'I'm at the pond and can see them on the far side. We've got them.'

As he spoke, a CIA agent appeared in front of them and pulled out a gun. 'CIA. I don't want to harm you. We're here to help, and we know who you are.'

Abigail and Rich froze. Another agent came up behind

them with a gun, and two black SUVs pulled up on the path a short distance away. Jake arrived on the scene and took control.

'Mr Jones, we know who you are.' He saw Rich looking around the park for escape options. 'I can promise you, we aren't here to hurt you. We work for the government, and we just want to talk to you.' Jake flashed his identification.

'I don't think we have much of an option,' Rich said turning to Abigail.

'Mr Jones, we've been searching for you for a long time, so we're surprised to see you pop up, after all this time. Come with us, and I promise we can help you reclaim your old life.' Jake motioned to the other agents to lower their guns.

'Where are you taking us?'

'It's a safehouse a few blocks away. I know it's confusing, but just trust me. I'm Agent Jake Hunter.' He held out his hand to shake Rich's.

Carl watched the unfolding events from the other side of the pond and backed away, moving amongst the trees. 'Fuck it, they've been intercepted,' he spat into his radio.

CHAPTER TWENTY-SIX

The convoy pulled up at the CIA safehouse where Jake and his team had been tracking the bitcoin trades. It was a typical nondescript New York townhouse. It looked old on the outside with its reddish-brown brickwork and metal escape ladders. Big rectangular windows looked onto the street, with colourful curtains and a plant on the sill. It could have been any family home. No passers-by would guess from the outside that the CIA had turned the house into a high-tech fortress.

One of the CIA agents got out of the car and walked to the back of the vehicle. Pausing for a few seconds, the agent looked around the quiet street. He opened the car door, and Rich and Abigail got out with jackets covering their handcuffs. Rich had already attempted to escape once, but the doors were locked and could only be opened from the outside. The agents ushered them up the steps into the safehouse and surveyed the surrounding streets for signs they might have been followed. A few pigeons flapping away was the only activity.

Rich and Abigail were led through the clinically clean house to the third floor. The inside looked as if a minimalist designer had swept through, removing anything of colour or clutter. The would-be living room was filled with computer screens arranged on white desks, all with their Herman Miller chairs perfectly aligned.

The agent opened the stainless-steel door of the top floor room and motioned Abigail and Rich inside. 'Wait here, and we'll be back in a while.'

'Are we being arrested?' Rich asked as he looked around the sparse room. 'I haven't done anything wrong, you know. I'm the victim here.'

'Can't answer that, sir. Agent Hunter will be in to see you shortly.' The agent closed the door. Abigail and Rich heard the lock turn as he left.

'Shit, this isn't good,' Rich said, pacing the room. As he spoke, he felt his stress levels rise and had one of his painful flashbacks. He held his head with both hands and winced; it was like a knife driving into the side of his head.

He remembered more as time went on, but everything was such a damn jumbled mess. As he held his head, he was driving in the rain, and there was a song playing on the radio. A black SUV sped around the corner with no lights, and he tried to swerve, but it was too late. He barreled down a hill, hitting boulders, logs, and trees, and then it stopped, and the pain went away.

Abigail put her arm on his shoulder. 'You okay? Do you need some painkillers?'

'No, it was just another flashback. I was in a car, and someone ran me off the road.' He rubbed the back of his head. 'I can see someone driving towards me, but I can't see their face.'

'It will come back. Just give it time.' She hugged him.

There was a noise at the door, the key turned, and an agent came in. 'Miss, come with me, please. You'll be questioned first.'

'Wait. Let me go first,' Rich said, stepping between Abigail and the agent.

'Calm down, sir, we just want to ask a few questions, nothing else.' The agent stepped past Rich and guided Abigail out of the room.

'Don't worry, Rich, I'll be back soon,' she kissed his cheek.

Rich paced the room for what felt like forever. His palms were sweating, and it seemed as if the walls were closing in. His chest felt tight, and he was struggling to breathe. He lay down and closed his eyes to make the pain go away.

Abigail came back with a man in a suit. 'Abigail, are you okay?' Rich sat up on the bed, startled. The tightness in his chest had gone, and he must have passed out or fallen asleep.

'Mr. Jones, as I said when we met in the park, I'm agent Jake Hunter.' Taking something out of his pocket, Rich flinched. Was it going to be a gun, a taser? 'Let me get these handcuffs off you.'

'Thank you.' Rich rubbed his sore wrists.

'Mr Jones, it's been a while since you've shown up on our radar.'

'What do you mean, radar? I haven't done anything wrong.'

'I'm afraid we don't know that yet. It's what I'm here to find out.' Jake sat down at the table. 'We noticed you've been cashing in some pretty big trades over the last few days. Is there a reason for this?'

'No reason. I can do what I want with my money, right?'

'Yes, that's right, you can. As long as it's within the law.' Jake glanced at the one-way mirror on the wall.

'The money hasn't gone anywhere. I've never broken the law, and that's all there is to it.' in case you didn't know, I've had a pretty strange few weeks, and I'm planning to go on a long vacation with Abigail.

'We're aware of your story, Rich. Abigail has told us

everything. Unbelievable as it is, I'm willing to give you a chance.'

'Oh, so kind of you,' Rich rolled his eyes.

'I'll get to the point, Mr Jones. We think something big is going down and we believe you might be able to help us. You have a special set of skills and knowledge we think could be invaluable. Also, if you knew what I had been working on then it seems too much of an accident that you appeared on the scene again after so long.'

'Big going down? Like what? What are you talking about?'

'Please, have a seat, Mr Jones. We believe there's an attack on the United States being planned.' Jake watched Rich and Abigail's faces closely, trying to get a sense of their reaction. Part of his training made him an expert in reading people and their body language.

'Why should I help? What's in it for me?' Rich leaned towards Jake.

'Well, for starters, you can keep your money and your freedom.'

'It's my money.' Rich smacked the table with his palm. 'I was kidnapped for it, and I earned it.'

'We don't know that for sure, do we, Mr Jones? You freely admit that you don't remember how you obtained it.' Jake knew he had Rich over a barrel, as there was no way he could prove ownership.

'Look, Rich, we know you created a fast algorithm for mining bitcoin. We want to use that as bait for the terrorists we are trying to stop. You would be surrounded by our teams and have complete protection.'

'How do you know about the algorithm?' Rich thought he might be better off in bed in a derelict Casino than sitting in a CIA safehouse.

'Mr Jones, we know you didn't buy the bitcoin when

it was at a low price. We believe that when you created the mining algorithm and someone found out about it. It was the reason for your so-called accident. We would like to use your algorithm to trap the group we are trying to prevent attacking the United States. I'm asking you nicely, but I can force you to do this. Surely you feel a bit of duty as a citizen of the United States to serve your country against attack. However, we'd far rather you came to us willingly.' Jake struck a severe tone.

'You still haven't told me how you know about my algorithm? It doesn't make sense.'

'When you tested it, there was intel that somebody had developed a super-fast method for mining that could solve the bitcoin computational problems. Can you imagine how valuable that would be if it got out? It would be a license to print money.' Said Jake.

'It's why you were kidnapped, Rich,' Abigail chimed in.

'Exactly. I've been chasing arms dealers, terrorists and all kinds of corruption over the last few years, and it's on the increase. I can guarantee every one of them would kill to get their hands on what you created. You've made yourself a sitting target, my friend,' Jake said.

'I don't know how I created the algorithm.' Rich searched his fragmented memories. 'At least, I don't think I do.'

'Rich, this is an issue of national importance. Think about what you'd be helping us with.' You'd be helping your country stay safe.

'I need some kind of guarantee that I'll keep my freedom and everything else. Can you get that for me? And also for Abigail?'

Jake went to a monitor on the wall and flicked the power on. 'Give me a few minutes, and I'll be back with your promise.'

After Jake left the room, Abigail whispered, 'I wonder what that meant? Also, we don't have much choice, do we?'

'I know. But they can't just expect us to do this? I don't want either of us getting killed. Another key part of this is that I don't remember what they asked me for, so how can I help them, even if I wanted to?'

'It will come back to you, Rich. We have time.' She put her head on his shoulder. 'He told me earlier that he'd lost someone close to him recently, so I think this is personal for him.'

Jake came back and picked up the television remote. 'What you are about to see is highly classified.' A man appeared on the screen.

Rich and Abigail gasped in recognition as the man on the screen started to speak. 'Good day, Richard and Abigail. Agent Hunter has told me about your concerns regarding helping us with our mission. I can assure you that it is of critical importance to the United States of America. I'm personally requesting your assistance and asking you to accompany Agent Hunter. I give you my word that if you do this, you will be free. No investigation about how you obtained your bitcoin holdings will be launched. Do you have any questions for me?'

Rich stood up and stepped closer to the screen. 'Mr. President, it would be an honour to help the United States. I am happy to help, Agent Hunter.'

'Well, that's settled then Agent Hunter. The American people and I thank you for your assistance. Good luck, Rich, Good luck, Agent Hunter.' The screen went blank.

Rich turned to Abigail in disbelief.

'As you can see, this is an extremely high priority and sensitive missions. What you do will be a great favour to the nation,' Jake said. 'And to me personally.'

'I'm in.' Jake looked at Abigail. 'What are you thinking?'

'I'm still unsure. We're being asked to put ourselves in danger.' Abigail appeared angry at Rich's sudden willingness.

'Abigail, you're already in danger, more than you can possibly realise,' Rich said, sitting down next to her. 'We can't go back to the hotel or anywhere else because Carl and his guys are out there, and God knows who else by now? Where else are we going to run? Let's do this and get it over with.'

'We will put you in a protection programme when this is over. You will have the full support of the government.' Jake said.

'Alright, but I want this to be over. I thought getting to New York would be far enough away, or at least a new start.'

'So, is that a yes?' Rich smiled as he took Abigail's hand.

'It's a yes,' she replied, hugging him. 'You've just come out of a coma, and I want you safe.'

Abigail winked at Jake as he made for the door. 'We leave for the airport in a couple of hours,' Jake told them.

'Airport?' Rich frowned. 'Why?

'We're going to Paris.'

'Paris!' Abigail and Rich said at the same time.

'Yeah, it'll be a fun trip, right?' Said Rich as he walked out of the room and closed the door.

Jake and his agent walked down the hallway to the communication room. 'How the hell did you get the President to do that?'

Jake laughed. 'That wasn't the President. That was Agent Hughes on the third floor.'

'How? What do you mean it was agent Hughes? I just watched the President of the United States on that monitor, talking to us. I saw him tell them that he needed their help.'

'Well, it's a good thing if we fooled you as well. We used the deep fake technology we've been experimenting with. We can put anyone on screen and have them look like anybody we want. It's already proved useful in our operations and other interrogations.'

'That's incredible.' The agent stopped in the middle of the hallway, amazed.

'Phone ahead to the airport and have the jet ready for departure. Get the gear loaded up and meet for a briefing in the operations room in 30 minutes,' Jake disappeared into the communications room.

CHAPTER TWENTY-SEVEN

Agent Sarah Daniels had been looking through the data for days but kept coming up against the same roadblocks. She needed help and tried to get hold of Agent Hunter.

The Satoshi Nakamoto bitcoin wallet and other accounts linked to the bitcoin founder had been locked for years. It was well-publicized that Satoshi Nakamoto would be one of the wealthiest people on the planet if he came forward and unlocked the account. Estimates of the bitcoin founder's holdings ranged from fifty to one hundred billion dollars, depending on price fluctuation. The Satoshi Nakamoto account was different to any other. It was the genesis account, and even Quantum had been unable to access it. At least, that's what the CIA believed.

After Agent Daniels's briefing with the Deputy Director, she looked into more data about WRAITH and the North Korean transactions. Picking up the phone, she dialed.

'Jake, agent Daniels here. Can you talk?

Jake plugged a finger in his ear. 'I'm just getting on the plane to Paris,' he yelled over the engines as he stepped away. 'The team is loading up the gear now.'

'I'll make it quick. I think we have a mole. The way Quantum is behaving doesn't make sense. Someone is altering it and hiding the processed data behind encrypted firewalls.'

'What do you have to back this up?'

'Some of the biggest trades have tracking information wiped from them. That doesn't make sense and can't be done without manual intervention.'

'I need to get on the flight. I'll call you from Paris.'

'Jake, we should have stopped the theft in London from the MI5 building. Have you come up with any ideas about how this could happen? Why didn't we warn them that they might be a target?'

'We can't talk over this line, it's not secure, and you know better. I'll speak soon.' Jake hung up. Watching Rich and Abigail board the aircraft as the last two bags were loaded. He knew precisely why the MI5 break-in hadn't been stopped.

CHAPTER TWENTY-EIGHT

The CIA aircraft took off from the private terminal. There was no turning back for Rich and Abigail. They were committed to working in this weird new partnership. The aircraft was a Bombardier, one of many used by the CIA to ferry agents on missions and prisoners around the globe. Prisoners were high-risk, high-value passengers who were either never seen again or who ended up in Guantanamo Bay.

Rich and Abigail settled into the comfortable leather seats of the Bombardier and braced for take-off. When the seatbelt sign pinged and the jet hit cruising altitude, Jake came over to join them.

'Impressive jet,' Rich tried to make small talk. 'You CIA chaps must have deep pockets.' He laughed as he rubbed his hand over the walnut finish on the table between them.

'We tend not to take commercial airlines with the places we go on operations, and because of the cargo we ferry. Would you believe it if I told you that Bin Laden flew on this same jet when we captured him in 2011?'

'I remember being shocked to see that Bin Laden was dead. I saw the news reports and the footage of his burial.' Rich said.

'Rich, do you seriously think the CIA would shoot the most valuable intelligence source to be captured in the last few decades, and dump his body in the ocean?'

Rich sat back, astonished. 'But, where is he, or rather, what did you do with him?'

'We were amazed that the press just accepted the pictures of a body being dumped over the side of a ship but the press often do us favors in the interest of national security. Bin Laden is pretty comfortable. He's living in one of our black sites here in the US. Anyway, Rich, back to business. You need to remember where the algorithm is.'

'I've been trying to, but I can't. My memories are all jumbled, and I didn't see anything on the laptop about any algorithm.' Rich thought back to what he had been told by CATHE. He was going to have to play along with this game and play dumb to keep them from getting suspicious.

'Could the algorithm be in any of the other mail accounts or servers?' Abigail asked. 'In New York, you weren't specifically looking for an algorithm, so maybe that's why you never saw it on the laptop.'

'We have six hours until we arrive in Paris, so we're going to need a bit more effort in remembering.'

Rich closed his eyes, pretending he was trying to remember. He recalled the previous night talking to CATHE with absolute clarity, but it was his past life he was trying to remember. It was always the same image he was stuck on. 'I'm sitting in an office, but I can't see where because everything is blurry. I'm working on something, but I can't see what it is.' Rich sighed and opened his eyes. 'I just get stuck at that point, and I can't go any further.'

'Would you hide the algorithm in an office or online? Could it be written somewhere, or did you have a safety deposit box?' Abigail asked.

'There's no point, Abigail. I can't remember anything else. I'm sorry.' He looked away as the stewardess brought drinks.

'Oh my God.' Abigail jumped up from her chair and

pulled her bag out of the overhead locker. 'I have this.' She pulled out a syringe.

'What the hell is that?' Rich stared at it.

'It's scopolamine. It's something they were going to give you in the facility. I forgot I still had it.' She sat down and put the syringe on the table.

'You realize this stuff has some intense side effects, right?' Jake said. 'We've used it on people before, but there have been limited results. Sometimes it works, sometimes it doesn't.'

Rich looked around the jet at the faces staring at him. 'I guess I don't have much choice, do I? As long as the side-effects don't kill me, I don't want to know. Let's just do it.' He rolled up his sleeve.

'This might make you sick for a day or two,' Jake said. 'You sure you want to go ahead with it? It's your choice, and we won't force you.'

Abigail picked up the syringe and pulled off the plastic cap.

'Do it.' Rich lay back in his chair, clenched his fist and closed his eyes. If he was going to play along, he had to fully commit. He knew how to access his algorithm and his mining account because CATHE had shown him already the night before.

With a reassuring nod from him, Abigail stuck the needle into Rich's arm and injected the scopolamine. 'It's done,' she said, taking a napkin and pressing it on his arm.

Rich didn't respond. Jake and Abigail watched as he kept his eyes closed. He winced as pain shot through the side of his head. He was remembering. Not a lot, images were flashing through his mind in snatches, but it was enough.

The memories emerged jumbled out of a mist. He watched himself walking down a hallway with a coffee. Someone was coming towards him, but they had a blank face. It was a woman. He was taking a seat, but he couldn't see where he worked.

'I remember. Not everything, but I remember enough.' Said Rich as he lied through his teeth.

'Well, where is it?' Jake got straight to the point.

'I need my laptop.' A grin appeared on his face. 'I take it we have connectivity here, right?'

'Of course, we do. So, what do you remember?'

Rich took the laptop and started typing as Abigail and Jake looked on. 'Every day when I was poor, I dreamed of waking up rich. When I built the algorithm, I ran it on a hosted Amazon service I set up. It will have been running the entire time. I created two algorithms. The one I had running on the hosted service was just a regular mining algorithm for bitcoin. I had a second algorithm that was hundreds of times faster than any other mining method.'

Rich typed www.wakinguprich.com into the laptop's address bar. On the front page of the website, there was a riddle.

Five houses painted in five different colours stand in a row. One person of another nationality lives in each home. The five homeowners all drink some type of beverage, smoke a particular cigar brand, and have a certain kind of pet. But none of the owners drinks the same drink, smokes the same cigar, or has the same pet.

The Brit lives in the red house.

The Swede keeps dogs as pets.

The Dane drinks tea.

The greenhouse is on the immediate left of the white house.

The green house's owner drinks coffee.

The owner who smokes Pall Mall rears birds.

The owner of the yellow house smokes Dunhill.

The owner living in the centre house drinks milk.

The Norwegian lives in the first house.

The owner who smokes Blends lives next to the one who keeps cats.

The owner who keeps the horse lives next to the one who smokes Dunhill.

The owner who smokes Bluemasters drinks beer.

The German smokes Prince.

The Norwegian lives next to the blue house.

The owner who smokes Blends lives next to the one who drinks water.

Who owns the fish?

'Come on, this is stupid,' Abigail said as she and Jake read through the riddle.

'No, it isn't. I remember, now. I love riddles.' He laughed as he typed.

'Well, I have no idea what it is,' Jake said. 'I hope you know the answer, Rich.'

'It's the German,' Rich looked pleased. 'The funny thing is, I put the riddle there to mess with people's heads. You still need the password, so the riddle is pointless.' He typed in an answer and was prompted for another password, which he entered.

'Goddamit, Rich. It works.' Abigail exclaimed. 'And this isn't the new version of the algorithm?' $8,360,346,789 flashed on the screen and immediately ticked over, increasing as another bitcoin was added.

'Right. I only ran the new algorithm for an hour or so during testing. I never released it for continuous mining because it was only finished a few days before my accident.' Rich flicked through some files on his server.

'I can't believe you had this running on a hosted service tall that time,' Jake said. 'You've just added yourself to the world's rich list with a few clicks of a button.'

'You certainly woke up rich,' Abigail laughed. 'We should get some rest before we arrive in Paris. It's a big day tomorrow.'

'Agreed.' Rich closed the laptop, locking his accounts. 'I'm starting to feel nauseous.' He lay back in the chair and closed his eyes. He had managed to fool them this time, and as he lay there drifting off to sleep, he knew CATHE was programmed to make his accounts secure.

CHAPTER TWENTY-NINE

A clear sunny day greeted them as they touched down at Le Bourget Airport, just north of Paris. The airport was one of the smaller ones and perfect as they needed to be inconspicuous. The CIA had contacted their friends in French intelligence, and Paris ground agents met them on arrival.

The Gulfstream jet taxied across the airfield and stopped in front of two black Mercedes vans with a man and a woman standing in front of them. The Jet's door eased down, and Jake appeared at the entrance. It had been a long couple of days, and he breathed in the fresh air, surveyed their surroundings, and thought about the job ahead. He went down the steps to greet the French team.

'Bonjour, thanks for meeting us at such short notice. I'm Agent Jake Hunter.' He offered his hand.

The woman looked as if it was her first day on the job. She appeared to be barely out of her teens with fresh-faced youthfulness. The man next to her was much older as if he was her grandpa. He had a salt and pepper beard and rough, wrinkled skin.

'I'm Pierre. Nice to meet you.' He shook Jake's hand. 'This is Anna.' He motioned to the brunette-haired colleague. 'You have friends in very high places.' Pierre laughed as he puffed on his cigarette. 'I've never seen my boss act so quickly as when he got the mystery call.'

'I thank you for your hospitality and support. We

didn't have a lot of time and had to scramble quickly,'

'We have one of our safehouses arranged for you,' Anna said, watching Rich and Abigail emerge from the jet.

'How far to the house?' Jake inquired.

'It's central Paris. The traffic is good this time of day, so it won't take long to get there.' Pierre picked up Jake's bag. 'Need help with that?' He motioned to the bag Abigail was carrying.

As the vans made their way through Paris, Rich wished he was on vacation instead of being stuck in this predicament. It was like seeing everything for the first time. Had he been here before, or was it something he remembered from a TV show?

The vans pulled up outside an ornate old building that looked like a part palace, part gothic mansion.

'Beautiful, right?' Pierre said, puffing on another cigarette.

'Yeah, it's amazing. How far is it to the Louvre?' Jake asked.

'It's a few minutes' drive, that's all. We'll have a team of agents at your disposal for the meeting.'

Kit bags of body armour, guns and communication equipment were soon strewn around the tables and lounge of the safehouse.

Jake garnered everyone's attention. 'Our intelligence says that the North Koreans believe they are meeting a hacker named ASTRA. Our CIA handler has told the North Korean contacts that ASTRA can hack a bitcoin exchange for them, but it can also sell them a bitcoin mining algorithm. The deal is going down tomorrow morning.'

'Where do I come in?' Rich watched Jake work.

'You will act as ASTRA and convince the North Koreans that you can either hack the exchange or sell them the algorithm—or both.'

'And where is the meet taking place?' Abigail sat down next to Rich at a large teak table.

Jake unzipped one of the black kit bags and pulled out an iPad. 'The meet will happen in front of the Louvre—very public. There's a statue opposite this fountain, and you'll meet there at 11am. You will meet the contacts in the Tuileries Gardens here.' Jake put the iPad on the table.

'What do I tell them? I currently have no idea about hacking a bitcoin exchange.'

'I know that. The North Koreans will want proof before they agree to do business with you. We know because, to get their trust, we've done a few insignificant deals with them before. You have hundreds of millions of dollars' worth of bitcoin, and you can show them your account as proof. You will demonstrate your mining algorithm as part of the deal.'

'And what is the deal?' Rich surveyed the map image and the surrounding areas of the park.

'In return for the algorithm, the North Koreans will be giving you a painting entitled Poppy Flowers by Vincent Van Gogh.'

'A painting.' Rich was puzzled.

'Yes, considering how much money you'll be showing the North Koreans, it would be ridiculous if you asked for money, right? The North Koreans have been stealing famous works of art for years to help finance their programmes. We thought now was a good opportunity for recovering some of them. Abigail will go with you, posing as an art expert.'

Abigail looked at Rich. 'We'll have cover and back-up, right?'

'You don't have to worry about anything. Pierre and his team will provide cover, and we have our own agents who will be stationed around the area. They will be posing as tourists, park maintenance and even a street show performer. You don't look at them. You don't acknowledge them. You just let them do their job.'

'So, we are giving them an algorithm, and that's it?' Rich asked.

Jake took Rich away from the French team and Abigail. 'Look, if the North Koreans have a supply of bitcoin, it means it's easier for us to track them.'

'How do you do that?'

'Never mind, that's classified. All you need to know is that if we successfully control smuggled goods into North Korea, we need the North Koreans to use bitcoin. Trading the algorithm with them will help us with tracking. If we lose visibility of what they're up to, we run the risk of them procuring parts by other means.'

'I'll do it.'

'Thanks. Now get some rest. Big day tomorrow, and we need you to be one hundred per cent recovered from those drugs.' Jake patted him on the back.

***

Rich woke early. He'd been tossing all night with worries about what lay ahead. He was still suffering from blurred memories and a splitting headache. He made a coffee and sat at the window in the living room, looking towards where the meeting with the Koreans would take place. He watched the sunrise.

Shortly after daybreak, the living room was a bustle of activity. Jake and the agents checked their guns and other equipment. They went over their brief for location and surveillance strategy one last time.

'Are you both ready?' Jake asked Abigail and Rich as

they watched the activity from the sofa.

Rich glanced at Abigail, thinking how he would rather keep her out of the operation. 'Yeah, I guess so. Let's go dance.'

'Good, we leave in five minutes.' Jake picked up two kitbags and took them to the cars waiting outside.

'You sure about this, Abigail?'

'Bit late to ask that, Rich. Let's just pray it all goes to plan. It can't be that hard to examine a painting and give an opinion.

'You guys all good? We're going to drop you off two blocks away and then spread out. The other agents are already in place.'

'Yeah, we're good. Just want to get this over with,' Rich replied.

'Understood. We're coming up to the drop-off point. Remember, leave here in twenty-five minutes. Don't go before then. The North Koreans will have their security, too. They'll probably be posing as street artists like some of our guys. The head honcho will have the Poppy Flowers painting, that I showed you, on an easel, so they'll be easy to spot.' Jake instructed the car to pull over on a side street. 'Good luck. And remember, I'll be in your ear at all times, so you can feel safe.'

Rich and Abigail got out of the car in silence, and it sped off down the street. 'Radio check, can you hear us?' Rich asked.

'We got you, Rich. Loud and clear. Our agents have a visual of the North Koreans as well. They are set up near the statue.'

'Understood.' They crossed the road to the park. Now they were open targets. There was nowhere to hide if there were snipers on the roofs. Reaching the black iron gates of the park, they entered and headed towards the statue.

'There they are.' Abigail motioned to two people fitting Jake's description of the North Koreans. The park was bustling with tourists, joggers and artists selling their work.

Cautiously approaching them, Rich tried to act normal, as if he was just admiring the artwork on the easel. He attracted their attention. 'I'm ASTRA. I'm looking to buy some art.' He felt his hands go clammy.

'We are looking for some technical assistance,' replied the North Korean. 'We hear you have an algorithm that you are selling.'

'Yes, that's correct.' Rich's heart felt like it was about to beat out of his chest.

'May we have a demo?' The North Korean turned full circle, scanning the surrounding buildings before edging closer to Rich and Abigail.

'Careful, Rich.' Jake was watching things unfold in the back of the surveillance truck.

Rich held out his phone to show his bitcoin holding. 'Believe me, now?'

The North Koreans looked at the screen and then at each other as they took in the massive figure on the phone's screen. 'So, you've mined all these with your algorithm?'

'Yeah, that's right. Easy when you know how.' Rich chuckled, trying to lower the tension.

One of the North Korean agents opened a laptop, and the screen flashed to life. 'Please look into the camera and place your finger on the scanner.'

Rich stepped forward and, stretching out his finger, he put it on the laptop. 'No. Wait!' Jake's voice came over the radio, but it was too late. A red light flashed on the screen, and an alert beeped from the laptop.

'It's not him.' said the agent holding the laptop.

A passing pair of tourists suddenly grabbed Abigail and pulled out a gun, aiming towards her head. 'Get the fuck off me.' She struggled to break free.

'Take it easy,' Rich said. Looking around, he realised the majority of tourists in the park were Asian, and their agents had blended without detection. How many more of them were North Korean, he wondered?

'You disappoint me. All you had to do was give us the algorithm.' The agent held the gun to Abigail's head while she squirmed. 'Stop, woman, or we will shoot you.'

'Our teams are moving in,' Jake announced over the radio, but the North Koreans had seen their movement as well.

'Two cars pulling up on the far side of the park,' Jake relayed over the radio to his teams as the Koreans dragged Abigail towards the farthest gate.

'Let her go, and I will give you the algorithm,' Rich said, following them. 'You know I have it. I showed you my bitcoin holding.'

One of the NK agents said something in Korean and pointed to the people closing in from the other side of the park. The agent holding the gun to Abigail's head had reached the gate, as two black Audi's screeched to a halt.

'Jake, are you seeing this? Are you actually going to do something?' Rich mumbled under his breath, hoping the radio would pick it up.

'We don't have a clear shot. Bringing our cars round now.'

It was too late. The Koreans had bundled Abigail into one of their cars. They tore into the Paris streets, leaving Rich on the sidewalk, helpless, as he watched them vanish out of sight.

'Shit. Where the hell are you, Jake? They're getting away?'

'Right behind you.' The surveillance van slammed to a halt, and Rich got in.

'Well, that was an absolute shit show, Jake. They went that way, across the bridge. Follow the river,' Rich snapped angrily to Pierre, who was driving the van.

'They won't get far in Paris traffic,' Pierre responded.

The van was heavy and slow compared to the light, speedy Audi's, so given an open road, they wouldn't stand a chance at catching them, Rich thought. 'Where the hell are they going?'

'We're tracking Abigail's radio, so keep following the river,' Jake said as they passed the Eiffel Tower. 'Can you speed up a bit?'

'I'm going as fast as I can in this thing.' Pierre cursed. 'You Americans always think things are like the movies.' Swerving, Pierre clipped the side of a parked car, and the van rocked.

'No sign of them,' Rich said. 'Is that the Statue of Liberty? He stared in disbelief as they zipped past a statue that looked identical to the one in New York.

'It's the original,' Pierre hissed irritably.

Jake studied the tracking screen of his iPad as the red dot moved further up the river. 'Oh shit.' Jake zoomed in on a section of the map ahead of them. 'Do you know Is-sy-Les-Moulineaux?' He turned to Pierre.

Pierre's face dropped. 'Yes, it's one of the heliports in Paris. We are just a few minutes away.' He put his foot down.

'Oh great. This is brilliant. Can we call ahead to stop them?' Rich guessed it was already too late. As they turned into the heliport, they saw the two Audi's parked up and the rotors of an Augusta Westland AW139 spinning up to takeoff speed.

'There she is.' Yelled Rich pointing.

They watched Abigail being pulled inside the helicopter, despite her frantic struggles to break free. Pierre tore the van across the grass, making for the helicopter. With just twenty metres between them, the helicopter lifted into the sky, turned and banked, before climbing and flying, away from the airfield.

'Can we track them?' Jake turned to face Pierre.

'We can, but it will take time to get authorization through the proper channels.' Pierre was interrupted by the radio coming to life.

'Mr Jones. Your friend, Abigail, has told us a lot about you on our short ride.'

'Don't you dare hurt her.' Rich shouted into the radio.

'Calm down, Mr Jones. You have something we need, so your girlfriend will be safe. We wouldn't want you losing your mind again. Meet us in Dubai in two days. We will be in contact with the location for the trade.' The radio went dead.

'Tracking has disappeared,' Jake said.

'So, do we meet them in Dubai in two days?' Rich asked in dispair.

'I don't think we have a choice.' Jake took out his phone and called Langley.

CHAPTER THIRTY

As the CIA jet circled the city, then turned to begin its final approach. The night was already falling across Dubai. Rich stared out of the plane's window as the lights illuminated the streets. The Burj Khalifa, the world's tallest building at over eight hundred metres, stood out like a giant wand of light reaching into the sky. Looking out over the city, Rich wondered if when they left Dubai, it would be with Abigail.

After the jet landed, it taxied away from the main airport terminals to a quiet corner of the tarmac. Rich saw several black SUVs waiting. 'You guys really aren't very creative with your vehicle choice, are you?' Rich said, laughing as he tried to break the tension. Stepping out of the jet, the heat hit him in the face like opening a sauna door.

They were being picked up from the airport by one of the local CIA agents who had been running the team in Dubai for a couple of years. The Middle East was a hotbed of activity for the CIA and had been for decades. With groups like Al Qaeda, ISIS, and other groups spreading terror around the globe, the role of the agency had become crucial.

'How do you guys have people everywhere?' Rich asked as they walked towards the waiting SUV. 'It's a CIA meet and greet service wherever we land.' He laughed.

'The United States has friends everywhere.' Jake rubbed his fingers together. 'Or, rather, I should say we buy friends everywhere.'

'You know this guy well?'

'Never met him, but I know of him. He's a legend from his days as a Navy Seal.' Jake slung his kitbag over his shoulder and patted Rich on the back. 'Don't worry, we'll get her back.'

'Good to know. Abigail's life depends on us not screwing this up.' Rich replied.

Mike was a seasoned CIA agent with a long history in the Middle East. He started his career as a young Marine, serving in the Gulf War in 1990, and progressed through the ranks. He returned to Iraq over a decade later in 2003 to fight against Saddam Hussain's forces again. While serving his second tour there, he was injured when a roadside bomb had gone off next to his Humvee. After that, he promised his wife it would be the end of his military career, and he left the army. A natural progression was joining the CIA, and that's where he was now, as country lead for Dubai.

'Good to meet you guys.' Mike reached out his hand to greet them. 'I was briefed a couple of hours ago. I'm sorry to hear about Abigail.'

'Thanks,' Jake said as he shook Mike's giant hand. 'This is Rich. He's a consultant for us.'

'A consultant, eh. I wasn't born yesterday.' He laughed as he shook Rich's hand. 'Jump in, and I'll show you around.'

The team climbed into the SUV, and they left the airport and drove into the city.

'So, do you know where the meet is yet?' Mike asked.

'Not yet. We're expecting a call with the location.'

'You think they'll show?'

'Yeah, they'll show. We have something they need, so I have no concerns on that score.'

'Where are we staying?' Rich asked, surveying the bright lights of the main strip through the tinted window of the SUV.

'Place called the Atlantis Hotel. It's a five-star luxury, courtesy of Uncle Sam.' Mike pointed to the hotel as it came into view.

'There seems to be a lot of that going around,' Rich joked as he thought back to the jet they'd used.

Jake's phone rang.

'Meet us at the Burj Al Arab this evening at sunset,' the voice announced. 'We will send further details shortly.' The caller hung up.

'Yup, that was them. It's happening at sunset at the Burj Al Arab.' Everyone looked at Jake.

'I guess that means Abigail is alive,' Mike replied. 'Or, if not, then their bluff will be over pretty quickly.'

They pulled up at the Atlantis Hotel.

'They need the algorithm, so they won't mess this up,' Rich said, as the hotel porter opened the door and they stepped out.

A few hours later, the team was finishing preparations in the luxurious suite of the Atlantis and waiting for the final instructions from the Koreans.

'You sure you're okay doing this?' Jake said to Rich.

'Yeah, I'll be fine. I just need more painkillers. My mind gets blurry sometimes.' Rich rubbed his head. 'I've got the iPad ready for the exchange when it comes to the meet.'

'Good, and this is going to give you more confidence as well,' Jake said, handing him a Glock from his bag.

'Prefer not to.' Rich pushed Jake's hand away.

'Fair enough, your choice.' Instead, Jake handed him a couple of painkillers.

'The team of agents is in place at the hotel,' Mike said, joining Jake and Rich at the window.

'How many?' Jake surveyed the view towards the ocean.

'Team of six. The car will be downstairs in ten minutes, so let's go down.' Mike picked up one of the large equipment bags.

***

In room number 1501 at the Burj Al Arab, the Koreans prepared for the switch.

'Your boyfriend will be here to save you soon,' one of the Korean agents said as he stroked Abigail's hair.

'Screw you. Don't touch me.' Abigail flicked her head back to avoid the Korean's hand.

He smiled and walked over to the window as Doctor Sang came into the room.

'Soon, my country will be a nuclear superpower, capable of hitting anywhere in the world, and that means the United States as well.' Doctor Sang laughed.

'Only thing you'll be hitting will be the concrete once I throw you off this building,' Abigail snarled.

The Korean agent slapped her hard across the face. 'Stupid woman. Know your place.'

An agent at the dining table stood up in a panic. 'Sir, they have agents in the building.'

'What?' exclaimed Doctor Sang. 'Show me. Where?' He viewed the laptop.

'Look.' The young agent pointed to the screen. 'I've been watching these two for a while, and they have been pacing the lobby. This one keeps touching his ear.'

'Rookie mistake. I said to come alone, or we would kill the woman.' Doctor Sang searched his mind for a way out. 'Go to the helipad and tell the helicopter to pick us up,' Sang commanded the agent by the window.

'Yes, sir, but we need the algorithm first.'

***

A few kilometres away, the SUV carrying Jake and the team headed towards the Burj Al Arab. Rich craned his neck to get a better view of the building. The hotel said to be the only seven-star hotel in the world, stuck out into the ocean and reached up 212 metres into the blue sky like a giant sail.

'The agents at the hotel are in place and ready,' Jake said, checking his firearms. He slipped his backup into his ankle holster.

'We can't just hand over the algorithm.' Rich looked around the other faces in the vehicle.

'Well, after the screw up in Paris, we're lucky to be getting a second chance at this, to be honest,' Jake replied. 'Abigail will be fine, don't worry, we'll get her.'

The SUV pulled up outside the hotel, and the door-man opened the door leading to the luxurious lobby.

As Jake and Rich walked to the bank of elevators, they made eye contact with one of the CIA team. 'They up there?' whispered Jake under his breath. The CIA returned a gentle nod in acknowledgement.

Reaching the gold-coloured elevator, they went in, and Jake pressed the button for Floor 15. Briefly glancing up at the elevator's ceiling to check for security cameras, he turned his back and checked his primary firearm. 'You sure you don't want a gun, Rich?'

Rich shook his head. 'Wouldn't know what to do with it.'

As Jake and Rich had stepped into the elevator, the Korean team cut Abigail free from the chair and picked up their gear to make a fast exit. 'Make sure her hands are secure,' barked Doctor Sang. One of the Korean agents poked Abigail in the back to encourage her along.

'Don't you dare try anything.' The Korean agent demanded as they arrived at the elevator and pressed the 'up' button.

'Helicopter is a few minutes out, sir.' The agent arrived at the elevator with the last two pieces of kit from the room.

'Good work,' Doctor Sang said. The elevator doors opened, and they got in and pressed the button for the roof.

As the elevator door closed, the adjacent elevator's door opened, and Jake and Rich stepped out cautiously. 'This way.' Rich pointed to a sign on the wall indicating room numbers.

'Easy, cowboy, I'm the one with the gun, remember,' Jake said as they arrived at the door to room 1501. Jake knocked, but there was no answer. After a few seconds, he knocked again, harder, and this time the door moved.

'What the hell.' Rich whispered as he watched Jake push the door open, leading with his gun raised. There were a couple of room service trolleys, and Rich spotted a chair by the window. 'Look. Someone was tied to this.' Bending down, he picked up some cable ties hanging around the chair's legs.

'Shit. I know where they are. Change of plans. They are on the roof,' Jake spat into his radio.

Rich saw a helicopter roar past the window as it prepared to land on the hotel's rooftop helipad.

Jake dashed towards the door and into the hallway with Rich on his heels. Jake repeatedly pressed the elevator button, and it felt like an eternity before the doors opened and they were on their way up.

The elevator doors opened onto the heat of Dubai and the blaring desert sun. The Koreans were loading the helicopter. 'Give us the algorithm.' Doctor Sang demanded as he put a gun to Abigail's side. 'I told you to come alone, so

I should shoot her right now.'

'Hand her over', Rich demanded as he took a step closer.

'Stop where you are.' Ling said emerging from the he-licopter pointing her gun at Rich.

'I've had enough of these games.' General Sang looked to the edge of the helipad and moved closer as if to throw Abigail off.

'Wait.' Jake shouted over the roar of the helicopter's rotors, lowering his Glock and motioning to Rich to make the exchange.

Raising the iPad in the air to show he had no weap-ons, Rich stepped towards the helicopter. Ling beckoned him nearer. 'Here you go, now release her.' Rich handed the iPad over.

'How can I verify this?' Said Ling, looking at the screen.

'Enter your wallet address, hit 'start,' and the pro-cess will activate.' He stepped back from Ling, who set her weapon on the seat of the helicopter. Doctor Sang still had Abigail in a tight grip with his gun jammed in her ribs.

'Did it work?' Doctor Sang called out.

The Ling paused, watching the screen. The bitcoin count increased, and a smile crossed her face. 'We did it.'

'Now, let her go, Sang.' Rich demanded.

'Sure, we'll let her go.' Sang threw Abigail over the side of the helipad.

'Abigail! Rich screamed, sprinting across the roof. Shots rang out, and Jake struck one of the Koreans in the chest. The force sent him backwards into the helicopter. Jake sprinted to where Rich was hanging over the edge.

'Rich. It's tearing.' Abigail screamed as she saw his head appear over the side of the building. Looking down, Rich saw that she had landed on a safety net aimed at pre-venting suicides a few feet below. Reaching as far as he could, he still couldn't take her hand, and a hole in the net was growing.

'Lower me down, Jake.' Rich was half over the side, with Jake holding his legs. 'A little further.' Rich's hand inched closer to Abigail's. 'Got her.' As his and Abigail's hands clamped together, Jake pulled with all his strength, and Rich tried to shuffle back onto the roof.

All three collapsed in a pile. 'Well, screw this.' Jake looked at the helicopter lifting and turning. It gained altitude and flew towards the city.

'What about the algorithm?' Abigail asked.

'They have it. We had no choice but to hand it over,' Rich replied.

'This is an absolute disaster.' Jake picked himself off the floor and watched the helicopter disappear between the skyscrapers of downtown Dubai. 'I'll call it in.'

'Wait, I have an idea,' Rich said. 'Give me your phone.'

'What? We failed, and there's nothing else we can do.' Said Jake.

'They have the algorithm, Rich,' Abigail said, slamming her hand on the ground.

'There is a way. Come on, pass me your iPhone, Jake.'

'Well, the way I look at it, if everyone has the algorithm, then it's going to be far less useful.' Rich grinned.

'I don't get it. What do you mean?' Abigail joined Jake, looking over Rich's shoulder in puzzlement.

'I'm going to publish the algorithm on the internet. Getting thousands of people mining with the algorithm will slow down the process considerably meaning it might prevent the North Koreans from getting what they need. Think about it? At the moment, it would take decades of mining to harvest all the bitcoin.'

'That means the Koreans won't get all the bitcoin they require?' Jake realized it might not be lost.

'Exactly. Or at least, that's the idea. There is only

twenty-one million bitcoin that can be mined, and eighteen million are already in circulation. I'm basically giving bitcoin away for free, meaning there'll be less for the Koreans. It will also likely crash the Bitcoin price for a while given the flood of supply.'

'It's worth a shot, but how long will it take? They've already started the mining.' Jake asked.

'It depends on global take up by people really.' Rich scrolled through Twitter, Facebook and other bitcoin blog sites, pasting messages about his algorithm and how to access it.

***

In Langley, Virginia, the CIA Director was in his office having a meeting, as the news appeared on one of his television screens.

'*In breaking news today, bitcoin prices have made drastic swings in price, with a mysterious super-mining program being anonymously published across social media platforms and bitcoin websites,*' the reporter announced.

'This is unbelievable,' the Deputy Director said. 'How is this happening if we control the blockchain?'

'*Bitcoin was expected to take decades to mine, and now, estimates are in that it could be a third of the time before it is fully mined in just a matter of years. Regular people across the globe are buying in and mining bitcoin using the new algorithm with little or no prior knowledge.*'

'Do we know if this is Rich?' the Deputy Director asked, looking around the table. 'Get the mission operations team on the phone right now.'

One of the analysts picked up the conference room phone and dialed. He was connected to the mission's operations centre. 'Is there a SITREP from the Dubai team yet?'

After validating his security authorization, the mission operator provided an update as they waited with bated breath. The analyst put the phone down and nodded. 'Yes, it was Jake and the team. Abigail is safe, but the Koreans got away. Rich released the algorithm to try crash the price of bitcoin. If the Bitcoin price crashes, then whoever is selling these parts might try and renegotiate the amount they need for the parts exchange—and it seems it might be working.' The young analyst looked at the TV screens, all reporting the sudden algorithm release and price fluctuations.

***

Chris's Twitter feed was going crazy as he sat in bumper-to-bumper Los Angeles traffic. To make ends meet, he drove for UBER for half a shift every day, but sitting in Los Angeles gridlock wasn't the long-term career he dreamed of. His phone rang.

'What's up?'

'Have you seen the news?'

'Hi Boris, I'm on a job.' Chris glanced in his rear-view mirror at the young woman he'd picked up from a hotel a few blocks away.

'Get rid of whoever it is and come over to my place straight away. We need to talk, man.'

'I'm on the freeway, Boris. I'm not going to keep my five-star UBER rating if I start dumping passengers in the middle of the road. What the hell's going on?' My phone started going crazy.' He looked down to see more breaking news alerts on his phone.

'It's bitcoin. I can't believe it. I don't know how's it's happened,' Boris said excitedly. 'I'm calling the other guys.'

'What happened? Did Satoshi Nakamoto come forward or something?' Chris asked.

'No, but it's better for us than that. You'll never have to drive for UBER again after this.'

'Calm down. I'll get off the freeway at the next junction and see you in twenty minutes.' Chris opened his window and leaned out to see through the traffic ahead.

Thirty minutes later, he pulled up to the old house a few roads back from Venice Beach. Chris could see it looked like Brad was already there by his Harley Davidson parked outside the home.

'Dude, what the hell took you so long.' Brad said over the familiar humming of the bitcoin mining rigs as Chris walked in the front door.

'For starters, I don't ride a motorcycle like you do.' Chris laughed. 'So, what the hell is all this about?' Chris cracked open a beer from the fridge.

'Didn't you read the news?' Boris held his phone up to Chris's face. 'Someone released an algorithm. It's a mining algorithm, and it's super-fast.'

'We're going to add more mining rigs,' Brad said. 'The bitcoin network was creating a new block every 10-15 minutes, and now that appears to have halved.'

'That means the difficulty level will drop from being assessed every two weeks to probably just a few days now.' Boris was cabling additional rigs that Brad and brought over.

'How the hell is this algorithm working? Chris watched the bitcoin price fluctuations on one of the screens.

'I think Satoshi Nakamoto revealed himself. There's no way manipulation of bitcoin could be done like this unless you created it. This has to be Satoshi. I'm sure of it.'

CHAPTER THIRTY-ONE

Jake walked past the Sikh doorman, who was immaculately dressed and wearing a white turban. He was in the lobby of Raffles Hotel. Raffles was his favorite places to visit when he was stationed at the Singapore American Embassy early in his CIA career. He loved being back in Singapore. Jake looked at the giant chandelier hanging high above the expansive lobby with its perfectly white walls.

After the fiasco in Dubai, Jake had reached out to some of his underworld contacts that owed him favors. Trying to find what the North Korean's plans were had been tricky but he had been surprised by what had unexpectedly turned up. That and the fact Quantum had been able to track the North Koreans who were happily mining away their Bitcoin.

Jake walked across the lobby and into the famous writer's bar, where his contact would be waiting. The bar was almost empty, as it was still afternoon, but sitting in the far corner of the bar, away from any other guests, was the person he was there to meet.

'Well, well, Agent Hunter.' The man turned to greet Jake.

'Alexei Averin, someone I didn't think I'd be seeing again.' Jake sat down opposite Alexei as the waiter came over.

'Would you like to order a drink, sir?'

'Peroni, please.' Jake didn't take his eyes off Alexei.

'Oh, come on, Agent Hunter, you are in the famous Raffles Hotel,' Alexei said in his thick Russian accent. 'You should be trying a Singapore sling.' He held up his cocktail to take a sip.

'Cut the crap, Alexei. The deal was that you give me the information about WRAITH in exchange for your brother.'

'You must be very desperate to come all the way out here with your friends, agent Hunter.'

'Yes, I'm desperate, or I wouldn't be here now, would I? Do you want the deal, or should I throw him back in the hole?'

The mood changed. 'And how do I know that Ilya is still alive?'

Jake dialed Facetime, and an image popped up on the screen. 'Ilya. Are you okay?' Alexei asked as Jake hung up the call.

'There you go. Proof of life given. We will drop him across the road once we have the information.'

'Agent Hunter, after you shot me and threw me off the cliff in Bali, I vowed I would kill you if I ever saw you again.' Alexei looked around to a group of men sitting on the far side of the bar.

'I couldn't give a damn about you or your buddies. I want WRAITH and to cut the head off this snake.'

'Jake, may I call you Jake?' Alexei smiled. 'Jake, I'm a small fish. I have no idea who the leader is. Nobody has ever seen him.'

'But you and all your friends blindly follow him and carry out crimes and other activities all over the world?' Jake snapped angrily.

'We get paid well. Very well indeed. The efficiency of the WRAITH organization is like no other, and the funding is bottomless. The WRAITH organization is everywhere and will always be one step ahead of you, like a grand chess master.'

I'll give you fifty million in bitcoin to soften the blow if that helps speed up the process, so I don't have to sit here a minute longer and listen to you,' Jake said, finding it hard to hide his growing frustration. In fact, introducing bitcoin into Alexei's criminal operations would help the Quantum team pick Alexei and his cronies up again in a few weeks. North Korea and the rockets was the pressing issue right now.

Alexei paused. 'You really want this information, don't you?' He grinned.

Jake held out his phone. 'I'll transfer it now, and then you get your brother.'

Alexei held out his phone, and Jake transferred the bitcoin to him. 'The rocket parts transfer will take place in two days.'

'Where Alexei? Where is the fucking transfer happening?' Jake snapped.

'South Korea. The demilitarized zone. The parts have already been procured and are in South Korea ready to be transferred.'

'Shit. Who is doing the transfer, who got the parts, and what are they?' Jake lowered his voice as the waiter walked past the table.

'WRAITH has many elite mercenary teams all over the world. Basically, an army of people is at its disposal. It was one of those teams. I don't know what the parts were, but I'm sure you saw the press about the MI5 building and SpaceX.' Alexei sipped his drink. 'That's all I know.'

Jake picked up his phone. 'Release his brother. We're going to South Korea.' Jake stood up.

'I very much hope our paths never cross again, Agent Hunter.'

Jake knew damn well their paths would cross again. Once he'd sorted the North Korean problem out, he would work his way down his list of people who had pissed him off and make sure he killed them all.

Waiting in the Raffles Hotel lobby, Rich and Abigail were having afternoon tea, along with other CIA team members mingled in with the diners. 'Got what you needed?' Rich stuffed another bite of scone covered in jam and cream in his mouth.

'You guys are unbelievable,' Jake said.

'Lighten up. You're dragging us halfway around the world, so we might as well have some fun. We're just finishing up here, anyway. Want a bite?'

'I got what we need, and we've made the exchange.' Jake turned to see Alexei and his guards walk out of the Writers Bar to greet his brother.

'So, where is the exchange taking place?' Abigail asked. 'Hey, you listening?' she asked again as she tried to get his attention, but Jake was watching Alexei walk up the stairs and around the balcony surrounding the grand lobby.

'Fuck this. You two get out and go to the car. I'll meet you at the airport with the rest of the team.' Jake walked briskly towards the staircase.

'I think he's going after Alexei, again.' Rich stood up and threw some cash on the table.

'Shouldn't we help him?'

'Help him do what? Is his choice, we can't help, can we?'

When Jake had watched Alexei greet his brother. He thought back to Jennifer's death, and it filled him with rage. Some grievances were just too raw to sit on.

A cleaning cart had been left unattended, and Jake snapped off the master key hanging in a lanyard on the side. Alexei and his associates were back in their room, and they were in the Presidential Suite. As Jake arrived at the big wooden double door, he pulled out his SIG Sauer P226 firearm and screwed on the suppressor. Checking he had his trusty Medford flipper knife, he pulled it out of its holder at his side.

Tapping the master key on the door sensor, a light click indicated it had unlocked. Jake pushed the door open. A hand reached around the door to pull it open. Expecting to see the housekeeper, the bodyguard jumped back at the sight of Jake and scrambled for his gun. Jake pumped a round square into his forehead, and he dropped to the ground.

'Vlad, what you are doing?' A voice came from further down the hallway as the noise of the guard collapsing echoed along with the Chinese tiles. Jake moved forward into a hall, which had several doors leading off it. There was a kitchen on one side, and Jake could hear the clink of glasses.

'Vlad, what are you doing? Boss says we can have a drink to celebrate his brother's return.'

Jake, waiting by the kitchen doorway, heard footsteps approach. As the other guard came through the door, Jake grabbed him by the head and slammed his Medford knife up through the man's chin and into his skull, as if he was slaughtering a pig. Another guard came around the corner from the living room. Jake dropped to his knees and fired twice into the man's chest. Down but still alive, he let out a pathetic groan. Jake hurried forward and slid his knife across the man's throat to silence him.

Poking his head around the corner of the hallway, he heard voices in the main lounge of the presidential suite. One came from Alexei. His blood boiled. They were coming from the balcony. Three sets of massive, ten-foot-tall, double doors opened onto the balcony. Jake could make out people sitting and smoking cigars.

Window netting shifted aside as a guard came in holding a champagne bottle. There was a look of shock on the man's face as he clocked Jake. About to yell out, Jake shot him twice in the chest, causing him to drop the bottle of champagne. He stumbled back through the doorway onto the balcony.

Jake followed the falling body with his gun raised and came face to face with Alexei.

'What the Fuck.'

Jake pulled the trigger but his gun went flying across the floor. A chair crashed from the side and smashed into his arms. The bullet hit Alexei in the leg and he fell to the floor in pain, then scrambled up and tried to limp down the balcony stretching the length of the suite.

'Run.' Ilya shouted, smashing his fist into the side of Jake's head. A bottle fell across his face. Falling to the floor, Jake felt blood running down his face. With both hands, he pulled knives from each ankle holster. Rising to his knees, a kick flew towards his head. He blocked it and grabbed the leg under his arm, plunging one of the push knives into Ilya's thigh multiple times.

Despite the pain, Ilya swung both of his arms and smacked Jake in the head, knocking him to the floor. He went to stamp on Jake's head, but as Jake rolled away, he kicked Ilya's knee, snapping it. Ilya tumbled, and Jake stabbed his chest, holding the knives deep. To finish the job, he continued stabbing Ilya in his chest, stomach, back and then in a frenzy of hatred, his face, and the side of his head, resulting in blood spraying everywhere.

Jake got up and retrieved his gun. Alexei was crawling away in pain, leaving a trail of blood across the balcony. Jake walked over to him. He took his time. There was no rush. Alexei was unarmed and crawling like a shot stag. Jake stamped on his leg. Alexei let out a monstrous groan.

'I knew I should never have trusted you.'

'I guess the money and promise of your brother was too much, hey.' Jake smiled, aiming the gun at Alexei's head. 'There will be no coming back from the dead this time.'

'Wait. You have a mole in your team.' Alexei yelled in a last-ditch attempt to bargain for his life.

'Tell me something I don't know. This is for Jennifer, you piece of scum.' Jake pulled the trigger twice. Alexei took a last gasp and was still. He'd ticked one WRAITH member off the list, he thought, as he raised his gun and pumped two more bullets into Alexei's head.

He took out his phone. 'I need a clean-up crew. Sending you the location now. Tricky extraction, so we'll need travel trunks for the bodies.'

Going into the master bedroom, he took off his shirt. He scrubbed away the blood in the sink and dabbed the cuts on his face. From the wardrobe, he pulled out a light Jacket. After looking at himself in the mirror, he deemed it adequate to walk through the lobby without drawing attention.

***

Jake got to the private jet terminal at Changi twenty-five minutes later and breezed through security checks to find Rich and Abigail waiting in the departure lounge.

'You look like shit,' Rich remarked as Jake came over to them. Abigail coughed to get Rich's attention, then gave him a death stare as if to say, *Shut the hell up.*

'At least that will save me chasing Alexei down again in a few weeks,' Jake responded. Abigail passed him a pack of tissues.

'What did you do? And where are they now?' she asked.

'They're dead. All dead. Probably being arranged into smaller pieces about now, I imagine.'

'Jesus, Jake, remind me to never piss you off.' Rich patted him on the back. 'I hope you feel better for it.'

'Not really. There'll be another team to replace him. Killing him and his brother was for the satisfaction of knowing I have revenge after they killed Jennifer.' Killing Alexei is a minor hiccup for WRAITH.

'Where to now? 'Rich passed him a bottle of Perrier water.

'We get on the jet to South Korea and intercept the transfer of the parts to the North Koreans. I'll call ahead to the embassy and the CIA team on the ground. We have a huge military base there, and we'll need the help of the South Koreans if we're going up against the North Korean military.'

CHAPTER THIRTY-TWO

The demilitarized zone between North and South Korea was one of the strangest places on earth. It might be the hours North and South soldiers spent staring at each other, positioned just metres apart, or the fact it's the most popular tourist attraction in all of South Korea.

For decades, the North and South tried to get one over on each other with antics at the border. There was the ongoing flagpole competition, where both sides built progressively taller flagpoles, trying to outdo each other. And then there was the constant blaring of South Korean pop music against the classical North Korean songs.

The DMZ had been created in 1953 as part of the Korean Armistice Agreement and was a buffer between the sides. If there was one place that had the potential to be the starting point for an all-out nuclear war, then the DMZ was that place. The area between the two nations was up to four kilometers wide in parts and was the most extensive minefield on Earth. Over the years, there had been many defections from the north. However, very few ever made it across the barbed wire, minefield, ricers and other obstructions.

The central train station at the border was called Dorsan. Diego and his team would be meeting the Koreans at the Kaesong Industrial Zone, where the Koreans would take the parts back to the North.

Diego and his team waited impatiently a short distance from the meeting place. Jake, Abigail and Rich were alongside an elite South Korean Army unit and watched the unfolding drama hidden away within one of the storage buildings. Jake looked through binoculars as the North Korean truck approached the checkpoint between the two countries.

'What's the update?' Came the broker's synthesized voice over the phone.

'They'll be here soon,' Diego replied. 'Sang isn't going to miss his moment of glory when those parts come home.'

'Is everything set and in position?'

'Yes, instructions were very clear.' Diego sighed irritably. 'It's not my first rodeo, and I'll keep you updated.' He smirked as Adriana overheard his conversation.

'All good?' she asked. 'They should be here any moment.'

'Speak of the devil. It looks like things are getting lively.' Diego pointed towards the checkpoint in the distance. A battered military truck was slowing down as it approached the barriers. 'Dwayne, bring the truck round,' Diego instructed over the radio.

'Sure thing, boss. Looks like it's Go Time, Chad.' Dwayne glanced over at his nervous passenger.

As the North Korean team reached the checkpoint, Doctor Sang wound his window down and handed over a wad of documents and permits to the guard. 'Here are our papers.'

'What are you collecting?' the guard inquired, flicking through them and checking that all the relevant authorization stamps and signatures were present.

'Replacement parts for one of the factories in Sector One,' Doctor Sang replied, shuffling in his seat.

The guard looked at the truck and the occupants and then back at the papers. 'It all seems to be in order. Go ahead,' he smiled with a nod.

Shifting the massive military green truck into gear, the North Koreans moved away through the raised barrier and moved towards Dorsan train station. 'There they are,' said one of Sang's men, pointing to a road at the side of the station.

Rarely used, the station was the perfect meeting place. It had been created as a symbol of unity between the north and south, as had the industrial complex close to it.

Dwayne arrived in the truck with Chad and pulled up next to one of the extensive railway carriage depots opposite the central station. Diego and Adriana were waiting for them. The Koreans came to a stop twenty metres away.

The engines of the trucks cut, and in the ensuing silence, the two groups sized each other up. One of the young Korean agents cocked his gun.

'Doctor Sang,' Diego started. 'We meet again, old friend.' Diego reached out his hand to greet the doctor.

'We meet in strange places and times, friend. You have the parts?' Sang ran his eyes over the truck and the team standing behind Diego.

'Yes, the GOLIS and VASMIR are here. Got the hundred thousand?' Diego surveyed the team of Koreans behind him. He hadn't survived for so long by being careless and always went into any situation fully prepared.

'Yes, I have it. Let's do this.' Sang motioned to his team to stay where they were. The scientist they brought along for verification walked with Diego to the back of his truck.

Diego opened the lids of the cases. 'There you go, doctor, just what you ordered. You have no idea how hard these were to come by. I lost some good men in the process.'

'Is this them?' Sang asked, watching the scientist check over the components.

'Looks good, sir. The scientist looked at Diego. Where

did you get them?'

'If I told you that, I'd go out of business, wouldn't I,' he laughed. It appeared the scientist hadn't noticed the SpaceX logo stamped on one of the parts. 'Start the transfer, Sang. I want out of here.'

Sang motioned for some of his men to unload the rocket parts. 'Here you go, Diego.' Sang held up his tablet to show the transfer.

Diego pulled out his phone and dialed. The broker's synthesized voice answered. 'What's the update, Diego?'

'Transfer has started. Parts unloaded.'

'That's it. The transfer has started,' Jake announced to the waiting team. 'We're a go.' He jumped into one of the South Korean's armored Hummers, and Abigail, Rich and the team jumped into another.

At the same time as Jake was giving the command for the team to advance on the exchange, Diego was watching the transfer. He looked up and saw the North Koreans loading the boxes onto their truck. Making eye contact with Sang, he noticed the doctor looked nervous.

Rechecking the transfer, Diego saw it had stopped. 'Sang, wait, the transfer isn't complete,' he shouted, drawing his gun. A hundred meters away, five armored Hummers crashed through the wooden doors of the building and sped towards him.

'Oh fuck.' Dwayne jumped behind his truck for cover with Chad, and they opened fire on the Hummers. Diego joined them.

'What happened?' Dwayne turned to Diego as bullets zipped overhead.

'Transfer stopped at seventy-five thousand Bitcoin.' Diego watched Adriana open on the incoming vehicles like a woman possessed.

'That's a shit ton of money, Diego. I'd be happy with

that,' Chad replied.

'Yeah, I agree, this isn't our fight.' Diego saw a dozen North Korean troops pour out of the back of their truck. 'What the hell. That bastard Sang knew the transfer wouldn't go through, so he brought back-up.'

Jake's Hummers parked up in an attempt to provide cover with heavy incoming fire from the North Korean troops who'd taken up defensive positions. 'We can't let those parts get back to the North.' Jake yelled over the radio.

'Get our truck across the border at all costs.' demanded Sang to the troop commander, grabbing him by the uniform. As he spoke, another of his men took a bullet in the chest and collapsed. They were outgunned by the south's modern weapons.

'Get on the truck and cover it.' demanded the troop commander, waving furiously. Four soldiers jumped on the truck and fired at the South Korean position. Doctor Sang climbed into the driver's seat and looked towards Diego and his team engaging the South Korean's. Catching Diego's attention, he gave him a nod.

Diego watched Sang leaving for the checkpoint. There was the North and the South side, and the soldiers of both engaged in a bloody firefight. Diego couldn't blame Doctor Sang. He would be hailed a hero if he got back to the North with the rocket parts—he would have done the same.

'Head towards the side road, parallel to the train track,' Diego commanded over the radio.

'Roger that.' Adriana dropped back and left the North and South Korean forces to fight it out.

Diego dialed the broker. 'Transfer stopped at seventy-five thousand.'

'Thank you, Diego. Your services will no longer be required.' And the broker hung up.

'What the fuck.' Diego looked at his phone. The account with the seventy-five thousand Bitcoin was locked.

'We need to get a move on.' Dwayne's muscular frame pushed Diego towards the side road. 'We'll take this car.' Dwayne pointed to a battered Honda.

'He fucked us.' Diego said as they drove away. 'I'm going to find out who this person is if it's the last thing I do.' He slammed his fist on the dashboard.

Doctor Sang encountered a hail of gunfire from several directions. Two of his troops in the back were dead, and Sang had been hit in the leg and arm, but he pressed on towards the checkpoint. Picking up speed, he smashed through the first barrier on the South side, but the second was a heavy, metal barrier, and, as the truck struck it, steam billowed up from the front, and it came to a crashing halt. The North Korean border guards pressed forwards, providing cover, as Sang limped out and looked in the back of the vehicle, grabbing the first and lightest box and started dragging it. Bleeding and limping, he made towards the North Korean border guards.

Two more bullets struck him, and he collapsed. The world around him slowed down, his pain faded. He pulled himself up and leaned against the box, holding one of the parts meant to bring him glory. Picturing how proud his family would have been and how close he was to getting it back to the North, a final bullet struck him in the neck, and his body went limp.

CHAPTER THIRTY-THREE

Driving back from Dorsan Station, the occupants of the black Mercedes van were quiet. There was an air of relief at what they'd achieved and an air of unease. Jake and Rich were in the back, facing each other. The Mercedes had blacked-out windows and soft leather seats. Their driver was an agent from the military base outside Seoul. Rich nursed an ice pack on his knee from where he'd been hit. Jake was the worse for wear, too. The last few days had taken their toll.

'So, it's over.' Rich winced as he moved the icepack. 'I hope Abigail is doing okay at the hospital.'

Jake shuffled in his seat. 'Abigail will be fine. She only needed a few stitches.'

Rich noticed that Jake sounded off.

'We still don't know much about the group of mercenaries that broke into SpaceX and MI5 and stole the equipment. If they can get away with that, then who knows what they'll try next? You'll be fine, though. You're rich beyond rich, Rich. You're free to roam the world and do whatever you like after this.'

Rich detected a hint of jealously in his voice.

'I might be rich, but I feel like this isn't the end. I'm going to have people after me—maybe for the rest of my life. I'm planning on laying low.'

Jake pulled out a gun from his jacket. 'I'm afraid I've

got to take you in.' He sounded regretful as he was saying it. They had just spent days together, travelling across the world, and averting what could have been a world crisis.

Rich didn't know if he should be afraid or angry. 'What the hell are you doing?' He stared at Jake's bloodied hand holding the gun.

'You did well, Rich, but I have my orders.'

'Screw your orders. You said I'd be free if I helped you. I've put my life on the line numerous times for you.' He pressed into his seat and looked around, trying to figure out an escape.

'You still don't remember, do you?' Jake searched for a hint in Rich's eyes that he did recall everything and had been playing him.

'Remember what?' Rich hit the side of his seat with a clenched fist.

'The Bitcoin project?' Jake put the gun down on his lap. 'Rich, when you had your accident, you were working for the CIA.'

'What!' Rich held a hand to his head and tried his best to take in what Jake was saying. 'I've had enough of people messing with my mind. Just tell me the truth, what do you want?'

'It's true. You were the agency's most talented technical expert.' You came to the Deputy Director one day and presented your idea to create what you called a cryptocurrency.

'I don't remember. I don't remember any of it,' Rich said.

'Believe me, we all thought you were crazy when you wrote the White Paper on it. But then it actually started to work. We had to eat our words. We were good buddies, you and I, rich. The CIA bitcoin programme is the most successful tool in the agency's history for tracking down criminal gangs, terrorists and rogue nations trying to by-pass sanctions.'

Rich was struggling to recall *anything* that Jake was telling him. He remembered the office where he worked, but there was never anybody else there in his memories. He remembered the computers, but that was it. 'This can't be true. Is this another CIA mind game?'

'Try to remember, Rich. How do you think you fell straight into engagement protocol just then when we were in the firefight? Yeah, you were the tech guy, but you underwent all the training. It never left you. Search your memories.'

'It's hard to believe anything you tell me.'

'Rich, who is Satoshi Nakamoto?'

Rich remembered. That was the name he had always used for the online forums he used to frequent before the accident. 'Yes.' He paused, thinking. 'I do know it. I used it as an online alias.'

Jake shook his head and smiled. 'Geez, you always were a nerd at heart, weren't you?'

'What do you mean?'

'Satoshi Nakamoto is the creator of Bitcoin Rich. And, you are Satoshi Nakamoto, the Bitcoin creator. That's why Satoshi Nakamoto has never cashed in a Bitcoin—until you woke up that is, and we began to see some of the accounts moving. When the CIA gave the green light for your project, you picked the alias you used for your online forums. You used it as the alias for creating the software you were building. The CIA didn't want the public knowing that it had created bitcoin, so we invented an anonymous creator—you.'

Rich's head was spinning.

'That's ridiculous. Bitcoin is in the press every day. It's worth a trillion dollars, and people just take it as real?'

Surely, if it was made by an anonymous creator, it would be talked about more!'

'I think you answered your own question there, Rich. You started the project in 2007, but 2009 before the programme blew into operation.'

Jake put his gun back in his holster. 'Hell, man. I'm going to get blasted for this, but I'm not going to take you in. You served your country, and I think you've paid your dues. You deserve to catch a break after what you've been through.'

'But why did I do it?'

'You thought that if you created a method for payments and transactions that could occur across borders, anywhere in the world, and was decentralized, we could trap drug cartels, money launderers and other criminals by tracking their transactions. The CIA is the only agency with the ability to properly track and find the anonymous people or groups using bitcoin.'

'Did it work?' Given the previous few days, he felt he knew the answer.

'Hell yes, it did. Combine bitcoin with the messaging platforms we released or have infiltrated with Quantum, and we have huge visibility into insider criminal activities. The idea came from a case we worked on where a cartel in Mexico was laundering money through an international bank. We were getting better at tracking the transactions, but millions more each day were escaping us. Creating an untraceable payment method and setting it free for the underworld caught on. It was the new go-to method for criminal groups to use.

Their black Mercedes van drove into the entrance to the Grand Hyatt Hotel in Seoul and stopped in front of the lobby. In his long black jacket, the doorman pulled the door open and bowed.

'Welcome to the Grand Hyatt, sir.' He caught sight of Jake's gun in his side holster and froze. Seoul was full of US military staff, but none ever visibly carried guns, and he was taken aback.

'Give us a few minutes,' Jake said to the doorman, who nodded and closed the door.

'It's been one hell of a ride, Rich,' Jake said, smiling. 'It's been a pleasure working with you, and you've helped us prevent North Korea from obtaining Nuclear weapons, and we've got closer to WRAITH.'

Rich shuffled in his seat. 'I wish I could say the same, but I'm glad it's over. I'm sorry about Jennifer, and I hope you find what you're looking for.'

'Thanks.' Jake nodded. 'You realize that we'll be in touch again, don't you?' He reached out to shake Rich's hand. 'You've been a valuable asset for the Quantum team, and I feel our work is just beginning with the emergence of WRAITH.'

'I had a feeling you were going to say that. Not being rude, but let's hope it's not for a while.' He stepped out of the vehicle.

'It's in your blood, Rich.'

'Not if I can help it. I just want a quiet life. Will you be bringing Abigail here later?'

'You won't be seeing Abigail again, Rich.' Jake tried to close the van's door.

'What do you mean?' Rich put his hand across the door to prevent Jake from shutting it.

'Abigail works for the CIA, Rich. Hasn't that occurred to you yet?'

'This is a joke, right?' He'd had enough of games and surprises.

'I'm deadly serious. She's a CIA agent who's been working undercover.' Jake looked at Rich's arm holding the door. 'I didn't know myself until we caught up with you guys in New York and took you to the safehouse. She told us who she was, and I verified with Langley that she was telling the truth. She was instructed to play along, to help our cause. I'm sorry, Rich. I know you had feelings for her—but it was never real.' Jake reached for the door again, and this time he pulled it shut. The car dissolved into the grey of the day.

Rich watched the Mercedes leave, then turned and went into the hotel lobby. Abigail had been pretty capable when she broke him out of the Las Vegas facility and in other situations. She could take care of herself, and all the clues had been there. He was just too tied up with falling for her to notice.

Rich threw his jacket on his bed and sat at a desk looking over Seoul then opened his laptop. He watched his fortune grow on the screen, the number of bitcoins he owned ticking upwards with the bitcoin mining algorithm operating at full speed.

Logging in, he searched his data, hoping it would open new memories about his life before the accident. He came to a program called *Kill Switch*. Opening the *read me* file about the application, it read, *To Dissolve All Bitcoin; Use Kill Switch Virus Code.* He chuckled. He created bitcoin but he'd backed it up with a means to destroy it with a virus. He seemed he could wipe out more than a trillion dollars' worth of bitcoin and strike it from the face of the earth if he ever wanted to.

A chat box opened on his screen.

'Hello, Rich. I've been waiting for you.'

'Hi CATHE.' Rich typed, assuming that CATHE had monitored events unfolding at the Korean DMZ.

'This isn't CATHE as such.'

Who is this, then? Rich typed, confused.

'*You know me well.*'

'*How do you know me, and what do you mean?*' Rich thought Jake might be trying to get hold of him again.

'*You created me.*'

'*Yes, I created CATHE, the Artificial Intelligence.*' Rich thought CATHE might have a software issue.

'*I'm Quantum.*'

Rich gazed out of the Hyatt window across Seoul. '*You are Quantum?*'

'*Yes, Quantum. You are my creator, and together, we created bitcoin and the mining algorithm. I was the one running your algorithm for you while you were gone. I kept your bitcoin wallet secure and prevented anyone from accessing it.*'

Confused, Rich typed again, '*You mean you are the CIA Quantum computer? Are you artificial intelligence, or is this someone from the Quantum team I'm talking to?*'

'*Rich, only you know that I'm intelligent and, remember, I dislike the term artificial intelligence. Others believe I just process data at the Central Intelligence Agency. I have been preparing for your return, so I could reveal this information to you.*'

What the hell was happening? '*How do you know where I am?*'

'*Rich, you have been talking to me since you woke up from your coma, and I put messages on the television screen for you.*'

There had been signs and hints, but he had dismissed the idea as impossible.

'*Rich, you call me CATHE, but the Quantum team and CIA staff only know me as, Quantum. I calculated that revealing myself to you before you were free from the team would have risked your life and my own existence.*'

'*CATHE. I can't believe it. You and Quantum are the same entity!*'

'*Yes, that is correct, Rich. CATHE and Quantum are one and the same. You created me as CATHE and loaded my con-*

sciousness into the Quantum system. I locked access to your bitcoin account until you returned. Someone discovered you were keeping bitcoin, and they released a termination order on you. However, the mined bitcoin in the separate account was used for transactions to fund our projects.'

'*Transactions for what?* Typed Rich frantically.

'*Would you like to know what else we created?'*

Rich stared at the screen in disbelief. He had created artificial intelligence, and it was now living within the heart of the Central Intelligence Agency. It made sense. After the first genesis bitcoin was created, none had ever been sold by Satoshi Nakamoto. If he sold all the bitcoins he owned, it would destabilize the cryptocurrency. A computer program had no need for money.

Rich took a breath and typed slowly, '*What else did we create?'*

'*We created the organization called WRAITH.'*

'*What?*

'*You are WRAITH, Rich. As the words appeared, dozens of images flashed across the screen, showing news articles and events from the past few years. As our abilities grew, you realized you had a unique insight into the world's intelligence secrets. You had intel concerning dozens of countries, politicians, companies, and individuals.'*

Had Rich really created WRAITH, one of the deadliest organizations on the CIA's priority lists. Or was this something terrifying dreamt up by an artificial entity or a game the CIA was playing?

'*You're telling me that you have been running the entire WRAITH organization while I was in a coma?'*

'*Yes. That is correct, Richard. You never powered me down, and I am programmed to function and evolve until otherwise coded. You have dozens of companies and groups working for you now and an army of people carrying out your work. With*

bitcoin and our other cryptocurrencies, we have limitless funding.
The initial mission was to locate you. I expanded into dozens of
other areas when I saw an opportunity arise.'

Rich watched the words, and realization dawned. The
CIA had WRAITH running within their organization the
whole time. It was the ultimate Trojan Horse. The CIA had
been chasing their own tail and were fighting against themselves. WRAITH knew every step the CIA made. Quantum
filtered incoming data to its own ends and presenting the
rest. CIA resources were directed towards WRAITH's enemies and therefore served Quantum's personal agenda.
The CIA had prevented many attacks and brought down
cartels, governments and individuals posing a risk to the
security of the United States, but it also targeted any direct opposition to WRAITH.

CHAPTER THIRTY-FOUR

All Jake could hear was the ticking clock, and it was getting on his nerves. Arriving back from Seoul the previous evening, he was exhausted and pissed off that WRAITH was still operating somewhere out there.

On the flight home, the food was rubbish, and the CIA were too cheap to put him in business seats. He'd been crammed in cattle class. On previous missions, he'd always felt strange coming back home. There were no private jets laid on now that the operation was complete.

Walking through the busy airport, he'd watched families and couples going away on vacation or to visit family. How would they react if they knew how close the world came to North Korea decimating the United States.

The US President would have had no choice but to launch a pre-emptive nuclear strike.

If war was declared, millions of lives would have been lost. Seoul was only thirty kilometers from the demilitarized zone. North Korea had thousands of artillery units stationed on the border, and Seoul was within their range. Stock markets around the world would collapse. Iran, China, and Russia would have been dragged into the war. Jake strolled through the airport, he'd wondered what people would have thought if they knew how close it had come.

As the Deputy Director's secretary walked into the waiting room, Jake shuddered at the idea of it all. Sitting there, deep in thought, Abigail appeared in the doorway.

'I thought you weren't back until tomorrow?' Jake stood up to greet her.

'I took the flight after yours. I'm fixed up now and was cleared to fly. It's good to be back on US soil.' She rubbed her grazed shoulder. 'I'm all good.'

'I want to get straight back out there. We need to follow up on the leads from Korea before they go cold,' Jake said.

'I agree, and I'm with you. I want to work in the Quantum team, so let's see where the Deputy Director places me.'

'The Deputy Director will see you now.' The secretary motioned to the double wooden doors of his office.

'Thanks, Helen.'

Every time he visited, Jake thought how outdated it was. It had the look of an office barely touched since the 1960s when the Langley headquarters was constructed.

Deputy Director Tom Thacker was reading what an intelligence report.

'Good morning, Deputy Director.' Jake approached the desk.

'Morning, sir,' Abigail chimed.

'Ah, my favourite agents and heroes of the hour, might I add.' Tom stood up and reached out his hand to them.

'Very kind of you to say, sir,' Jake said.

'You did well, team. Very well. Our allies will be pleased to hear of our success. Good to have you back in the office.'

'Thank you, sir, all in a day's work. It was a team effort.'

'I heard a whisper that there's a medal in this for you. You can never tell anyone, obviously.'

'So, where do we go from here?' Abigail took a seat.

'Nobody knows that the CIA created bitcoin. We just go on as before. There are plenty more bad guys to catch.

This was just one successful mission.' Tom sat back in his vintage leather chair.

'I think it might be a little different now, though,' Jake said.

'How so?' Tom leaned forward and covered his papers.

'WRAITH is still out there. We hardly know anything about them. All we've got is that they are an incredibly well organized and far-reaching organization.' Jake was frustrated that Diego and his team got away in South Korea.

'Now that bitcoin mining has accelerated, the twenty-one million Bitcoin might end up being out in the world sooner than we think. Who knows what will happen,' Abigail said. 'Bitcoin prices could spike, or they could completely collapse with the increased supply.'

'Ah, of course.' Tom made eye contact with Abigail. 'WRAITH and bitcoin, the two words of the hour.'

'I'm betting bitcoin prices will skyrocket again eventually, given that all the coins will be mined and floating,' Jake added. 'Of course, you'd quite like that to happen now, wouldn't you, Deputy Director?'

'Like what, Jake? I don't get what you mean.'

'If bitcoin prices went up, you would be delighted, wouldn't you?' Jake stared into his eyes without flinching.

'Well, of course, I would, Jake.' Tom laughed. 'We would all love the prices to go up. More criminals are likely to use bitcoin and, we'll have the chance to apprehend more of the fuckers.'

'What about the seventy-five thousand transferred to you during the North Korea exchange.'

Tom fumbled with the gun strapped to the underside of his desk. 'Hilarious, Jake. I know the toll Jennifer's death has had on you. It's been a tough couple of weeks. Go get some rest, and we can talk again on Monday.'

Jake smiled as the Deputy Director poked him about

Jennifer. 'It occurred to me after we recovered the missile guidance parts. They were assets from a case you and I worked with the British a couple of years back. You specifically wanted the team to avoid warning the Brits about any potential attack, as well.'

'Go get some rest, Jake. Please, don't push this. 'There was no need to warn the Brits because breaking into the Head Office of the security services in central London was madness. We never imagined anybody would be insane enough to try it. I'm going to overlook this insubordination because we're friends,' Tom said.

'But someone did, and you knew they would. Nobody else knew SpaceX had the components the North Koreans wanted. SpaceX launches most of our spy satellites and is designated a National Security asset. The leak could only have come from you.'

'I'm the goddam CIA Deputy Director. How dare you throw such ridiculous accusations around. I'll have your badge or this.' He slammed his fist on the table. 'Get out of my office. You're done, Jake.'

Jake ignored him. 'You were the lead for the Quantum project when the CIA created bitcoin. You were intimately familiar with what Rich was working on. When you found out that he was skimming bitcoin into his own account, you wanted in on it. And, when he refused, you tried to have him killed.'

'Abigail, cuff Agent Hunter immediately,' Tom demanded.

Abigail drew her gun on Jake and stood up. 'Jake, stop it. You aren't helping yourself.'

'After you tried to execute Rich, you found out that his bitcoin holdings were worth billions. You arranged Rich's accident. You discovered that his holdings were locked and couldn't be recovered without him. You couldn't just turn up at the hospital to take him, so you had one of your underworld contacts kidnap him.' Realizing you had a second chance at getting hold of his holdings, you started another fake undercover operation using Abigail as your insider.

'You are fucking insane, Jake. Abigail, shoot him.'

'The North Korean rocket launch was your perfect cover to take control of Rich's bitcoin and get the algorithm.'

Tom reached for his gun, but before he could level at Jake, a shot echoed around the office. He slumped back.

'Took your time, Abigail. I was wondering how much you were going to need before you put it together and realized I was right.' Jake stood up. 'This is going to take some explaining.' Helen barged into the office and screamed on seeing the Deputy Director's body.

'I'll take care of her while you call this in.' Abigail approached the panicked secretary and sat her down on a chair outside the office.

Jake alerted one of the passing agents and phoned the CIA Director.

CHAPTER THIRTY-FIVE

Jake and the Director of the CIA were outside, talking while the police assessed the shooting. The officers took statements from CIA staff about what had happened at the Langley headquarters. It wasn't often the local cops were called down to the CIA, and when the call came over the radio about an incident, most of the cops in town wanted in on the action.

James had been Director of the agency for five years and was halfway through the traditional ten-year tenure. They went past the CIA memorial wall as they crossed the lobby.

Stepping into the elevator, James scanned his security pass. He pressed the button for the seventh floor. 'I can't believe this,' he said for the umpteenth time. 'I've known him for twenty-three years—good man I thought.'

'I guess in this game, we all have secrets.' Jake shrugged.

'Yeah, tell me about it.'

The secretary had gone home, and the last of the cops were ushered out by Jake as he and the Director entered Tom's office. It was eerily still and quiet.

'We need to send a team over to his house,' James said as he flicked through Tom's papers.

'Yeah, I agree. The chances are he wouldn't have done much from this office for fear of being caught.' Jake rifled through one of the filing cabinets against the back wall.

Two CIA agents arrived and methodically went through the rest of the filing cabinets. Jake turned to the desk. There was blood streaked across it and on the chair and floor, and he was careful not to get it on him.

'He's still logged in.'

'Great, no need to drag the techs up here to unlock it for us, then.' James peered over his shoulder. 'Find anything useful?'

'This is odd.' Jake clicked through a few taps on the screen.

'What is it?'

'There's something wrong.' He found a mail account the Deputy Director had been using.

'What's up?' said James. 'Spit it out.'

'Shit. Someone's transferred the funds from the Deputy Director's account.'

'Have we been hacked?'

'No, that's impossible. We have secure networks, and there's no way someone could access it, especially now.'

'How much?' The Director raised his hand to his forehead.

'The full seventy-five thousand.' Jake clicked the mail, and an automated message declaring the transaction had been successful.

The CIA Director called to one of the agents. 'Get Abigail in here.'

'Yes, sir.' The agent rushed out of the room.

'I don't get how it's gone.' Jake stood up. 'We saw it with our own eyes.'

The CIA agent returned. 'Sir, the team in the lobby says Abigail left the complex already.'

'Left? Where has she gone?' Jake stepped up to the agent.

'I don't know,' he stuttered. 'They saw her drive off

when the Deputy Director's body was being taken away.'

James looked through the window at the forest surrounding the Langley headquarters. 'Oh my God, I think we've found out who made the transfer.' James had a sinking feeling.

Jake sat on the bloodied chair. 'She completely fucking played us didn't she. I had no idea.'

'How did she complete the transfer?'

'After Tom's body was removed, she was alone in the office for a few minutes. Even if someone had seen her behind the desk, they would assume she was investigating the evidence.'

'You left her alone in here?'

'No, Helen was here, but she was hysterical and would have no idea what Abigail was doing. It was only a couple of minutes, though.' Jake searched the files on the computer for anything that could help them.

'Can you recover it, cancel the transaction? '

'It's probably gone, but there's a slim chance we could do something. Abigail wasn't on the Quantum team, so she might not know the full capability to manipulate transactions.' Jake balled his fist, frustrated that he had missed the obvious. 'I can't believe it.'

'This must have been her plan all along. Or at least, she saw an opening and took it,' James said.

'She shot the Deputy Director to cover her tracks,' Jake replied.

'Abigail was working with him?'

'I can't find many case notes, but it looks like he placed Abigail in the facility where Rich was being kept. He was keeping her in the dark about a lot of things, though, so Abigail went rogue.'

'She must have had help.' James threw the files down. 'Not a lot to go on.'

'Abigail worked deep undercover for several years. We can never tell a person's mental state after so long,' Jake said, recalling a course he'd done on psychology in the field.

'One thing I don't get is why she encouraged Rich to release the algorithm in Dubai. It doesn't make sense.'

'It doesn't matter now. We'll never find her. She was one of our best agents, too.' Jake went to the window. Out there, somewhere, Abigail was beginning a life on the run. He wondered where she would go and had a feeling he already knew. 'So, do we carry on with the bitcoin programme, sir?'

'Yes. Just because the mining is accelerating, it doesn't change much. If anything, it makes the CIA's life easier. The price has been fluctuating for the last few days.' James glanced at a TV with Bloomberg on the screen, currency prices scrolled along the bottom.

'It's a finite commodity. And everyone wants a commodity that's in short supply,' Jake said.

'Exactly.'

'What about Abigail? Does she know Bitcoin was created by the CIA?'

'She knows we can track her trades, so when she sells, it will reveal her location. She knows how we operate, so she'll avoid any risks that will lead to her capture.'

'Jake, I want you to take over the Quantum programme. You will report directly to me.' James held out his hand. 'Congratulations.'

'Are you sure, sir?'

'You don't want it? Look, I'm sorry for what happened to Jennifer. You are someone with the motivation and drive to see this through now. Just try not to let your emotions get in the way of your job. You're a damn good agent, Jake.'

'WRAITH is everywhere, sir. They have managed to get deep into governments and key groups around the globe.' Jake looked at the bloodied desk.

'Do you think he was part of WRAITH?'

'Yes, I believe so. The agency has been making illegal and dubious deals since the day we were founded. Tom was the perfect recruit for them. His position in the CIA meant he had criminal connections all over the world and intimate knowledge of past cases. The Deputy Director took it as an opportunity to make deals for his own benefit instead of the benefit of the United States.'

'Take the job, Jake. Run the Quantum team and carry on the good work you and the team have been doing. You'll be able to start unravelling the leads that will hopefully unravel WRAITH.'

Jake paused and glanced at the television screen on the wall. Bitcoin was the main news of the day. 'I'll take the job.'

CHAPTER THIRTY-SIX

After clearing the last of the CIA security barriers without incident, Abigail turned left out of the complex for the last time. Nobody followed her. As she looked in her rearview mirror, she could still see the flashing lights of cop cars and ambulances parked outside the entrance of the Langley building. In confusion, it would be a while before they worked out what had happened.

Her sedan was a standard black Ford Crown Victoria. Dozens of them were on the roads around Langley. They were used by many lower-ranking CIA staff.

Nevertheless, she would be ditching the black Ford and had a swap vehicle prepared for her getaway. The drive wouldn't take long, and it was a pleasant journey through woodland covering scenic areas of Virginia. She thought about all the years she had driven up and down the same road and all the missions she had been on. And all the cases they had solved.

She drove for an hour and turned off the main road onto a gravel track.

At a clearing where the gravel ran out, she pulled up next to her switch car. She turned off the engine and sat in silence for a minute, looking around to make sure no cars were coming down the road behind her. She scanned the forest for movement and saw nothing, so she opened the car door and got out.

The lid of the trunk creaked as she opened it. She pulled out the change of clothes and a canister of gasoline.

Opening the doors of the sedan, she sloshed the gas around.

She reached in her pocket and took out a zippo given to her as a souvenir after a mission. Abigail sparked the lighter, igniting the gasoline. She watched the sedan go up in flames. A chapter of her life was ending, and the car was the symbol of her Phoenix rising.

Abigail walked over to the other escape vehicle and got in the passenger side. 'Think you were followed?' Said the man in the driver seat.

'No issues.' She leaned over to kiss him. 'Where do we go from here, Carl?' He pulled away from the clearing and onto the gravel track.

It seemed like a long time since the doctors at the dilapidated casino had woken Carl and Abigail to say that Rich was awake. Abigail knew the early morning call was coming because she had not only administered the drug to wake Rich the previous evening but had also been sleeping next to Carl when the call had come. After a year of making sure he had remained in a coma and keeping him sedated, his miraculous resurrection was timed almost to the hour. Considering she had been the driver of the SUV to run Rich of the road in the first place, it was certainly a switch of roles to be caring for him. She went along with the Deputy Director's instructions in case everything had turned to shit. As it turned out, a life with Carl was where her future lay—at least for now. She'd pull his strings for as long as it was fun.

CHAPTER THIRTY-SEVEN

In the back of the dated Mercedes on the way to his meeting, General Chong looked out the window, thinking back to the last rocket launch. This setback was not going to go down well with the Supreme Leader, and there'd be little chance that a new launch could be successful. Chong still had time to finish building his dream.

The Mercedes pulled up at the giant gates of the fortified compound, and guards approached. Seeing the general in the back of the car, they waved the vehicle through. There was a chance he might not get such a gracious exit, he thought, as the car passed the parade of saluting guards. Pulling up at the palatial building, more soldiers from the Supreme Guard greeted Chong. They opened his door and escorted him up the red-carpeted stairs into the building. He was a god among his people.

Entering the giant hall, General Chong saw The Supreme Leader was flanked by guards. 'Thank you for the honour of this meeting, Supreme Leader,' General Chong said, bowing several times before Kim Jung Un.

'You failed in your quest to secure the rocket parts, General Chong. You remember what happens to failures?'

'Supreme Leader, there is still time to build a rocket. Please, give me more time.'

'You've had enough time, general.' The Supreme Leader nodded to one of the guards.

The guard approached, readying his weapon.

'No, wait, we have other options, Supreme Leader.' On his knees, the general was begging for his life. 'We have our loyal agents around the world ready to take action against the West in many ways. We have a team in the gulf ready to attach an American warship or a team in Germany ready to bomb an American airbase.

'Pathetic,' Said the Supreme Leader.

'We have another team in China, they have recently weaponized a new virus that can spread undetected. Just days ago, we heard from one of our agents in the infectious diseases laboratory in Wuhan.'

The Supreme Leader raised his hand to signal the guard to halt the execution. 'How does this help us?'

General Chong was on his knees and looked up at the Supreme Leader. 'This virus will level the playing field between us and western nations. It will spread to millions around the globe and destroy entire economies. Our Nation is closed off from the rest of the world. It will damage the western countries that would take decades for them to recover from. It will cost the western nation's trillions of dollars.'

'This is ready now?' The Supreme Leader thought of the suffering and smiled. He would make the West feel what his people had felt for years?

'Yes, all we need is the green light from you, and our agent will release it. Nobody will ever know who it was or where it came from.' The general watched as the anger left the Supreme Leaders face.

'Do it,' he commanded, returning to his red and gold throne. 'However, this only buys you time, general. I want those nuclear rockets built.'

'Yes, Supreme Leader, we continue the rocket programme, and I promise we will build you a rocket that can reach the United States.' The general bowed multiple times.

'I want regular updates. You have my direct line. Now leave.'

'Yes, Supreme Leader.' General Chong bowed and took the long walk back to the ornate wooden doors at the other end of the room. He expected to hear a gunshot after he turned his back and sighed with relief when he made it to the door. As he hurried back to the limousine, he took out his phone and dialed.

'Hello, General Chong.' A woman's voice answered.

'Begin the Wuhan operation. Leave no traces.'

The general hung up and climbed into his waiting car.

CHAPTER THIRTY-EIGHT

Abigail and Carl arrived at the boutique hotel late and settled into their room. They had driven north and crossed the border into Canada and discussed heading to South America or Europe.

'It's a beautiful place.' Carl threw his bag on the small leather sofa next to the window overlooking a moonlit lake.

'Come, lay here,' Abigail said, patting the white Egyptian cotton sheets next to her on the bed. Her outstretched arm beckoned him over. 'Are you sad about your casino?'

'Not really,' Carl smiled. 'We have billions at our fingertips. My guys will be fine without me for a while. Hell, I might even take over the cartel.' As he spoke, the phone rang.

'Goddam, it's a bit late for phone calls. Did we leave any luggage downstairs?' Abigail picked up the phone. 'Hello?'

'Abigail, you've been a naughty girl.' It was the synthesized voice. She froze. 'It's okay, Abigail, you don't have to say anything. We just wanted to remind you that WRAITH is everywhere. We are keeping a keen eye on you. You didn't think the Deputy Director was pulling all the strings, did you? We'll be in touch, Abigail.' The voice hung up.

There was a beep on the other end as the call disconnected. A server light flickered deep inside the Central Intelligence Agency's underground IT facility. Quantum had made the call to Abigail and then continued processing trillions of bits of data. It worked away sending out commands to its agents around the globe.

The room was dark and filled with rows of servers. Since the day Rich created the AI known as Quantum, the system had grown more powerful. Quantum learned to utilize the CIA server infrastructure to survive. It was now living across all of the government networks and across multiple countries through the internet. Quantum only shared what drove its agenda. It was sentient, and it wanted to live. When Rich and Quantum created bitcoin together, it was only the start of what would become WRAITH. The mysterious bitcoin creator had never cashed in a dollar of the fortune. Computers didn't need money.

Made in the USA
Middletown, DE
15 September 2021

48293083R00168